I0634662

the
March Hare
Anthology

Edited by
ADRIAN FOWLER

BREAKWATER BOOKS LTD.
100 Water Street · P.O. Box 2188 · St. John's · NL · A1C 6E6
www.breakwaterbooks.com

Library and Archives Canada Cataloguing in Publication
The March Hare Anthology / Edited by Adrian Fowler.
Poetry and short stories from The March Hare festival.

ISBN 978-1-55081-228-2

1. Canadian literature (English)--21st century. 2. English literature--
21st century. I. Fowler, Adrian

PN6014.M37 2007   C810.8'006   C2007-900204-8

Copyright © 2007 Adrian Fowler

ALL RIGHTS RESERVED. No part of this publication may be reproduced
stored in a retrieval system or transmitted, in any form or by any means,
without the prior written consent of the publisher or a licence from
The Canadian Copyright Licensing Agency (Access Copyright). For an
Access Copyright licence, visit www.accesscopyright.ca or call toll free
to 1-800-893-5777.

The Canada Council | Le Conseil des Arts
for the Arts | du Canada

We acknowledge the financial support of
The Canada Council for the Arts for our publishing activities.

Canada

We acknowledge the financial support of the Government of
Canada through the Book Publishing Industry Development
Program (BPIDP) for our publishing activities.

ACKNOWLEDGEMENTS

I am indebted to many for their support in the task of editing this anthology. The March Hare Committee (Rex Brown, Nick Avis and Randall Maggs) have been unstinting in their efforts to supply me with information and advice. Dr. Wade Bowers, Associate Vice-Principal of Research, at Sir Wilfred Grenfell College has been unfailingly helpful and encouraging, and Grenfell College has been supportive in many other ways – I must especially acknowledge the assistance of colleagues Martin Ware, the late David Freeman, Ken Livingstone, Linda Carroll, Pam Parsons, Linda Humphries and George Maslov. David Morrish generously lent his professional expertise in photographing March Hare images. In addition, financial support was provided by Grenfell through a Principal's Research Grant and through two SWASP (Student Work and Service Programme) grants that enabled me to hire two research assistants. I am grateful to Al Pittman's wife, Marilee, and his daughter, Emily, who gave me access to a collection of papers specifically related to the March Hare, and to Rodney Mercer who made available his collection of March Hare posters and portraits. Stephanie McKenzie of SCOP Productions and John Ennis of the Waterford Institute of Technology graciously gave me permission to use biographical information collected for their Ireland/Newfoundland and Labrador anthology, *The Backyards of Heaven*. At Breakwater, I have been fortunate to have had excellent colleagues in Clyde Rose, Rebecca Rose, Wade Foote, Kim O'Keefe and especially designer, Rhonda Molloy. The following provided invaluable assistance as copy editors: Joanne Barber, Madeline Fowler, Sherry Boone, Stephen Bolt, Sharon Warford, Kelly Humber, Terri Lynn Mullowney, Andrew Bowers, Adam Baker and Adam Kelly. Finally, I must salute the dedication of my research assistants, Michelle Deluney and Caroline Crocker, whose enthusiasm for this project was genuine and infectious.

INTRODUCTION

The March Hare, Atlantic Canada's largest poetry festival, originated probably in 1988 as an innovative but inauspicious winter entertainment at the Blomidon Golf and Country Club in Corner Brook, Newfoundland.[1] That an important literary event should owe its birth to three golfers attempting to generate business for their local club during the bleak days of March might seem unlikely, but given that the begetters were poet Al Pittman, organizer Rex Brown and club manager George Daniels, it perhaps should have been expected. The March Hare was one of a series of events they concocted to enable the club to stay open during the long winter months – the Swish, Swallow and Swill Gournament, the Blomidon International Night, and the Great Tack's Beach Growl Tournament – its original purpose not substantially more noble than theirs. Unlike the other events, however, the March Hare survived – survived the deaths of George Daniels and Al Pittman and a change of venue downtown to the Columbus Club – to become a unique trans-island celebration of words and music, involving seven events in three towns over five days, attracting writers from all over Canada and indeed the world, and featuring the best traditional musicians in Newfoundland and Labrador. In its twentieth year, the 2007 March Hare was scheduled to take place not only in Corner Brook, Gander and St. John's, but also in Toronto and at seven venues in Ireland, including Waterford and Dublin.

Although much is known about the origins of the March Hare, after twenty years memory doesn't always serve and research only recovers so much. The original plans did not anticipate the long-term development and success of the event and the preservation of documentary evidence was not a priority. To some extent, therefore, the early origins are lost in the mists of time. Was 1988 actually the date of the first March Hare? Was the first March Hare called the March Hare? Who performed at the First March Hare? These questions can only be answered in probabilities, not facts.

The March Hare of 1994 was the first to be designated with a number, the programme indicating that it was the seventh. Even though systematic record-keeping may not have been a priority in those days, Al Pittman had a good memory and an eye for history and Rex Brown was formally trained as a historian. It is a good bet, therefore, that in counting back from 1994 and locating the first March Hare in 1988, they were on the money. Furthermore, the 1988 March Hare was almost certainly called the March Hare, although there may have been earlier poetry readings using the Blomidon Club as a venue. The English Department at Sir Wilfred Grenfell College, led by Al Pittman and John Steffler, had established an energetic programme of readings by visiting writers from the opening of the campus in 1975, and, in fact, the tenth anniversary of that tradition was celebrated by the performance of eleven writers over a two-day period at the Holiday Inn in 1985. University-sponsored reading events were therefore well-established in the community by the late 1980s and they took place off-campus as well as on. Although it undoubtedly drew on this tradition, however, the March Hare was different in that the Blomidon Club was not just the venue but the sponsor of the event.

No documentary evidence has been found of the 1988 programme. It is even possible that there was no printed programme, although this seems unlikely given Al Pittman's love for ritual and his tendency to introduce it even into social events among intimate acquaintances. As for who performed, it was probably pretty much the same line-up as the following year. According to a 1989 March Hare flyer, that year David (Smoky) Elliott, Rosalie Elliott, Nick Avis, Adrian Fowler, Randall Maggs, Al Pittman and John Steffler read from their own writing; David Freeman, Maria Bourgeois and Patrick Monaghan performed an excerpt from *Twelfth Night*; and David Freeman was Master of Ceremonies. Music was probably a feature from the start, but it was not listed on the programme until the third March Hare of 1990, when Lorna Hart, Susan Kent and Emily Pittman performed as *Two Rode Together*, Art Griffin, Wayne Muggeridge and Vicki Pike performed as *Polypudjum*, and legendary club and provincial golf champion John Ledrew played the piano and, memorably, whistled. Visual art was not formally introduced until 1995 when George Maslov, master printer in Grenfell's Fine Arts Programme, nominated a student, Frances Thoms, to create the poster for the March Hare dedicated to Smoky Elliott. Nevertheless, early March Hare programmes, dating from 1990 and created by Nick Avis, featured a striking fusion of image and word, juxtaposing delicate line drawings and haiku.

The March Hare moved to the Columbus Club in 1994. The following year, in honouring Smoky Elliott, the tradition of dedicating the annual event to celebrate the work of special artists, or supporters of the arts, was initiated. The tradition wasn't resumed until 1998, when the enormous impact of Al Pittman was properly saluted, but since then the March Hare has paid tribute to the contributions of Des Walsh, Clyde Rose, Pamela Morgan, David Freeman, Daniel Payne, Bernice Morgan, Irish poet John Ennis, and in 2007 John Steffler. In 2002, in a departure from the singling out of one individual, the mystical influence of Inner Placentia Bay was acknowledged. The formalizing of the annual tribute led to the commissioning of portraits to commemorate the occasion. Since 1999, Gerald Squires, Grant Boland, Dave Sheppard, Corey Gorman, Melissa Martin, Darren Whalen, and Rodney Mercer have all produced art works for the March Hare.

1998 was also the year the March Hare expanded to four events. The traditional Saturday evening performance was supplemented by a Friday evening reading at Casual Jack's Roadhouse, a Saturday afternoon matinee for children, and a Sunday afternoon musical event in King Henry's pub at the Glynmill Inn. The package was advertised in the Corner Brook *Western Star* as "a weekend of words and music," a formulation that had been used conversationally for years and succinctly summed up what had by then become one of the defining qualities of the March Hare.

Al Pittman died in August 2001. But in the spring of that year, the first St. John's March Hare had been organized by Nick Avis and by late summer plans for the 2002 Hare were essentially complete. They included two new venues: an event in Gander, organized by Eric Norman and Sheldon McBreairty, and a reading at the Sir Wilfred Grenfell College Art Gallery in Corner Brook. The concept was that a core of four or five writers from outside Newfoundland would perform at events in St. John's, Gander and Corner Brook, supplemented by local artists in all three centres. Although Al Pittman did not live to see the 2002 Hare, in the last months of his life he oversaw its culmination in the seven-event trans-island festival that it is today.

There are many poetry festivals around the world and quite a number in Canada. Many of them are bigger than the March Hare. The large urban centres of Canada – Toronto, Montreal, Vancouver and Ottawa – all host international literary festivals that attract hundreds of writers and thousands of aficionados. But the March Hare is unique. It bears no resemblance to a convention, a conference or a circus. There are no panel discussions or workshops or competitions. It does not privilege the professional interests of the writers; nor is it aimed at an audience of the elect. There are no prima donnas mumbling into the microphone or droning from the podium while earnest spectators assume a stoic posture struggling to convince themselves that although it tastes awful it does you good. At the Columbus Club on Saturday evening in Corner Brook, poets, musicians and patrons sit around tables, bar-style, and break during the intermission to replenish their glasses or line up to partake of the Hare soup. After the readings, the stories and songs go on, as they would in a kitchen party, until the wee hours of the morning. The occasion is, in Al Pittman's words, "a gathering."

The origins of the March Hare provide a clue to the meaning of that term. The event was created to fulfil a social purpose. It was conceived as an enticement to bring people together. It reached out to people who did not think of themselves as poetry lovers and it promised them stimulation and entertainment. At the core of Al Pittman's aesthetic was the uncompromising conviction that good literature could be appreciated by ordinary people, and that, in fact, it should serve the broad community. Not even Milton Acorn was more naturally or more truly a people's poet than Al Pittman. This article of faith on his part was complemented by the fact that poetry and song are deeply embedded in the tradition of popular entertainment in Newfoundland and Labrador.[2] The variety show, the soup supper and the community concert were all social events that invited broad participation and performance. Recitations, rhymes and ballads provided opportunities for both social bonding and social commentary. These events, identified as signature features of popular theatre in Newfoundland and Labrador, are the archetypes of the March Hare's unique blend of music and words. They also explain its improbable success: the audience recognises the genre and understands its social purpose.

The roots of the March Hare go deep and they extend beyond the locale in which the idea originally germinated, drawing sustenance from a larger sense of shared community in this part of the world. Early in its evolution, friends and acquaintances from St. John's and elsewhere started turning up to take in the event. Des Walsh, Clyde Rose, and Larry Small were among them. Being writers or performers themselves, they were sooner or later invited to participate onstage. Established artists like Pamela Morgan, Michael Crummey and Stan Dragland have made their way to the Hare just to be part of the scene, without any expectation that they would perform.[3] And although it may flourish in this place, the sense of community is open-handed and freely shared. The young Newfoundland poet Ben Hynes described the March Hare as "a reaching of arms."[4] This is why Lorna Crozier, Patrick Lane, Susan Musgrave, Stephen Reid, Glen Sorestad, Louise Halfe (Sky Dancer), Michael Ondaatje, Alistair MacLeod, John Ennis, Paul

Durcan, Emiko Miyashita, Eiléan Ní Chuilleanáin, and many other writers from other parts of Canada and the world have gravitated to the March Hare – not just to flog their wares (although certainly books are launched and sold) but to participate in a ceremony that feels like a party.

Like the traditional variety show, the March Hare originally drew on the talents of people living in the local community. The event has gone way beyond that now, but the elements of the original formula have been faithfully, even lovingly, maintained. Performers are handled as though they were all guests in Rex Brown's home from when the Hare begins on Wednesday evening in St. John's until when it ends on Sunday afternoon in Corner Brook. At the same time, writers are chosen for their interest in getting the words off the page and they are reminded that the patrons of the event are an equally important ingredient in its success. It is expected that audiences will be challenged as well as entertained, but the March Hare insists on the importance of the exchange between performer and audience. Rex Brown has often said that every year he is as excited to introduce the patrons to the presenters as he is to introduce the presenters to the patrons. The ethic of the March Hare is that presenters owe audiences their very best attempt to communicate and audiences owe presenters their open-minded attention. It is a powerful combination of mutually undertaken obligations. As Stephanie McKenzie has observed, at the March Hare literature is treated as a live art form.[5] This is why it combines so naturally with music in the programme.

From the start, the March Hare has demonstrated a strong commitment to the quality of the experience. The programme was always planned many months (in recent years, over a year) in advance. Great care was taken to ensure that the balance between the various 'acts' was right. Presentations and performances were timed to the minute and going over time was seriously frowned on. Professionals were hired to handle lighting and sound. Such high standards continue to characterize all aspects of the March Hare and it is reciprocated by the attention of the patrons. Although the Saturday evening event takes place in a bar packed with hundreds of people, there is no talking or moving about during the presentations. In the words of Glen Sorestad, there is "a reverence for the word, whether it's sung or whether it's spoken. The audience is just so attentive. They're holding onto everything and very respectful of the music and the words."[6]

The March Hare attempts to create the conditions under which it is the quality of the whole experience that is being sought, and it is being sought not just by the organizers and the performers but also by the patrons, who are made to feel that they are an integral part of the enterprise. A populist, democratic philosophy prevails. Traditional stories alternate with contemporary poems, emerging writers appear alongside established writers, local performers share the stage with performers from all over the world, and all of them are accorded the same courtesy. While long-term achievement may be given the nod of respect in the form of an extra two or three minutes at the podium, the time allotments are tight and more or less equal. There are no stars at the March Hare.

It is paradoxical that an event that is so rooted in tradition should be so open to change and so open to the world. This has been the great achievement of the March Hare. Cultural identity, like individual identity, cannot be protected by staying the same. When a culture is alive and well, it is dynamic, re-discovering and re-asserting its essential integrity while embracing the world. It cannot protect itself by preserving the past; it must draw on the past to re-invent itself in the present to take on the future. This has also been the great legacy of Al Pittman. In his life, even more than in his work, he exemplified how this act of creation can take place.

Today the March Hare continues to be a labour of love for the organizers. In 2001, Randall Maggs and Nick Avis succeeded Al Pittman as artistic and programme directors respectively. Randy is primarily responsible for the line-up of out-of-province writers and he oversees the Corner Brook programme. Nick collaborates with Randy and Rex on the overall design of each year's Hare and organizes the St. John's event. Sheldon McBreairty still puts together the Gander programme, and in 2007 John Ennis and colleagues provided direction for the Ireland leg of the March Hare. As always, Rex Brown is responsible for the overall organization of the festival. He is also, more than anyone, the guardian of its spirit, the keeper of the flame.

As such, one of his concerns has been to prepare for the passing on of the torch to a new generation. In 1998, at the March Hare dedicated to Al Pittman, Al's daughter Kyran, read from her work, and the following year a new tradition was established of making room on the programme for one or two emerging writers. Through this process, the March Hare has become a venue, or set of venues, in which new writing is featured side-by-side with established work. This represents an infusion of new blood into the event and provides a valuable forum in which emerging writers are introduced to experienced practitioners and to a broad audience. This inter-generational cross-fertilization is critical to the future of the March Hare, as it is to the future of the arts in general.

In creating the *March Hare Anthology*, I have tried to remain faithful to the spirit of the event. As many former participants as possible were identified, tracked down and asked to submit work. Editorial judgement was exercised in the selection and arrangement of material, but I have attempted to utilize the same elusive principles of balance and eclecticism that have always shaped the development of the March Hare programme, sometimes gathering together works of similar styles or themes, inviting comparison, at other times juxtaposing difference to emphasize contrast. Although there is some variation in the amount of space allocated each writer, in this too I have attempted to imitate the variation in time allotted to writers in an actual March Hare event. Absolute equality is not insisted upon, but a spirit of egalitarianism prevails. Furthermore, the full spectrum of approaches to writing, from the traditional to the avant garde, is here presented without apology.

Although the March Hare may not be the best known literary festival in Canada, it is surely one of the most interesting and innovative. The Hare reframes traditional forms of entertainment embedded in the culture of Newfoundland and Labrador so as to showcase writing from all over the world in a way that appeals to a popular audience. In managing this, the organizers have made a very important statement about cultural transition, about the ability of ordinary people to appreciate good writing, about the human striving for expression and communication that are at the core of all the arts, and about the need to build and re-build communities that welcome and encourage such aspirations in order to draw nourishment from them. The organizers, participants and patrons that constitute the true essence of the March Hare have shown how such communities can come together. It is a lesson and a legacy of no small significance.

– Adrian Fowler

[1] Stephanie McKenzie, "Interview with Rex Brown," in McKenzie, O'Dowd-Smyth and Thackray, eds., *Living at the Edge, Living at the Centre* (Waterford and Corner Brook: Waterford Institute of Technology and Scop Productions, 2006), 40.

[2] See Ches Skinner, "Newfoundland Amateur Drama – Historical Sources," in Lynde, Peters and Buehler, eds., *Proceedings of the Workshops on Newfoundland Theatre Research* (St. John's: Memorial University of Newfoundland, 1993), 88-93.

[3] "Interview with Rex Brown," 44, and personal interview with Randall Maggs, 21 November 2006.

[4] Ben Hynes, *The Current*, March 2004.

[5] "Interview with Rex Brown," 61.

[6] The Corner Brook *Western Star*, 13 March 2000.

TABLE OF CONTENTS

Two: "When the sun and the tide were the keepers of time"

Three: "a cat / climbing the tree"

Four: *"like a hunter mapping his path in the dark"*

Five: "rocks over rocks tumbling / towards Ireland"

Six: "butterflies dreaming they were men"

The March Hare

CODE OF CONDUCT

"The March Hare will be much the most interesting, and perhaps," Alice said to herself, *"it won't be raving mad."*

– Lewis Carroll

RITES OF PASSAGE

Whatever little time we live, time
in the end, adds up to no time at all.
Sadly and gladly there are things
to be seen in the sun and missed
in flight along the way.

We take to wing, fly a while, ponder
all that circles below us and descend
to earth. We look up to see where
we've been. We measure the spaces
we inhabit inside, out and about.

The ground beneath our feet
is our foothold for as long as we
can stand and hang on. The sky
is where birds and angels dwell.
We've all been visitors there and come
back home to the back yards of Heaven.

The sky is where we've been when
we've gone to sleep undreaming
or been wide awake, night and day
alert to our own mortality.

But however low below the slow clouds
we strive to thrive, the sun burns above.

And keeps on burning.

– Al Pittman

The
March Hare

A Special Tribute to Smokey Elliott

Host: Rex Brown
Master of Ceremonies: David Freeman
Prelude: Al Pittman

Place: Columbus Club

Date: Saturday, March 11, 199?

Time: 8:00 p.m.

Admission: $5.00 ($2.50 for students with I.D.) Includes
March Hare soup, ... Cash Bar

"Drunk with the moth and the bee"

ONE

David Elliott

TALKING TO TREES

I like talking to trees
And they say they like talking to me.
Their speech delights me:
The heavy utterance of elms and pines,
The sensible remarks of maples,
The banter of birches,
Even the idle chatter of the giddy aspens.
There was an old spruce who taught me much poetry,
And in a far country an oak tree
Told me the meaning of patience.
But especially I loved the old poplars in my back garden.
How courteously they would interrupt their meditations
To answer my greeting.
I told them about us mobile folk,
And what strange lives the unrooted undergo.
They told me stories of air, wind, water,
And the slow riding of the midnight world
Towards the stars
They died last winter.
This week I cut them down.
Some day, through various stages of ashes and dust,
We shall be back in earth together,
And resume our conversation.

AFTER THE SNAKE

I came to Eden after the Snake took over,
So I don't remember the old days.
They tell me angels lifted above the trees
Like soaring rainbows, and the unmoving sun
Blessed all the garden with his shining love.
Lambs played with lions, nobody carried a gun,
And the four rivers that flowed in Paradise
Reflected paradise in every pool.
It was all right, I guess, but yet, I think
I'd find that kind of living rather dull.
What could you do but sing and eat and sleep?
Sing hymns, eat fruit, and sleep without a dream.
Things are much different now.
You have to scramble to come out on top,
Lambs are for eating, lions are to hunt.
No angel hangs about this neighbourhood.
The spinning sun
Is veiled in smoke and dust. The rivers are blocked
With crap of all kinds, not excluding bodies
Of those who were too slow with knife or gun.
There's always something to get you interested.
The new boss likes to keep everything stirred up,
And, I must say, he's got the right crowd for it.

BAMBOOS FLOWERING

In Sichuan the bamboos are flowering,
The giant stems sprout yellow blossoms
Gilding the mountain side.

Twice in a hundred years that calm eruption
Gladdens the eye and lifts the clouded spirit
On shining perfumed wings.
In Sichuan the bamboos are flowering.

In Sichuan the pandas are dying,
They cannot eat the procreant trees:
The harsh and bitter grass cannot sustain them.

Slowly they starve, and sifted blossoms
Wrap them in fragrant shrouds.
The golden heaps are clustered in the forest.
In Sichuan the pandas are dying.

RIVER IV
for Al Pittman

One time, late in the day, at Second Pond,
I wanted to go home.
In layered trees, sleepy birds trilled briefly,
That sound that bids farewell to afternoon
And welcomes evening.
A warm wind drifted from the melting sun,
And darkness flowed like another river,
over the folded hills.
A bittern thundered on my left hand,
and a loon sobbed toward sunset.
The day died suddenly, night came alive.

I had no reason to travel by night
Except that I wanted to go home.
I have noticed that we need reasons for everything
Except going home.
I put my battered tent in the canoe.
An evening mist blotted out the world.
I saw nothing, but knew where everything was
In this place, my home of four centuries.
So, even in darkness I knew I was drifting the Steady
Where Betsy Tizzard, a hundred years ago,
Ran over the water to escape her murderous husband,
Sustained by her faith in God and her ignorance of physics.
I kept away from Sand Point
Where Beothuks killed Corn Hiller in 1790:
Those who have seen his ghost do not travel the river again.
Then I felt the quick lift and fall of Minnie's Rattle,
And rushed into Sea Pond.
The mist lifted and stars marched over Indian Hill:
Orion leading his Hound,
The Bears, Big and Little,
And a thousand others whose names I do not know,
But whose shapes I have known from infancy.
Then I heard the sea snarl, gnawing the bones of the world,
And broke into the harbour.
Across the cove, the light in my father's house
Led me towards home.
I sometimes think and always hope that it may still do so
When I have travelled in a greater dark
Down the last river
To that unknown sea.

Patrick Lane

FOR AL PITTMAN

Dear Al:
    Somehow everything for you came down to the sea.
It was your father's boat, the one that sat in the field
Rotting in the sun long after he died, and you sitting
In the wheelhouse with your drink, staring across the withered
Summer grass, both of us drunk, you telling me
Through tears of the outports and the years. What I remember
Is the sadness of it all, that boat pulled out of the water, the hull dry,
The cabin windows broken. You tried to turn the wheel
But it was frozen by the sun. It was like you
To be running rough water in your heart, the right tears
In the wrong place. Too many years. We could both find a metaphor
In all that now, or I could, now you're gone. The last time I saw you
You didn't want to talk. You sat huddled over your drink in the bar
In Corner Brook and couldn't be moved. There were too many echoes
Of all the other poets I saw die with their hands clenched
Around a glass or puking booze and blood into a toilet bowl.
Echoes of my own terror, the bottles as long as the years.
Christ, we went back a long way. I think it was '66 we met,
You in Montreal, and me the first time in the East. Did we fight?
Probably. You Newfies were always troublesome, proud and vulnerable,
With a gift for the insult of love, the tender touch of hate. I thought
    your
Wife a pretty one and likely made a pass at her. Those days I wasn't
Much good for anything but trouble, and poetry. I felt it was the same
    with you.
The many times together, the dawn you locked yourself out of our
    house
In Regina and got lost in the alleys as you searched for a cigarette butt
To light. That you were naked but for your underwear made little sense

8

To the neighbour who guided you back. You passed out on a lawn
    chair.
When I found you hours later you were sunburned to a salmon. I
    think it was
The only time your skin was ever touched by the sky. Jesus, Al, I loved
    you
And I couldn't bear your dying, the steady day and nightness of it.
I was dying too, but that doesn't mean much now. I'm still dying,
Just more slowly. We were always drunk together, Al. Always,
With Nowlan or Newlove or Acorn, or just whoever happened
to be around, and at the end no one but ourselves. I remember
    guiding
You off the stage in Vancouver. The audience was laughing at you,
Your jokes and stories. I knew you were dying up there,
That you'd got lost and couldn't find your way back.
I put my arm around you and you whispered in my ear,
Thank Christ, and then you asked, *Where are we?*
I still don't have an answer. Some questions leave me reeling.
Maybe where we always were was in a boat in a dry field far from the
    sea.
Maybe that was the best we had together. If I close my lids
I can see you in the red light the sun makes of my eyes. You're up
    there
At the wheel with a good sea and a fair wind. Someone's laughing,
Your father, me, and we're heading in to harbour, the last light falling
Across a Canada far to the west, and there's a life to be led on the
    waters,
In a dry field, with no one to hurt us, and tears enough to go around.

HOPE AND LOVE

The spider
weaves her web
in the window
at dawn.
The night has been
cold and she moves
slowly, filament
to filament,
drawing from
herself a cage
that is
beauty to me
and to her
her only life.
It is the seventh
morning and she
has caught
nothing all week.
This is her last
web and it has
nothing to do
with hope
or love, only
that she must
sit in the centre
of her making
and know that
what will feed
her is to come
or not come,
the sun
on the far flowers
and nothing
rising in the frost,

no sound among
the false blossoming
this cold, this
early spring.

Not Going to the Nitobi Gardens, Choosing Poetry Instead

In the white coffee mug a yellow flower, nameless,
picked at dawn, her sleeping in the muscled dark, bright hair
thick with sweat. Him sitting in the wicker chair, silent,
staring at the flower with the old regret. A wasp
rages at the window, the glass between its wings and paradise,
crashing its helmet head against what it can't reach, cedar trees,
magnolias, penstemon, and the last blooms of the foxgloves.
In the redwood tree a gray brain thinks among the branches,
a wasp nest where eggs lie in cells, each one a thought, each one
what he can only imagine. He does not open the window,
wonders instead at her dream, the click of the wasp's blunt head
    on glass,
what she is translating now, what dream of hell she holds,
the *click, click, click, click* of the wasp, and her shifting,
the hair falling across her cheek. All this and waiting,
the wasp resting in fury on the flower, the only thing
resembling its other life, nectar pooled below, the flower
alive in spite of its death, and her waking, slow to the morning,
him in the wicker chair, its brittleness creaking, and
not going to her, the wasp under its bright wings, watching.

AUGUST LIGHT

White sand and the gold running deep in the sun
at the far bend where a spring run jammed the wrack,
branches and leaves, an old tire, and a bit of cloth caught up
like a sail flung hard against still air, the bed of the creek deep
where no wind moved. The path did not wander. It followed
the land, each footfall as much animal as man,
around the hill, not over, stump and root, rock and hump
as distance, not discovery. This way, the worn bridge
over the creek old, the boards ground grey and curved
by foot and paw, hoof and claw, how many years, and how
many bridges over this dry creek and through this wood,
the path one path so one could in the old days
follow them from the north to the south or east to west,
an intricate map that covered the continent – so long ago,
as I moving south of the Netchako followed the trails
safe through the last mountains to the Cariboo plateau
and how I sat there in the forest looking down upon
the first man I had seen in a month and did not move,
gone feral, on my haunches behind alder leaves,
my rifle butt in the dust, and watching him,
as he moved from barn to house to truck and down
the road away and how I slipped back into the trees
for three more days, my fire small in the night, thinking
my way back into being a man again – the last
coffee brewing in the pot, a Blue grouse baked in clay
broken open, the meat of the bird I thanked the land for.
And now this creek bed, deep and waterless, white sand,
and going on through the wood behind Faulkner's Rowan-Oak,
and on to Oxford in the far Mississippi I never thought
I'd see. I'd read *Light In August* in the hotel
and found the creek in his book exactly as it was,
the trail he took from town to home and back again how many
times? The time I sat behind alder leaves, a feral man,
who watched another of his kind, afraid for three days,
thinking by the fire that he might kill someone and not

knowing who. That man followed a path south leading him
I knew, even as he wished to be lost, back to himself,
The Cariboo, late August light – now long ago, as I
see again the sand shot with gold in that dry creek bed, the
journey old as the trail that led me back again to the world.

Joan Clark

from
LATITUDES OF MELT

*Francis St. Croix spotted it first, a black dot floating in an ocean
of water and ice. When he and Ernie rowed alongside for a look, they
couldn't believe their eyes. There was a baby inside a makeshift cradle
on an ice pan, bobbing like an ice cube on the sea. How had a baby
come to be in the North Atlantic? Francis wouldn't have been out here
himself but for having signed on to a Lunenberg schooner, the* Maria
Claire. *The fishermen had been hauling trawl lines into the dory when
a thick fog rolled in, obscuring their view of the schooner as well as her
marker buoys. All day long the men had rowed through fog looking for
their ship and that evening, when it lifted and there was still no sign
of the* Maria Claire, *decided to head for Newfoundland and rowed all
night. Early next morning they came upon the child.*

*The cradle was a basket on top of a wooden chair. Black rubber
sheeting was wrapped around the basket and tied with some fancy
gold rope. On top of the sheeting was a woman's veiled hat. While
Ernie steadied the dory, Francis removed the hat and lifted the chair
and the basket into the boat, noticing how the sheeting had been
rucked up at one end to make a hood. When he pushed back the hood,
he saw the baby's face, white as the Virgin's. A girl, Francis knew it
was a girl. Her eyes were closed. Was she dead, or asleep? He held his
hand in front of her face, felt a wisp of breath warm his palm. May
the Holy Mother keep her asleep. If she awoke they had nothing to feed
her except hard tack and a bit of cold tea.*

*An angel must have been guarding the child, for she slept until
the next day, and when she awoke there was no cry, no whimper or
discomfort or distress. It was as if she understood that the men were
delivering her to land as soon as they could. The sea cradle was on the
dory bottom between Francis's legs where he could see the baby as he
leaned to the oars. How long had those eyes been open? Blue they were,
a clear regarding blue. When he looked again, they were brown. After*

she had memorized his face – so Francis liked to think – the baby closed her eyes. By the time she opened them again, Ernie was at the oars and Francis was kneeling beside the basket. The baby poked a finger into her mouth and sucked. Francis groped among the cradle cloths to test her warmth and found a jar of sweetened water and a bit of bread wrapped in a lady's handkerchief. This in turn had been wrapped in two flannel napkins and tucked at the baby's feet then covered with rubber sheeting, well away from sharp-eyed gulls.

They were too far out for gulls. So far they had only seen puffins, a small flotilla riding the swell. Though the worst of the ice was behind them, the air was cold. Francis slipped the jar beneath his shirt to warm it. The child was wet. He bent to the task with chapped and calloused hands. When his sons were babies, he had occasionally changed their napkins but he had no skill with such things, much less with a female child. But it had to be done. He chucked the soiled napkin overboard and fumbled a clean one between her legs. Before he bundled her tight, he rubbed her vigorously to bring up the colour but her pallor remained. He softened a pinch of bread in water and slipped it into her mouth. She smacked her lips and swallowed. Then she smiled. She had teeth, four miniature accordion keys. Twelve month old she was, maybe more. She was so little, her age was hard to guess. He fed her more bread and she closed her eyes while they rowed beneath a sky where a celestial compass guided them home. It was a two-day journey to Newfoundland, with each of them taking a turn at the oars while the other dozed.

Francis put ashore in the Drook with the cradle and the hat, and Ernie continued to Trepassey where he boarded a schooner that took him back to Nova Scotia, leaving the dory and the chair behind. Albert Sutton claimed the dory and his wife the chair, a collapsible wooden frame with a woven cane seat. Her mother sat in the chair for years to watch passersby, until a fire destroyed both the chair and the house.

Because no one was expecting Francis, his family was doubly astonished to see him walk into the kitchen with a baby in his arms.

"Mother of God! What have you there?" Merla St. Croix put her hand on the baby's forehead. "Ice cold."

"I found her on a bergy bit."

"A girl, is she?"

"As pretty as you please."

Four sons crowded around while Merla unbuttoned a wool bunting.

"Her little legs are that thin, they're like candle sticks," Merla said.

"She's been without food for a time," Francis said. "She'll be hungry."

No one thought to ask Francis if he was hungry or how he'd happened ashore earlier than expected. All that was told later, after the child had been changed and bundled in the basket, which was put on the oven door like bread set to rise. Merla dipped a cloth in warm milk and squeezed it into the baby's mouth. The child swallowed the milk and went back to sleep. Three days later she opened her eyes, one blue, the other brown, and looked around.

They named her Aurora because Francis had come upon her in a gleaming dawn. When word come from Cape Race that after colliding with an iceberg, a White Star liner, the Titanic, *had sunk southeast of the island with most of its passengers aboard, Francis, thinking that the child might have been cast adrift before the ship went down, gave her particulars to the wireless operator at the Cape who sent them to the White Star office in New York.*

Merla had advised Francis to describe the child as being between one and a half and two years of age. Despite the youngster's size, she was fairly well along, being able to walk and talk, though until now it had been mostly gibberish. It was only reasonable to assume that a child so lovingly entrusted to the arms of the sea had parents, one or both of whom might have survived. There were bound to be grandparents, maybe sisters, brothers, cousins. A youngster as beautiful as this would certainly be claimed.

Father Murphy, the parish priest, placed a notice describing the child – approximate age, sex, appearance – in the St. John's Evening Herald *and requested that information be sent to J.T. Mulloy at Cape Race. Copies of the newspaper were stuffed into suitcases and satchels and carried on trains and ships as far as Montreal and New York where they collected dust in pastorates and libraries. Still, no one inquired about the child and she remained on the island of Newfoundland.*

Though the waters of the island were often filled with ice and its shores hidden in mist, it was not the fabled Vinland or the Island of the Blessed, and it was not newly found except perhaps to an Italian explorer. The island was so large that for centuries fishermen had made use of its shores without even encountering each other or seeing the red people who had sprung from arrows shot to the ground. The shoreline of the island went on at such length and in such a configuration of coves, inlets, harbours, tickles, bights and bays that it was possible for a child who had been rescued from the ice to grow and flourish in splendid isolation.

Mary Dalton

HEADLONG (A KIND OF ODE)
i.m. Al Pittman

Quick as a flanker,
he could mimic a
slouching insouciance.

But he burnt his candles at both ends.
And he burned fierce:
white heat of someone colliding into
the spinning planet.   Headlong
he tumbled into each moment –
the gravelly voice,
the rumbling authority,
the tremble beneath.
And dark laughter at Professor Pittfinck
and his parade of follies.

Headlong into the moment –
the rum and the river –
arms thrown open.
A warm-handed clasp against
Death and his solemn sidekicks,
Death and his dirty tricks.

RAVISHED

The old chrome chair holds her up
as a boat over the mystery of water,
its rubber-tipped legs lost in
the dizzying shift and sway beneath.
The hill-meadow is thick and teeming:
flame-spikes of the sorrel – feather and fire;
sun-clusters of hawkweed, buttercup;
pink-purples and creams of clover.
Timothy. Its small bulrush gesture
assents to the wind's choreography,
ignores the near season of mowing.

Metal, geometry, vinyl
are bearing her up; still
she is being drawn into
that riot, down into
the deeper reaches of the firmament:
the starry asterisks of the chickweed;
campanula, Lilliputian –
a miniature world that seethes,
that spins with laughter at
barren, at *bleak*,
at *I*, at *it*.
The hill readies to loose its seed,
broadcast its next year's assertions.
She is spilling out into
its tumble. Her brain a nest of bees.

She pulls back, all askew,
leaves the dazzle, the chair,
stumbles into the cool shaded house –
inside her the sun's glamour, part of
her gone, adrift over the meadow.
Drunk with the moth and the bee.

KITCHEN

Open the porch door.
When you enter,
her smile and the blast
from the woodstove
heat you –
to the marrow.

She brings the flowered plate,
the Christmas cake,
the gold-rimmed
glass of sherry.

Seal, pigeon,
buxom galleon
she slides her bulk
behind the table.

Twenty-five widows in this cove –
we get together and play cards.

She's had two offers,
one from the cabbage man;
he knocked one day,
took out a wad of money,
asked her if she'd marry him.

The other she didn't know at all –
he came to the door,
asked if she had cows to sell,
then – just like that –
she laughs, crinkles
at her remembered surprise –
asked if she'd marry him.

She shuffles the deck –
in the stove with a thud
a junk collapses into
the inferno beneath –
the air ripples, in waves of heat.

IN THE WIDE ROOM

In the wide room a radio is playing.
A woman in a blue cotton dress
Walks out on the verandah, down to the terrace,
In her hands a shawl and a bowl –
Or is it a gun and a book –
At this distance, in this light
It's impossible to say. She teeters

Slightly; perhaps the high heel of her shoe
Has caught in the crazed pattern of slate.
Even in this light her hair scintillates,
A drift of fire along her shoulders.
She tilts forward, as if she is reaching
Into the evening, alert for some
Sound about to ripple across the lake.

A small brindled terrier trots over towards her,
In its jaws a scrap of red paper.
The people on the bench watch intently –
Where will the poem go at this point:
Will the woman stop, bend down to the dog,
Fondle its whiskery little snout? Or
Will she shudder at the clue in its mouth?

The woman – let's call her Alba –
Starts for the slope at the back of the house.
A whale-gray plane in the lessening light.
She's shaking now, enough to drop the bowl.
Time slows – it takes forever, it seems,
To clatter onto the pathway of gravel.

Once it strikes the ground, there's a rattling
Of pages as they fall away from a spine.
White moths flutter up from it, pale confetti in motion.
Her face is chalk, a white of moon on the
Ice floes in March. The notes from the radio
Are softer now. There will be a crescendo
Eventually but not yet. The woman pauses, goes on.

The dog hurries after her. Together they climb
Away from the house, the watchers, the radio.
A thick grove of alders obscures them from view.
The woman has begun to sing, a clear low contralto:
If I were a blackbird I'd whistle and sing,
I'd follow the ship that my true love sails in.
Soon nothing but her voice, fading away in the dark.

On the top rigging I'd there build my nest
And I'd pillow my head on my fond lover's breast.
Those left below are restless, on edge. They turn
To each other, the air thick with questions unspoken. What was
It meant to mean: that radio, the dog, the woman,
Her song? And the slope? The alder grove? The vanishing?
Was it simply a trick of the light, a play of sound?

Kevin Hehir

REASONS TO CELEBRATE

Today is my birthday.
And I have reasons to celebrate.
If 40 is the new 30 or the new 20
Then I am a new man

New and improved.
Stays fresh longer
Econo-sized
Instant in store rebate
As seen on TV

Not like Paris Hilton but without the talent.
Not with the cultural depth of a Leah MacLaren column.

But another year older and deeper in doubt.

But I do believe in Honky Tonk Angels
In clown colours and leather boots
We were well launched at the Ship that night.
I met you in the strum and the twang.

Then we were
married by a gardener.

You were pregnant with a broken leg.
Knocked down then knocked up, you said.

Now the bump has been born

A new stocking by the chimney.
A new supergreat kid
Where in that second it takes to pull on a t-shirt
He tries to launch himself off the bed

Pull yourself up by my face
Reach your little hands into my nose
Open up your alphabet
get in touch with the inner alchemy of the word
Sing me your sound poems
Yayayayaynggheehakhjfi
Muma's at the MOMA and Dada's into Dada

And when they say,
Your father was a CFA
And, that's not a Newfoundland name

Invite them to your language toybox
And build bridges with words
Syntactical structures to walk over and play under.

Your very first library card.
Your very first steps.

You'll need to be handy with language, My son
You'll need to decode the signs
For sale signs. Signs of the times.

In this city where oil is the new cod
where City Hall's
not so civil servants
advertise from Signal Hilltops
"don't let building codes stop you.
Battery not included."

The developer's wetdream.
A confidence trick.
A figure of speech.
A letter to the editor.

An angry phone call.

If you are concerned about the loss of green space in the city
    press 1
If you believe that your call is important to us
You must be delusional.

So they keep us indoors.
With no sidewalks for strollers, the babies are kept at home.
The city becomes impassible. Impossible
For those with walkers and those learning to walk.
A city of shut-ins.
With nothing to do but read and breed.

A city of new parents.
An army of new fathers under the watchful eye of the womenfolk.
"Poor thing, needs his mother
Here, give him to me."
He's too hot. Too cold. Too quiet. Too loud.

We'll bring our babies to book launches
Take our toddlers to openings.
Dance in the grass of Bannerman Park.

What will our new city look like?
Where wonder? and what weight?

We must think outside of the big box store
The irresistible urge to imagine
The irrefutable power of dreams.

I see a city that is illuminated by pure creative energy.
The beams of a thousand children
Reaching over the city like Cabot Tower's star.

I have reasons to celebrate.
My city, my wife and my child.
Another year older and deeper in love.

LEXICON LAKE

After the dream this part comes. This part comes after the dream.
After the dream, this part. Part of why. Part of the head space where
you feel like a stranger in your own mind. Part of feeling like a lost
kite floating over indifferent suburbs. Over dog shit and swimming
pools. Down every street that has hosted a bicycle accident. Have
you been lifted out of a dream and allowed to watch yourself sleep?
Tracing the contours of your scars without making yourself flinch.
You remember a memory. A smell, an odour, a broken bottle of
cologne. It has soaked into the fabric. It will not leave you and you
will not ask it to leave. It leaked in to your dream this morning and
it has remained all day. Floating like a question afraid of the wrong
answer, you are tentative. If you close your eyes in your sleep will
vision become visions? Bring your arms in tight and feel the speed.
Swoop down. Spiral out. Fast. Are you terrified? *I love it.* Slip in to
the wind. Trapped in an alphabetic labyrinth like swimming in
language. The lexicon lake. Call out and listen for: Stroke. Stroke.
Stroke. Sink. Think your way out of it. Get higher. Let evocative
notions be your guide to awareness. Emotions like motions owe
prayers to the source. Seek out. Wear trust like a blanket knit by the
woman who raised your favourite uncle. Wrapped up in wonder.
Feel yourself as if stitched into a seam, simultaneously in and out. In
and out of control. Is there control? Are there elastic bands glued to
your teeth that snap your jaws shut when you scream? Is there a
wooden broom handle behind your elbows causing you to stumble
when you run? Don't fall. *But I'm flying*, you remember. Does this
part come after the dream? After this part comes the dream.

NOW THAT YOU ARE LIVING
for al pittman

my god my god why have you forsaken me
  matthews jesus

now that you are living
with the poets who are dead
the ones you would complain about
who they always teach in schools

i imagine you in heaven
in your favourite heavenly bar
waited upon by angel barmaids
who love you as they do on earth

you are talking to god   telling him
to get the fuck out of the universe and leave
the earth alone
especially newfoundland

you blame him for the garden of eden and the great flood
taxes poverty war and death
resettlement the fishery and joey smallwood
beaumont hamel and the massacre of the beothuck

all the darkest nightmares
our lives have ever known

god listens to you with the equanimity of a mountain
and the calmness of a mirrored lake   he lays back
with his hands behind his head and leans on a galaxy
too far away to have a name

he rests his feet upon a star that collapsed
so long ago its light will never reach the earth
and no one will ever know
it happened

he takes your cigarette and draws on it
slowly   for what seems like an eternity

then he blows smoke deep
into the emptiness of space and burns
another billion stars into the illusion of
the night sky that will always be above us

al my son he says with a smile
on his face like the moon   as he shrugs
his shoulders only the way you can
all this   over an apple   a woman   and a man

YOU AIM TO LOVE

summer solstice
                the thin white line
                around her suntanned hips

her mind changed
                in the ocean breeze
                dragonflies rustle

touching her sunburnt breast   robin song

she gives me her tongue   waterfall

after love
      her heartbeat
   summer rain

      she combs my hair
with her hands
            mist among the trees

      naked she rises
out of the lake   the moon
            in her hair

   cool night
                  the heat
from her sunburnt legs

dawn window
                  sunlight in the shape
                  of her body

autumn begins
            after making love
      her nose still cold

in her sleep
she whispers a name
                  night deepens

too angry to speak
            a chainsaw rips through
the frost filled air

spring morning
            still the cold touch
            of her wedding ring

we say we're sorry
            the easter lily begins
                                    to open
            we talk of our past
she picks wax from the candlestick
            burns it in the flame

            starfall
            she holds my hand
more firmly

after love
a faint smell of burning wax
from the candle's flame

she raises the hem
of her new dress
            the day now longer

Michael Ondaatje

TO A SAD DAUGHTER

All night long the hockey pictures
gaze down at you
sleeping in your tracksuit.
Belligerent goalies are your ideal.
Threats of being traded
cuts and wounds
– all this pleases you.
O my god! you say at breakfast
reading the sports page over the Alpen
as another player breaks his ankle
or assaults the coach.

When I thought of daughters
I wasn't expecting this
but I like this more.
I like all your faults
even your purple moods
when you retreat from everyone
to sit in bed under a quilt.
And when I say 'like'
I mean of course 'love'
but that embarrasses you.
You who feel superior to black and white movies
(coaxed for hours to see *Casablanca*)
though you were moved
by *Creature from the Black Lagoon*.

One day I'll come swimming
beside your ship or someone will
and if you hear the siren
listen to it. For if you close your ears
only nothing happens. You will never change.

I don't care if you risk
your life to angry goalies
creatures with webbed feet.
You can enter their caves and castles
their glass laboratories. Just
don't be fooled by anyone but yourself.

This is the first lecture I've given you.
You're 'sweet sixteen' you said.
I'd rather be your closest friend
than your father. I'm not good at advice
you know that, but ride
the ceremonies
until they grow dark.

Sometimes you are so busy
discovering your friends
I ache with a loss
– but that is greed.
And sometimes I've gone
into *my* purple world
and lost you.

One afternoon I stepped
into your room. You were sitting
at the desk where I now write this.
Forsythia outside the window
and sun spilled over you
like a thick yellow miracle
as if another planet
was coaxing you out of the house
– all those possible worlds! –
and you, meanwhile, busy with mathematics.

I cannot look at forsythia now
without loss, or joy for you.
You step delicately
into the wild world
and your real prize will be
the frantic search.
Want everything. If you break
break going out not in.
How you live your life I don't care
but I'll sell my arms for you,
hold your secrets for ever.

If I speak of death
which you fear now, greatly,
it is without answers,
except that each
one we know is
in our blood.
Don't recall graves.
Memory is permanent.
Remember the afternoon's
yellow suburban annunciation.
Your goalie
in his frightening mask
dreams perhaps
of gentleness.

THE GREAT TREE

"Zou Fulei died like a dragon breaking down a wall...

this line composed and ribboned
in cursive script
by his friend the poet Yang Weizhen

whose father built a library
surrounded by hundreds of plum trees

It was Zou Fulei, almost unknown,
who made the best plum flower painting
of any period

One branch lifted into the wind

and his friend's vertical line of character

their tones of ink
– wet to opaque
dark to pale

each sweep and gesture
trained and various
echoing the other's art

In the high plum-surrounded library
where Yang Weizhen studied as a boy

a moveable staircase was pulled away
to ensure his solitary concentration

His great work
"untrammelled" "eccentric" "unorthodox"
"no taint of the superficial"
    "no flamboyant movement"

34

using at times the lifted tails
of archaic script,

sharing with Zou Fulei
his leaps and darknesses

*

"So I have always held you in my heart...

The great 14th-century poet calligrapher
mourns the death of his friend

Language attacks the paper from the air

There is only a path of blossoms

no flamboyant movement

A night of smoky ink in 1361
a night without a staircase

Al Pittman

WEST MOON

In all the dark world there is no darkness like the dark of an outport night. Here on the coast of Newfoundland, darkness comes in all seasons as sudden as sudden death, comes coasting unannounced from its hideaway over the hills, sweeps silently down upon the seaside settlement of St. Kevin's, and covers the quicksilver, looking-glass sea like a shroud thrown from the sky to fall on the face of the funeral earth.

No human eyes can pierce the eternal darkness as it lies like death upon the dead village. And in St. Kevin's now, this November All Souls' Night, there are no human eyes alive and shining where once, not too dark a time ago, fishermen returning from their dreams upon the sea could see with blazing eyes the firebrands waving the way for livyers moving from house to house upon the hills, their bright kitchen visits over for the night, as they blinked their way, with caution, curses and prayers, home to their wide-awake beds.

Tonight, with no human eyes to see them, the only fires alive are the fires in the eyes of the animals as they go about their animal business in the dead dark, in a wilderness of ruins.

The sleek otter gliding over the cold stones in Middle Brook, a quiet gurgle splitting the village in two as it runs unseen down from the warm wooded hills, leaps at a quick spark of silver somewhere in the sound of the brook, and comes up with a tiny otter-appetizer of sparkling brook trout.

The rabbit, running erratically down the grass-grown road to or away from God-knows-what, stops suddenly at the grey decayed gate on the edge of Jack Leonard's hayfield, perceives some rabbit threat in the black breeze, and leaps – a silent flash of fur swallowed by the meadow in one grassy gulp.

A forlorn fox laps at the chill water of the spring at the foot of the scrape behind the cathedral ruins of Bill Sullivan's house and, by the light of his eyes, sees his amazed self in the gun-metal gleam of the pool. One look is enough, and away he races to the shelter of the woods pursued by his own vicious image of himself.

In Chapel Pond the arrogant frogs croak their solemn sermons to the night as the trout doze irreverently, a faithless congregation heeding only the dreams they inhabit as they lie suspended in sleep among the lily pads.

On the beach below the old beach road (below the grey-green skeletons of stages and stores standing like amphibian invaders from worlds beneath the sea, their crooked strouter legs wading in the shallows, their grotesque headless torsos thrust lumbering in the air) a million crabs crawl lopsided over the rocks rolled round and smooth by a million years of wave break, swish and roll.

In the graveyard below the waterfall of Ladore the mice run hunting or playing hide-n-seek among the headstones which announce mutely to the living night all that matters concerning the dead decayed lives of those buried in the sinking soil below.

LUPINES
for Frieda

Across the ditch by the graveyard fence
a groundbound rainbow of purple and pink.

Triumphant yesterday in the Trinity Bay sun.
Courageously upright today
in this day's torrential downpour.

I come upon them suddenly
at a quick twist in the twisted road.
Whatever the weather, they are here
this summer season like a bright ribbon
of light, not quite, but almost
out of sight.

Behind and above them, sleeping deep
in the rainsoaked earth, the dead rest
deep in peace.

Below, the waves wash
in their eternal turn upon
the Goose Cove shore.

Making my way to Trinity
in this morning's morning deluge
(soaked to the skin and bereft of love)
I would tip my hat to the trinity
of the sea, the dear departed
and the lupines blooming between.

I don't happen to have a hat on my head
but I do wear a prayer in my heart.

I make a secret Sign of the Cross
and say silently inside to the one god
who doesn't believe in me, "God bless
the long and just gone dead, the sullen
slate-grey sea, and especially (now)
I pray, please bless the lupines blooming there
upright (purple, pink) and right as rain.

ATLANTIS

Now at run-off time
the river sleeps deep
in the dark woods, drowning
in its depths my daughters'
fond places. Fish swim
in paths they danced along
last summer. Eels swarm
where they played out
the truths of their childhood.

A week from now, the river
will be back in its own bed.
The paths and clearings
in the woods will sprout
new grass and curled ferns.
My girls will be there
as lovely and familiar
as flowers.

Today their deep wooded world
is the haunt of gilled things.
Because they know every twist
and turn of season here, they
are not disturbed by this.
They play at the water's edge
and wait patiently, with love,
for the turning world to give
them back their little lost
Atlantis.

HER PORTRAIT OF ME

Until today
I'd been nothing more
than a lovable scribble
that's you daddy
that's you she'd say
quite certain that I'd never know otherwise
today however without any fuss
she drew me with a head
and two bulging eyes
a splash of a nose
a lopsided mouth
and whiskers going every which way
and when she was finished
made no announcement of any kind
but slyly left it lying around
where I'd have to see it
while she waited nearby
ready to measure my reaction
not quite sure I'd find it
as pleasing a portrait
as the scribbles she had grown to realize
I loved

FINAL FAREWELL

This final farewell
might be as a moth's wings
melting in candle wax.
A reservoir of lava fossilizing
fragments of burnt membrane.
The disintegration of flight.

Or it might be as the death of lilacs
clinging to the end of their own scent
as they go colour-blind out there
on the sunlit, rainswept, windblown tips
of their tombstone twigs.
The grey branches as cold as granite.

Or it might be nothing as neutral
as either of these. The dead-end flight
toward light. The quiet decay of purple.

It may be a denial of death
and downfall. A defiant dedication
to light, flight, bloom, and blossom.
A benediction of being.

Or for the moth, the lilacs, and
for our love, all this may be nothing other
than an end. Where
at the end of things
everything else begins.

THE March Hare

A celebration of words and music

The
Columbus
Club

8 p.m.,
Saturday,
March 8, 1997

admission at the door only $ 5.00 Adults
                              $ 3.00 Students
(Includes March Hare intermission soup, etc.)   Cash Bar

*"When the sun and the tide
were the keepers of time"* | TWO

Sheldon McBreairty

JABBERWOCK ENVY
On the occasion of the 4th annual March Hare, 2005
(Gander Jabberwock), Gander, NL

I envy them
this night,
their patience,
their pain,
their snow falling,
their letters burning,
their view of the cove.

I envy them
this night,
their courage,
their memories,
their cards on the table,
their journeys for a word,
their gracious surrender.

I envy them
this night,
their longings,
their doubtings,
their days on the islands,
their houses at road's end,
their buttering of toast.

I envy them
this night,
their confessions,
their pardons,
their rendering of excess,

their parsing of pretense,
their rocking chair evenings.

I envy them
this night,
their colors,
their canvas,
their strokes in the air
their theft of the moment
their payment in full.

David J. Shaw

BEACHCOMBING
for Sarah and Jeremy

Hand in hand we walk across the timeless sand that lines the shore.
Child of my child, blood of my blood. Teacher and pupil. Both in
wonder stroll.
Picking. Turning. Pulling. Examining. Selecting. Discarding. Saving
the treasures.
What is this? Where did it come from? How did it get here? Is it any
good? Can I keep it?
From three to thirteen and beyond, we walk and share this precious
time.
One with a view to infinity. The other glad of heart to see the
horizon.
One thinking this will always be. The other knowing it will not.
Dreading the time when he can't. Or worse, when the other won't.

Bill Butt

KEEPERS OF TIME

He rests on the bank as he looks 'cross the bay
The chores gone undone will await a new day
While he ponders his plans, he goes back in his mind
When the sun and the tide were the keepers of time

His work keeps him busy from the spring until fall
And he takes time to talk when friends come to call
And the children delight in the stories he tells
Of ghosts and of shipwrecks, of lights and ship's bells

He has scores of plans for the things that he'll do
Never pausing to think that his years may be few
He's had a good life, few regrets has he known
But again to tell stories to kids of his own

Those things done as boys bring a gleam to his eye
Giving way to a tear as he silently cries
For each of those memories that runs through his mind
Recalls an old friend who's slipped over the line

He rests on the bank as he looks 'cross the bay
The chores gone undone will await a new day
While he ponders his plans, he goes back in his mind
When the sun and the tide were the keepers of time

He recalls his grandfather from when he was a boy
And the legends of old that were told with such joy
When the old harbour witches were sketched upon rocks
And their spells quickly broken with a muzzle-load shot

His big, calloused hands tell their own kind of tales
Of the hauling of lines and the punching of gales
But such hands will no more mark a man and his trade
In the modern-day world, few things are hand-made

A call from the porch brings him back from his thoughts
Just a short hesitation and he climbs o'er the rocks
And he makes his way back to the love of his life
Through thick and through thin, through good times and strife

She can tell he's been thinking, it's a look that she knows
So she smiles and she pours him live tea from the stove
It's so funny, he says, how the time slips away
Whether over a lifetime or just in one day

> When he rests on the bank, he looks 'cross the bay
> The chores gone undone will await a new day
> While he ponders his plans, he goes back in his mind
> When the sun and the tide were the keepers of time

Isabel Blackmore

Tongues and Common Sense

Somewhere there exists a well turned-out young man who has by now attained a full measure of success and perhaps renown. This I know although I but once had occasion to make his acquaintance, not so long ago, but before the cod moratorium, before roller blades, baggy duds and reversed baseball caps became the status symbols of youth.

On that day, the seven- and the ten-year-old perched on my front step, unabashedly taking stock of each other, verbally sparring in the manner of many young fellas on first acquaintance. Chad, the town child, owned the sporty MX which lay in the driveway facing us, while Neddie the visitor had been pleased to use my bike, a relic of a kind that could only belong to a sixty-something matron.

Neddie wore long unfashionably pressed pants and his hair was combed and parted, the very model of a proper outport lad making his annual visit to town relatives; it had been established that he lived at home with his Nannie.

"Got a bike home?" Chad was getting in the first oar.

"Yeah, but it's a old one. Gettin' a new one, though, gettin' a big one, bigger 'n yours"; then with the slightest suggestion of bravado, "mine's gonna be the biggest one ye can git."

"What kind?" So far the new MX had been the envy of the neighborhood, and Chad in his baseball cap and Hawaiian shorts had enjoyed much prestige and envy, circling the block on his latest model wonder, bedecked as it was with flashers, buzzers, lights and horn. "What kind?"

"Don't know yet. Best one I can git."

"Who's gonna buy it for ya? You don't have no Dad."

"Nobody. Gonna buy it meself."

"How? You got lots of money?" In obvious disbelief, Chad glanced at the out-of-place dark pants, the plain leather shoes. Clearly he had come across an odd breed of creature, surely one to be reckoned with. New interest lighting up his freckled face, he prodded, "How?"

"Gonna make it, b'y. Cuttin' out cod-tongues." (What else? he seemed to imply.)

Now, then! Chad's jaw dropped. He could see that this was no joke, though, so with a let's-get-this-straight look, he moved closer to the strange specimen.

"CUTTIN' OUT COD'S TONGUES??"...each word a loaded question mark.

Nonplused, Neddie replied, "Yes, b'y; we gits dollar seventy-five pound fer 'em. Last year we on'y got dollar and a haff. Made a hunnerd dollars all same." Warming to a subject he could relate to and perhaps expecting a little more interest from someone more worldly than this greenhorn, he turned to me and went on, "Fishin's not so good the year though, water's too cold. All the same, when the boats come in we makes lots of money cuttin'. I got a hunnerd dollars sove and I'm gonna buy meself a new bike when I gets enough." He was cool and matter-of-fact, and even I was a little abashed in the face of such implacable confidence.

The younger lad was certainly at a loss for words, perhaps struggling with the concept of an alien world where boys without doting dads made money on their own and bought flashy bikes for themselves; where by some barbaric process he had never associated with any fish he had ever eaten, out on the wharves of busy fishermen, boys could be a part of the process and learn to talk the talk of fishermen.

"Gee," he almost whispered, "do cods have real tongues?"

Some dumb remarks don't merit answers.

"How do you do it?" he prodded.

"Fish knife." (Simple!)

Again, a little suspicion. "Are you 'lowed to have a knife?"

"Course, b'y, you gotta have that." There was pure disdain in his words.

Now, then, this was getting out of hand. "How do you do it?" And Chad visibly braced himself for what he feared was coming.

Neddie at last was in his element. With the fine flair of a dab-hand cutter and using all the appropriate sound effects he slashed the air this way and that in clear demonstration of a job well understood and executed...no amateur, he.

Chad was duly impressed and, if I'm not off the mark, a little shaken. After a considerable pause, his only comment: "Yuk." Product of another civilization, the only contact he had ever had with a cod was a tasty fillet served to him on a dinner plate, often crisp with golden fries. That such a thing would have had a...tongue...which somewhere between the ocean and his plate would be yanked out, was not welcome news. He actually paled so his freckles stood out. But he had to be sure. "Is THAT what cod tongues are?"

Neddie declined to answer. He rose, tired of all this foolishness. He looked at the city slicker as if to say, "what a stunned one you are, at all!" Then he picked up the rusty bike and once again rattled off, his long trousered legs and straight back describing a young fellow well on the way to the top. He looked over his square shoulder and thanked me for the use of my bike. "I'll have her back directly," he called.

The younger lad in his cool duds picked up the MX and with considerably less panache than before pumped away too, calling out for the benefit of all, "Me and my dad's goin' fishin' soon!"

Yes, somewhere, I suspect, Neddie is doing quite well.

Tony Collins

DISQUALIFIED

Like a lot of Newfoundlanders with a rural background, my friend Hayward seems to be able to do just about anything he sets his mind to.

While the rest of us mere mortals deem ourselves lucky to possess one marketable skill, Hayward is blessed with an aptitude for everything, whether that be installing kitchen cabinets, paunching a moose, or rebuilding an engine and not ending up with a box full of leftover parts.

Hayward didn't go to university or what used to be called the trade school. In high school his teachers all said he lacked ambition, an opinion with which Hayward was in complete agreement.

You see, Hayward figured he didn't need ambition, considering he was already happy living where he was, and was more than capable of doing the things that had to be done, like building his own house, fixing his own car, and growing vegetables to get himself and his family through the winter.

Among his many talents, Hayward has an amazing gift for coming up with the simplest possible solution to virtually every problem. It's what's referred to as Occam's Razor, whereby all unnecessary facts or constituents in the subject being analyzed are to be eliminated. Hayward does that almost instinctively and quite nonchalantly, as if the right answer should be perfectly obvious to everyone else as well – which it isn't.

One of the questions the computer software giant, Microsoft, asks of its prospective employees is why manhole covers are round. It's supposed to test intuitive thinking and the ability to reason logically.

52

Hayward didn't need to think about it. As far as he was concerned the answer was as plain as the nose on his face.

"Well, b'y," he responded immediately, "if they were square they could fall down the hole and land on your head."

I didn't tell him I'd spent the better part of an afternoon wracking my brains trying to come up with the answer.

The other day I sought Hayward's advice on how best to fix an old ping pong table I had lying around in the basement. The wooden table top fits down into a metal frame but most of the screws holding it in place had come loose or fallen out altogether. For the life of me, I couldn't figure out any way of repairing it short of buying a whole new top, at considerable expense.

He thought about it for 30 seconds.

"Why don't you just drill new holes?" he asked. "Shouldn't cost more than a dollar or two for a few new screws."

Eureka!

Hayward built a cabin up in the woods a while ago. He cut all his own logs and had them sawed on the halves. He was most of the summer getting the frame and roof up, in between working on an Employment Insurance top-up project, fibre glassing his boat, wiring his next door neighbour's house, paving his driveway with second-hand asphalt he'd scrounged off the highways department, and putting a new motor in his Dodge pickup.

Hayward also does his own painting and plastering, and can wield a chainsaw with the dexterity and finesse of a surgeon. His skills as a plumber are legendary, and on occasion he's been known to try his hand at welding. At the moment he's busy refinishing some chairs for his wife, and the volunteer fire brigade wants him to do some renovations down at the hall (on a volunteer basis, of course). He told them he can't do anything until after he gets his moose, which may not be any time soon, seeing as how he's got a bull-only licence for Area 23.

Before the moratorium Hayward used to fish with his two brothers. They built their own longliner and after the trap voyage was over they'd go handling and jigging on the Offer Banks. Usually they'd make enough money to see them through until early spring, when the seal hunt started up. Hayward's a crack shot with a rifle and can skulp out a seal in under five minutes.

Hayward also knows which way is north, and when the rabbits are starting to change colour, how to castrate a pig (an art in itself), where to find the best berries, and exactly what to do in any and all emergencies. And when his children were smaller he used to make up little poems for them, every night before they went to bed.

When his youngest brother was killed in a car accident up in Alberta last year, Hayward delivered the eulogy.

Yup...Hayward can do just about everything. The only thing he hasn't been able to do lately is find a job.

They say he lacks the necessary qualifications.

MELVIN – ANOTHER TALE
FROM NORTH HARBOUR

Part I

Melvin left the two-room school at North Harbour in grade eight. He wasn't kicked out, he just gave it up. He quit. I don't know how old he was. I just remember that he was older than the rest of us because he had failed a few grades along the way and had to do them over again, so the rest of us caught up with Melvin.

The teacher considered him to be a "slow learner" and a bit of a "hard case" – someone who would never make it in the higher grades. For the rest of us in the classroom – from grade six to eleven – he was pure genius entertainment and we knew we would miss him a lot when he left.

For us, Melvin was half the fun of going to school. He was different. He was tall and lanky with a full head of black curly hair like Bunga of the Congo in the grade four geography book. His teeth were half black, he had a slight stoppage in his speech, and bunions on his feet from walking the two miles to school from his house on the other side of Goose Cove. He was a fierce fella for bologna and for cocoa. We made fun of him everyday and he made fun of us and everyone else; teachers, preachers, shopkeepers, neighbors and strangers.

We would try to tease him with such things as his mother Jenny might say to him while sending him out the door to walk his two miles to school – "Drink your cocoa tea, Melvin, and eat your bologna meat, you can't walk very fast with those bunions on your feet." Melvin's response was always quick and something like "Go on ye young fellows is still shittin yella."

He taunted the teacher with his answers to their exam questions. In grade six geography, in response to the question "What do you understand by 'the rotation of crops'," Melvin wrote "I understand nothing by the rotation of crops." In history when asked "Who was Pontiac?" Melvin replied – "That's Roy Gilbert's new car."

But he loved literature and could retell any story in exact detail and recite any poem in its exact entirety. His favorite poem was John Gilpin – forty-two verses long. "John Gilpin was a ci ci citizen of credit and renown. A famed band captain eke was he of famous London Town." Ask him to start a poem, a story or a ballad and he just wouldn't stop til the end.

Melvin's love of stories, rhymes and songs kept us entertained well beyond the classroom antics. On Friday nights, young fellas and girls would walk in around the bottom of Goose Cove and sit on the wooden rails on the Nook bridge and listen to Melvin. He knew every Pat and Mike joke on the go, every rhyme ever written on a shithouse wall and songs we never heard on the radio. He would sing "Quare Bunga Rye" and "The Pub with No Beer" to us young fellas who didn't even know what a pub was.

Melvin had an amazing ability to totally transform popular country songs played on the radio by changing just a few words – like heartache to hard on, lonely to horny and heart to arse. To our juvenile minds, this was hilarious, and is still to my still juvenile mind, when I think of him launching such new hit songs as "I'm in the middle of a hard on – half out – half in," or "How can I write on paper what I feel in my arse."

Melvin lived next door to the Gilberts, a large extended family headed by the patriarch – Albert Gilbert – known as Ab – who never worked because he claimed to have a bad arm. Ab would say "Melvin b'y, the arm is some bad today. I can't get en above me shoulder. Now yesterday, I could get en right above me head, way up there," lifting and waving his arm above his head. Ab always said he would have been rich if that Englishman looking for the relatives of Sir Humphrey Gilbert hadn't turned around at Come-by-Chance and come no further. Melvin, having listened to Ab's lies most of his life and watched Ab's wife and family get into many colorful schemes and rackets, sat down one day and composed the Gilbert alphabet. It included the entire Gilbert clan and anybody they had anything to do with.

A is for Ab with the pain in his arm
B is for Bill, was the brother of Darm
C is for Car, they all liked to use, and
D is for Don who goes on the booze

I used to know all of it at one time, but my memory has faded as the Gilberts have faded.

When the resettlement program started, the new people who moved from the Islands and western side of Placentia Bay to North Harbour hauled their houses up into the meadows and gardens around Melvin's house and became new neighbors for Melvin, his mother and father and his brothers and sister, Ivy, who happened to be married to a man known as the Anglican sinner, because he wasn't of the Pentecostal faith.

One Friday, there was a great scandal in the harbour when one of the newly established fishermen from Port Anne – a married man himself – ran off with sister Ivy to his brother's place in Baine Harbour. The scandalous news went on for days until the man's employment cheque ran out and he had to come home to fill out a new form.

When asked what he thought of all this, Melvin replied "Ivy had it too good, that's all. She had everything from a baby fart to a clap of thunder."

After that, Melvin gave it all up, left North Harbour and took off for Toronto, like so many Newfoundlanders at that time. He got a job taxi-driving in Toronto where he met a woman from Trinity Bay and started having youngsters. He always said he only made enough money to pay his traffic tickets so after a couple of years he gave it up and came home and moved into his father's house with his new wife, Annie, and his new youngsters.

They were building the oil refinery at Come-by-Chance at that time and Melvin was determined to get a job. He went into St. John's to see the Premier, Frank Moores. Melvin had no appointment with the Premier but waited all day to see Mr. Moores outside his office. Moores finally agreed to meet this determined fellow at the end of the day. "Well, young man, what can I do for you." Moores said. Melvin replied "You got to get me a job at Come-by-Chance, sir."

"Why should I help you get a job any more than any other man, Melvin?"

"Well sir, I got a crowd of youngsters and the big ones are starting to eat the little ones." Frank Moores actually got him a job at Come-by-Chance and he worked there til the oil refinery was built and stayed on until she closed down for the first time after the big Japanese bankruptcy.

Melvin, like many of his fellow laid-off workers, then took off for Western Canada and found work digging the Tar Sands at Fort McMurray in Northern Alberta. He has been there ever since. I haven't seen him since he left North Harbour but I still miss him and I think of him often.

Part II

At a reception at an International Mining Conference in Toronto at the Royal York Hotel, I once met the Director of Human Resources for Syncrude – a stunning Norwegian woman called Kjersti. I thought she was beautiful; she thought I was interesting. When she learned I was from Newfoundland, she became more interested and started telling me what great workers the Newfoundlanders are and how Syncrude could not possibly have built the Alberta Tar Sands Project without them. "I really like the way the Newfoundlanders talk," she said, "how they interact with each other in such a jovial manner. They remind me of my own people in Northern Norway where I grew up; they make me homesick. To me, they are hardly like Canadians at all."

At that moment, I knew two things. I loved this woman; and I wanted Des Walsh here to witness this.

I took a chance on it. "Did you ever meet a Newfoundlander called Melvin Stacey?" I asked. "He's from my home."

"Why, yes I did" she answered. "He's one of our best employees, certainly our best drag line operator – you know these super long excavators that cost millions."

"What would a guy like that make?" I asked.

"Oh he'd make about ninety-five thousand a year with overtime. He works lots of overtime because he's so reliable. When we have serious difficulties in our operations, we always call Melvin."

"Not a slow learner." I said.

"No, no, not at all," she said. "And the reason I remember him most is that, over the years, his sons and daughters have won all our company scholarships. Melvin would always come to the awards ceremonies. That's really how I got to know him. Most of his children have now left and gone on to university. One of his sons is particularly brilliant and winning many academic awards at the University of Alberta. But I remember them all as such fine young men and women."

"Good thing the big ones didn't eat the little ones." I said.

"You said Melvin is from your home. You should really come to Fort McMurray and visit him and see our operations."

"Thank you." I said. "I'd love to do just that."

Because I can't remember who comes after Roy in the Gilbert Alphabet; but I do remember that

> A is for Ab with the pain in his arm,
> B is for Bill, was the brother of Darm,
> C is for car, they all liked to use, and
> D is for Don, who went on the booze.

Don Downer

from
LAST NAIL

Sitting alone at the large bare table, Fonnie looked around in wonder that it had finally come down to this. After today, he would not come back and Sandy Point would be left to the piping plovers, the black-headed gulls and the dolphins, to the sand dunes with their blackened saltmarsh grasses, to the wind and to the sea.

He pushed back the wooden straight-backed chair and stood up. He was not a tall man, but there was good health and vitality in his big frame. He looked around the room and out to the back-kitchen door. There, two battered suitcases sat. These contained the last earthly possessions that he and his mother would take from the island.

He called to Mrs. Swyer who was resting in her upstairs bedroom.

"It's time, mother."

"For what, Fonnie? Where are we goin'?"

"Leavin.'"

He could hear her shuffling around upstairs.

"Should I take my good coat, Fonnie?"

"Yes, mother, take everthing."

"Where's my suitcase, Fonnie...have you seen my suitcase?"

He listened for her heavy unsteady walk from the doorway of her room. She paused. Her breathing was laboured. Should he go to help?

"Fonnie, have you closed the wood shed door? Might be stormy before we gets back."

"Yes, mother."

She faced him in the doorway leading from the foot of the stairs.

"Tink them stairs gettin' steeper."

He helped her on with her sweater. She walked out the back door, a large black handbag held in the crook of her right arm.

"Fonnie, have you seen my good black gloves?"

60

"They're here, mother. Right here."

He handed her the gloves and then held her arm as she walked slowly down the path to the stage. She tentatively put one foot ahead of the other on the narrow wooden walkway. A small skiff was tied up at the old wharf. Mrs. Swyer stopped at the head of the wharf.

"Fonnie, did you take my good pot?"

"Yes, mother."

"And the suitcase?"

"I'll bring it, mother."

She took one quick look around, stepped into the boat and stared out over the bay.

Fonnie picked up a hammer and a handful of four-inch nails. After he had lifted the suitcases through the doorway, he turned and nailed the door shut putting a nail in the top and bottom corners. He then placed wooden shutters on the two remaining windows on the ground floor. The shutters fitted well and he nailed these tightly with nails in the corners and sides. As he did so, he muttered under his breath about the futility of doing such a thing, since anyone wishing to break into the wooden structure could easily do so with the help of nothing more than a crowbar and a hammer. That had happened already to several other abandoned houses in the community.

After these chores were completed, he turned towards the boat moored and loaded down at the wharf. His mother sat patiently. Fonnie jumped in and threw the fly wheel of the small gasoline motor. It caught and propelled the skiff forward. Fonnie and his mother turned their backs on their world and steamed towards the mainland.

The Swyers were the last to move from Sandy Point. They moved at the urging of relatives in the United States who feared for their safety. They settled across the harbour at Barachois Brook, where Mrs. Swyer died shortly after their arrival.

Larry Small

THE BAY FROM LONG POINT

Families climbed the cliffs in June
To watch the schooners round Cape John,
But now, no schooners sing the song of fish.
The southwest wind blows down from Fridays Bay
But finds no trapmen on the grounds,
The berths without their moorings,
Their names vanishing from the lexicon.
The Old Sow weeps
While Western Head stands vigil
To the sea and ice.
And what about the winds...
Are they lonely now
Since those who knew the nuance
Of every breeze
Have shipped into another life?
Who will be a soulmate to the wind
And who will give benediction
To the Bay?

CHRISTMAS

Christmas is only five days old
And I am already lonely.
The earth has new snow.
The sky,
Patches of white and blue,
Sending shades of light on hills
That are not mine.
But it is in the language of
Light and darkness on the landscape
That I look for the symbols of solitude
That once made all days special,
Especially Christmas.
The men and women who gave meaning
To the season
Have vacated their homesteads
In search of the final solitude;
Their houses fading from the landscape
Or filled with strangers.
I have no place to go.
I am left with my memories,
Telling stories to men and women
Who do not know my people.

Stan Dragland

COME ALL YE

Agnes and I were talking – this was in Coffee and Company – we'd
been talking about the great holes in our lives and Ag had said
"sometimes I just stand in the middle of my living room and I look
up and say 'Dear God, is this it? Am I going to be alone for the rest
of my days?'" And we went on to talking about the need for
solitude we share (Ag calls it "aloneness" in one of her poems), the
deep need to look about us and think and wonder and write, so I
said, "You know, Ag, I always have lots going on in my mind.
I'm always having a relationship with myself, a stormy one at that,
positively tempestuous, and sometimes the commotion gives me the
impresssion that I'm carrying on a relationship with someone else."
I was just trying to tell her how things look now, what I might as well
face up to (absent while present, driven: bad risk as a partner), but Ag
laughed and laughed. "You'd better write that," she said. "I'll steal it
if you don't." Go ahead, Ag, and welcome. Your version won't look
like this.

And Agnes said to her therapist, who was really not grasping the
problem, she said, "You can look out your window at the beautiful
snow falling there, and just enjoy it, can't you?" "Yes," he said.
"Well," said Ag, "I can't ever look at that beautiful snow without
having to search and search for words. I have to write it down." And
he looked at her funny. Which gave her serious doubts. Was he the
therapist for her? Which of course made me chuckle. You'd better
write that or else I will, I should have said. But of course I'm a dab
hand at keeping things to myself.

I'm writing myself into Ag's life for love of her and her writing.
It won't help to fill the abyss that sometimes has me standing
supplicant in my own living room. Might as well face up to it: that

64

hole can't be filled. It's not only the struggle to find satisfactory words for that wondrous blizzard raging out there, it's knowing that those words *always* lead to others. It's a path. It's the way – now I wasn't expecting this – it's the road to market with the scrawny cow, and it's selling the beast, hell, *giving* her away to the flim-flam man for a handful of beans, which is absolutely the last straw for mother, who fires the goddamn beans out the window. Scarlet Runners. I have a thing for Scarlet Runner beans. Anyway, this is a very low point in seriously disadvantaged lives, so very low indeed that recriminations ensue. How under blistering heaven could you be such a dunderhead! How could you be such a perishing dolt! Losing poor old Bossy for a bloody handful of bloody beans!

But but but. Here comes the turn. Now it's the morning after the night of despair and something is different about the kitchen today. It's that chlorophyllic light filtered through the thick green stalk grown up the side of the house, the stalk you shinny up until – your sentence taking an unexpected jog, as if somebody grabbed aholt the verb and snapped a kink in it – your head pushes through the clouds and everything you've known and everything you've been – realigns. You can almost hear the click. How familiar it is up here – solid rock and grass and blue sky and cloud, though yet no wondering what might be discovered up there if ever the means, the beans, were found to lift you to it – how familiar and how very different. And you're moving forward now, moving on alone.

Come all ye bold heroes
Lend an ear to my song...

*

Come all ye fair and tender maidens...

*

Come all ye damsels past your prime
with holes in your lives to fill...

s'w'M, old enough to know better, well, just plain old and still no better than a fool, decrepit in mind and creaky of body but not quite dashed in spirit, seeks SF between the ages of 20 and 80, high romantic with proportionate sense of irony, for "quiet times" (meaning let us infiltrate and suffuse each others' lives but hold the speech, please, while in silence I gaze out the window at the snow and blowing snow so insistently calling to the blizzard within). Unless I'm completely wrong. I have been wrong before. Yes, the window is also a mirror and now it's not the storm I'm seeing, but *her*, in reflection, and a queue of conversational subjects begins to form, and ardently I turn to her. Let the storm rage to itself tonight. "You know," I begin, and she raises her eyes, "you know, I've been remembering the first time I walked up to an automatic door and it opened. This was in Great Falls, Montana, when I was just a kid. Well, I was astonished. I couldn't believe it. I had to back up and go again, make sure it was opening for me. And I wanted to tell you, love, there are days even now when I feel so full, you know, full to bursting with expectation. I'm in for a surprise or I'm going to figure something out. Those first times – they keep coming. Know what I mean?" She nods, full stop. Which means Yes, yes, I hear you, Buzzard. Now scram. Think you're the only one in this house nursing a reverie?

MR. ICEBERG

Another blizzard. There has already been over 500 cm of snow. We have a shot at last year's record. No point going down to the Duke, really. Very doubtful Gordon will try driving in from Mount Pearl. Even walking is a struggle. Trudging across Bond to Cathedral, down Cathedral to Duckworth, down Duckworth to the Duke of Duckworth. Because I need a change. Because the house is a mausoleum on weekends and I really should set up some mirrors to multiply presences, angle them this way and that, increase the sense of domestic traffic. Because the Duke is always impossibly noisy, music cranked up high and patrons shouting over it. Because green baize. Because death by second-hand smoke. Because poor old harlequin. Because three pints will kindle me. Because I'm a sweet drunk.

No Gordon – no surprise. But Peter. I know him just well enough so he trusts me to help him watch women. His looking is non-predatory, appreciative, tender. A lover of women without a woman. "I'm leaving it in the hands of God," he says. Like God's going to fix him up. I shouldn't take that tone; Peter's not the only one. But God helps those who help themselves, right? That's free will. I don't think God is backing us passive souls.

Peter has told me that he played so much pool at one time, and played so well, that he could hold the table all night. Then he got to mistrusting success at pool as a source of affirmation, and he quit. If he could play, then, though, he can play now, so I'm a little apprehensive as he racks 'em up. I'm not a bad loser, but I like to be in the game. A few decent shots would be affirming enough, but having my ass kicked might make me wish I'd never left my empty, unreflecting house. Now, maybe it's punctiliousness, or maybe it's strategy, but the first game is hardly begun when Peter comes over with a guarded expression on his face. "Don't take this wrong," he says, "but a point of protocol." "What?" "You only chalk when you're the shooter." Hm! I've been chalking up my cue whenever the mood takes me throughout my long but sporadic pool-playing career. I'm out to lunch with cutlery too. Arbitrary rules and rituals. But nobody likes to be caught out. So now I'm reaching for the chalk and stopping myself. Only the shooter. Reaching for the chalk and – no, shooter only. And with such distraction detracting from my so-so skills, I ought to be losing. I ought to be having my ass kicked by a man who once upon a time never lost control of the table. But I'm not losing. I'm in the zone, where there's no calculating a shot, only sensing it. I'm playing all the angles. Pythagoras is my middle name tonight. Which is nothing. Which is doodly-squat in the big picture. Peter was right. Why would I even bother to set this down? Because I'm so cool and efficient tonight, potting ball after ball, that Peter starts calling me Mr. Iceberg. Mr. Iceberg: that's a good one.

Who's behind the eight ball? Not Mr. Iceberg. Eight in the corner, one bank. Boom. Game over. Mr. Iceberg.

Is Mr. Iceberg ever obliged to compose himself? *Please*. Mr. Iceberg is composure itself – to the point of affliction. Never discomposed, ever combobulated: that's your Mr. Iceberg. Mr. Iceberg is every bit as cool as God, and no whit needful of assistance divine. Mr. Iceberg is cucumber-cool. *Concombre*, we absently murmur as he passes, even those of us without any French. And the legend of Mr. Iceberg is a paradox of fire-in-ice. Though cool, you see, Mr. Iceberg is

> All that a woman could ever possibly dream of;
> Gentle, wild, soft-spoken, courteous, sad;
> Angular, awkward, candid, methodical;
> Humorous, passionate, angry, kind;
> Entirely sensitive to a woman's world.

And sometimes, out of the mauzy chill that deepens far across the mysterious barrens, an exhalation, a velvet-soft susurration, may be heard. Some kind of a boo? Some kind of a bibe? No no, nothing of the sort. It is wind-borne spirit-voices of women, keening their long-pent longing for – all together now – *Mr. Iceberg*.

Arch Bonnell

HELPLESS

I cannot bear this hour
I cannot bear this scene
The loneliness, the barren waste
A man inside a dream

I cannot take these moments
When nothing fills my soul
But longing for the morning
And lies that leave me cold.

For I am but a soft man
Not made for worldly slight
I scream out loud and whisper
Through the unforgiving night

I need to hear your voice
But I dare not call your name
For the beating of your heart
Will only bring me rain

I cannot bear this hour
That comes upon me now
When night absorbs my soul
And you absorb my power

Derrick Earle

THE FLAGMAN

The screams last for hours on some nights.
A man comes tumbling out the screen door
with a bad cough fingering his lighter,
twisting and clutching it about with calloused hands
like it was something that offended him –
a few puffs
as smoke pours out his pointed nose
and his broad shoulders lower.

The next morning he's wearing an orange vest,
standing in the street with a sign.
Stop. Slow, and switch.
The traffic murmurs by.
The sun must move so slowly holding that sign
for a living:
Stop. Slow, and switch.

Tonight his children will be playing in the back yard
making snow men with carrot noses
but never eyes or ears
while he'll be slapping her around the kitchen counter
and clutching her like he might
clutch a sign,
or light a cigarette.

Kerri Cull

RED

our fingerprints float in wine
undulating on the surface
between curves of the oversized glass

I drink up mixing life, family, love lines
pressed on the folds of my hands
an extension deep and ripe with age

stealing the last drop
heat resonates within me
your mark will slide over my insides
and I will blush red

HOUSES

are funny things
and I imagine you dance in yours
in the buttery light of dusk's beginning
again in the morning when dawn
is draped in the sky like
sadness hanging

caramel sweet
long and slow as forgiveness

Lynn Coady

MEAN BOY

The reading, in fact, was like nothing I'd ever seen. By the time we got everyone chairs, and ran back and forth between buildings a few times to make sure there were no confused souls lingering outside the Sociology seminar, the hour was closing in on 8:00. Janet showed up accompanied by the very same sweet-faced old woman who was so indulgent of my tea-drinking at Carl's. This turned out to be her landlady, Mrs. Dacey. I shook Mrs. Dacey's gloved hand and took a moment to compliment her on her raisin pie because it has occurred to me that Janet's house is going to be available after she graduates this year. Then I led them to a couple of good seats close to the mantelpiece.

That was our crowd. The eight of us from Jim's seminar, a couple of strangers, Janet, Mrs. Dacey, Bryant and Ruth Dekker and Charles the-sore-thumb Slaughter. I kept waiting to see Doctor Sparrow come slinking around a corner to take in the show. But he never did.

Schofield just sat down in a chair by himself until Jim went up to him and told him he could start.

When Schofield stood and turned to face us, I thought he was sick. His eyes were squeezed shut behind his glasses, and his head was down. In his right mitt, he held an untidy clutch of paper that must have been shoved in his jacket or pants the whole time I was with him this evening.

"I would like to thank," he said.

Schofield's face blossomed red the instant he started speaking. I never saw anything like it except in grade six when Joey Cahill got so pissed off at the math teacher he blurted she could kiss his ass. An instantaneous faceful of red, just like Schofield now. I nearly stood up and walked over to help him to a chair.

"I'd like to thank my good friend Jim Arsenault," Schofield managed to finish, "for inviting me to be here today and exerting such a profound and felicitous influence on myself and, I would have to say, Canadian poetry as a whole. We are all of us the better, for the likes of Jim Arsenault – I say that with all sincerity. He makes me proud to be a fellow practitioner. I would also like to thank the department of English, one Larry Campbell who was kind enough to keep me company this stormy evening, and, as ever, the Heritage Arts Coalition, which made this and so many other wonderful events like it a reality. I am deeply grateful for the opportunity to read to you today. I thank you all for being here."

Schofield did not raise his head, shift his position, or open his eyes once during this entire speech.

He's having a heart attack, I thought to myself, watching his face pulsate as he chewed out every syllable like a series of minuscule light bulbs.

And then, Schofield raised his head, eyes open, looked directly out at us, and recited his poetry for twenty minutes. It was like he was possessed by gods. Or demons. It was wonderful. It was riveting. He started with the man word/woman word poem. He did not consult the twisted sheaf of paper in his right hand at any time during the recitation, although he did pause to shuffle the pages, for some reason, between each poem. He *performed* the poems, giving them exactly the right cadence, emphasizing precisely the words and phrases he wanted us to most notice. His reading voice was nothing like his speaking voice. It was an actor's voice, and not the least bit reedy. He was a muted, less-stagey Gregory Peck.

And yet, it wasn't as if he were acting – there was no sense of remove, like in a play how everyone pretends the actors aren't standing there in front of you but are somewhere else, oblivious to your presence. Schofield was by no means oblivious to our presence. He leaned toward us as he recited, he looked us in the eye, he harangued, he appealed, he explained. That was especially how the man/woman poem struck me – as a patient, meticulous explanation of something ineffable. It's the same kind of feeling I sometimes have listening to classical music, or even staring at the lines in the palm of my hand, sometimes. The sense that there's a language there, that something is being expressed, communicated. Something infinite, beyond words.

But Schofield did use words.

My cousin's landlady raised her hand the moment Schofield finished his recitation, having dropped his head again and thanked us. She sat there with her entire arm in the air like a septuagenarian schoolgirl while everybody else clapped hard and long.

"Hello," said Schofield when he finally peeped through his scrunched eyes and noticed what Mrs. Dacey was doing.

"Hello," she said back.

"Did you have a question?"

"Yes I do," said Mrs. Dacey in a clear and rather youthful voice. "I would like to know," she continued. "Why is it people feel they have to concern themselves with matters of the bedroom so much lately."

Schofield looked around as if not quite sure where he was.

"Do you mean people...in general?" he asked after a moment.

"I suppose I do," said Mrs. Dacey. "I suppose it's something you see quite a bit nowadays. But I thought you might be the man to ask considering the nature of some of those poems you were reading."

Schofield blinked a few times behind his glasses. "They were *my* poems."

"Yes I assumed that," Mrs. Dacey snapped, sensing condescension. "You're the man of the hour, so to speak."

Jim interrupted at this point.

"I think," he said, rearranging his limbs in his chair in a pertinent sort of way, "with the storm and people needing to get home and everything, we may have to keep the questions to a minimum this evening."

Mrs. Dacey responded to Jim, but kept staring at Schofield. "Storms don't bother me," she told him. "I walked here from my house and I'll walk back. I'm not bothered by any storm, never have been. I grew up on the Bay of Fundy with the wind coming straight off the Atlantic ocean every winter, you'd never see me bat an eyelash in a storm."

Schofield pursed his lips and nodded at this.

"All the same," said Jim, and didn't finish the sentence – as at a loss as I've ever seen him. No one came to his rescue.

"So let's hear it," said Mrs. Dacey to Schofield.

"*Bedroom matters,*" repeated Schofield.

"Yes," said Mrs. Dacey. "You tell me: what's the story on that, now?

"Well I can't speak for others," Schofield began.

"I understand that," Mrs. Dacey assured him.

"But I can say that love...and poetry, historically, have always gone hand and hand. Um. Shakespeare, for example – "

Mrs. Dacey was having none of it.

"Love is one thing," she interrupted. "But I'm talking about things that go on, or should only go on, in the privacy of the bedroom. *Bedroom...matters.* Love is fine, and I think it's just wonderful if a poet wants to write something about love, I have no problem with that at all. But here's my question:"

We waited. Nobody could look at anything in the room except their own twiddling fingers in their laps.

"Why is it that people think there's this need these days to discuss private and intimate things for entertainment? For the amusement of others? You see," said Mrs. Dacey, shifting her weight forward, "what people don't seem to understand is that *that* is basically the definition of pornography. Entertaining others, in the public arena, with private and intimate things. And I'm just afraid that people get so caught up in their art or selling their books or whatever that they don't realize when they are crossing certain pornographic boundaries."

Mrs. Dacey sat back and folded her hands, keeping her bright little eyes pinned on Schofield. Dermot's own huge mitt was resting against his heart as if to quiet it down.

As the seconds passed and we all sat waiting for Dermot's defense, the entire English department began to vibrate with the noise of what can only be described as a guffaw – a guffaw in the truest sense of the word. In fact it onomatopoeically came close to sounding like the word *guffaw*.

"*Hawg!*" It went. "*Hawg, hawg, hawg, hawg!*"

It was the loudest, rudest laugh I've ever heard. It was coming, I noted, craning my neck along with everyone else, from Charles Slaughter, seated sprawl-legged in the back.

"*Hawg, hawg, hawg, hawg, hawg hawg, hawg!*"

The furniture shook with it.

Mrs. Dacey straightened her delicate shoulders once Slaughter was finished. It took him a moment or two.

"I beg your pardon if I've said something funny," she said, not fazed, not taking her hamster eyes off Schofield. By this time I was somewhat in awe of Mrs. Dacey.

Schofield, meanwhile, had used the eternity of Slaughter's mirth to get himself together. He gazed straight back at Mrs. Dacey and assured her she had said nothing funny at all. Then he even managed to apologize for the laughter without being accusatory toward Slaughter – as if Schofield himself was somehow responsible. Then he answered her question.

Bernice Morgan

from
POEMS IN A COLD CLIMATE

The poet jumps onto the platform, begins arranging material on the piano stool – his file folder, three magazines and his published collection of poems. All have little markers of coloured paper. In a conversational tone he tells them that the coloured markers are his wife's idea. Different colours indicate poems for different moods, so that he can suit his reading to the audience. But, he says, looking up with a happy smile, he will not tell them what the colours indicate. He also has extra copies of his book, which he hopes they will buy later. He takes his time, moving the sound equipment back, tapping the mike with the tips of his fingers. He asks the waitress to please turn off the music and, if possible, dim the lights. The woman, Sarah notes, obliges with the first kindly look of the night.

Eventually he begins to read. He has a confident, pleasant voice. Even the regulars sitting at the bar seem to listen.

The readers are always good-looking, either handsome young men or handsome older women. Sarah mulls over this phenomenon. Where are the plain young women, the ugly old men poets?

Julian Grant is good. He gestures a lot. Sarah, who notices hands, likes his. They are tanned and long fingered. Between poems he talks about how he gets ideas, about his place in Nova Scotia – an old farm house overlooking the river – about his wife Teresa and his five year old daughter Amanda, about the pets they shelter in the winters and free in the springs. Sarah suspects this easy involvement. He and Teresa do not seem to get stuck with dogs in the early stages of prolonged death or neurotic cats who want to live on top of the fridge. She resents this ability, which she totally lacks, to garner all the blessings of caring without any of the messiness. Is it just very good luck, or are some people more selective in their loving?

Or maybe the secret is Teresa. Sarah imagines a beautiful Irish woman with dark red hair and pale, pale skin that gives her a fragile look. But Teresa is not fragile. She drowns the cats, dogs and birds when Julian is in town talking to his publisher. He doesn't know this of course, and continues to write poems about them foraging through the summer countryside.

He tells the audience he has just put in a flush toilet, a real sign of success, he says, for an Atlantic Canadian poet. Then he reads a wonderful poem about this acquisition. Leaning back, his hips just out, the muscles at the back of his legs make a long strong line in the grey cord. He is the only person in the room with hip bones.

"If I had a daughter I would lock her up," Sarah thinks.

She turns her head slightly to study the faces around her. As always, the audience is made up of middle-aged women and a smattering of men, one or two obliging lovers and husbands who have grown to accept the eccentric activities of their partners. Sarah once heard Andrew, Mary's husband, tell Ted, "Well, it's better than Valium…"

In the dim blue light the ageing faces tilt upward, moon-like, adoring, held captive by the beautiful young man, by the words that flow down, so neatly, so cleverly contrived, so charmingly delivered.

Sarah thinks she might be ill. She can feel bile rising at the back of her throat. She hates Julian Grant. She hates him more than she has ever hated anyone. She begrudges him his apple tree, his Teresa, his Amanda, his view of the river, even his flush toilet.

There is a lot of applause when he finishes. People get up, mill about looking happy and relieved; happy for the audience that the poet was so good, happy for the poet that the audience was so good. They chat, buy more drinks, buy the poet drinks.

"He was great – even Andrew enjoyed it!" Mary whispers to Sarah.

Beth and Mike go up to talk to him, and Beth buys one of his books which she brings over to Sarah. He has written, "To Beth of Newfoundland, fellow poet. From your friend Julian."

Sarah decides she will not, after all, ask anyone back to the house tonight.

Mike, Beth and Sarah walk up the hill together. Mike recites a few of the poet's lines. There is a long pause. Then Mike says, "You know, the likelihood of anyone publishing a first book of poetry after the age of forty is one in 600,000."

They are all quiet.

The night has turned clear and still. Snow scrunches underfoot. Inside their clothing their bones are ever so fragile, thin as the shells of sea creatures bleaching on rocks. They move closer together, the heavy cloth of their winter jackets touching, so aware of the cold flesh underneath, that had they been another race, they would have embraced and cried in each others' arms.

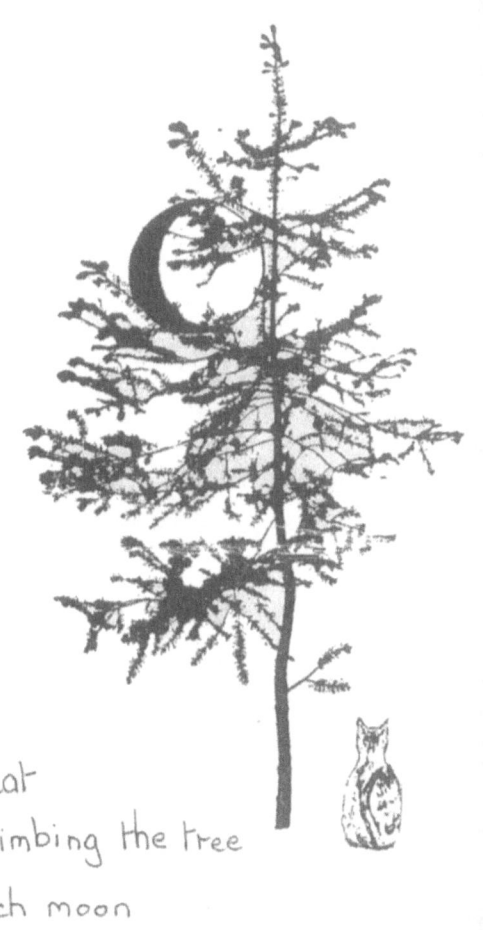

a cat
  climbing the tree
the march moon

Lorna Crozier

WHEN I COME AGAIN TO MY FATHER'S HOUSE

When I come again to my father's house
I will climb wide wooden steps
to a blue door. Before I knock
I will stand under the porchlight and listen.
My father will be sitting in a plaid shirt,
open at the throat, playing his fiddle –
something I never heard in our other life.

Mother told me his music stopped
when I was born. He sold the fiddle
to buy a big console radio.
One day when I was two
I hit it with a stick,
I don't know why, Mother covering
the scratches with a crayon
so Father wouldn't see.
It was the beginning of things
we kept from him.

Outside my father's house
it will be the summer
before the drinking starts,
the jobs run out, the bitterness
festers like a sliver buried
in the thumb, too deep under the nail
to ever pull it out. The summer
before the silences, the small
hard moons growing in his throat.

When I come again to my father's house
the grey backdrop of the photos

my mother keeps in a shoebox
will fall away, the one sparse tree
multiply, branches green with rain.
My father will stand in his young man's pose
in front of a car, foot on the runningboard,
sleeves rolled up twice on each forearm.

I will place myself beside him.
The child in me will not budge
from this photograph,
will not leave my father's house
unless my father as he was
comes with me, throat swollen
with rain and laughter,
young hands full of music,
the slow, sweet song of his fiddle
leading us to my mother's
home.

LEAVING HOME

When he left New Orleans for Chicago
at King Oliver's request, Louis Armstrong's mother
packed him a trout sandwich and no one met him
at the train, though he could blow his trumpet
and be heard across state lines. I don't know why,
but I love to think of that trout sandwich he carried
in his pocket and later ate, the wheels spinning him
into fame, though it took some years and at least
two women. When my dad and I went fishing
Mom laid roast chicken from the day before

between slices of store-bought white. Was there mayonnaise?
I don't remember, but in the boat, a few fish biting,
our fingers shone with butter as if we'd dipped our hands in fire
then treated them for burns. The sun was bright but weaker,
the afternoons so long I watched the hairs on my father's arms
turn gold. If I'd been called away by someone other than myself,
years later, that's what I'd have wanted, chicken on white bread,
and the thing that turned my breath and body into music.
Leaving home like Louis Armstrong, though there's no one like him
and his trumpet. And the sandwich he saved until he reached
the outskirts of Chicago, savouring the Southern taste of what
his mother made him. Imagine those fingers, that mouth.

THE DARK AGES OF THE SEA

Because we are mostly
made of water and water
calls to water
like the ocean to the river,
the river to the stream,
there was a time when
children fell into wells.

It was a time of farms
across the grasslands,
ancient lakes
that lay beneath them,
and a faith in things
invisible, be it water
never seen or something
trembling in the air.

We are born to fall
and children fell,
some surviving
to tell the tale,
pulled from the well's
dark throat,
wet and blind with terror
like a calf
torn from the womb
with ropes.

Others diminished into ghosts,
rode the bucket up
and when you drank
became the cold shimmer
in your cup, the metallic
undertaste of nails
some boy had carried
in his pocket
or the silver locket
that held a small girl's
dreams.

In those days people
spoke to horses,
voices soft as bearded
wheat; music lived
inside a stone. Not to say
it was good, that falling,
but who could stop it?

We are made
of mostly water
and water calls to water

through centuries of reason
children fall
light and slender
as the rain.

SAND FROM THE GOBI DESERT

Sand from the Gobi Desert blows across Saskatchewan,
becomes the irritation in an eye. So say the scientists who
separate the smallest pollen from its wings of grit,
identify the origin and name. You have to wonder where
the dust from these fields ends up: Zimbabwe, Fiji,
on the row of shoes outside a mosque in Istanbul,
on the green rise of a belly in the Jade Museum in Angkor Vat?
And what of our breath, grey hair freed from a comb, the torn
    threads of shadows?
Just now the salt from a woman's tears settles finely its invisible kiss
on my upper lip. She's been crying in Paris on the street that means
Middle of the Day though it's night there, and she doesn't want the
    day to come.
Would it comfort her to know another, half way round the world,
    can taste her grief?
Another would send her, if she could, a few of the rare flakes of snow
falling here before the sunrise, snow that barely fleeces the brown
    back of what's
too dry to be a field of wheat, and winter's almost passed. Snow on
    her lashes.
What of apple blossoms, my father's ashes, small scraps of sadness
that slip out of reach? Is it comforting to know the wind
never travels empty? A sparrow in the Alhambra's arabesques
rides the laughter spilling from our kitchen, the smell of garlic
makes the dust delicious where and where it falls.

Anne Ferncase

CATCHING THE KLONG BOAT

Thai Tourist Guide:
To get to the
Grand Palace of Thailand
take a klong boat.

First rule:
The Klong boat
has no schedule.
Shaped like a wooden slipper,
it is swifter than a tuktuk
as it sails the last canal
of Bangkok.

Second rule:
It never stops for passengers.
To board, stand prominently on
the edge of the dock;
lock eyes with the captain;
dare him to come closer.
Then jump
to the railing!
Hold tight to the cord.
If you misstep,
if you lean *back*
instead of *into*
this open shoe,
I hope you can swim
because no one
will come after you
no one would dare
disturb the water spirit

who has filled this klong
with stench and sewage
just to keep you out.

Third rule:
If you have successfully
hauled your wide western ass
into this water taxi,
move to the middle
so the lady in high heels
and the slight
man with his child
have space
to land.

Last rule:
To disembark from moving boat
climb out on the railing
assume crouch position
let go of cord
and jump!
Please mind
the other jumpers.

On your way back,
I advise
a land taxi.

Louise Halfe (Sky Dancer)

DEAR MAGPIE

Dear Magpie,

Your crouched frog that holds its legs against its body
wishes to return. For two weeks its insistence sat
on the tip of my ear. It started after I found many of my own.

I have one, whose left leg curls its belly,
The other leg still pushing forward,
I don't know what killed him.
There, safe on the hot road. No wheels to squish him.
I've see others, headless, so still in movement rushing
Out of the way. Perhaps it was exhaustion, far from the slough
Miles of hopping for a frog though
For us it is five hundred footprints.

I hope you are well. The frog tells me you are so
Though age eventually catches us
Mirrors our tired lines. Our youthful spirits
Naughty and reflective lie to our bodies.
At least this is what I feel and see.

I hope you are well. Your book shares its story.
I was absorbed in the garden of your journey.
The spilled spirits who haunted your living
Dissipated as your charge took life
And hugged it to your soul.
These days ancient legends work their way
Into how I've experienced my life.
I reframe them, hope they will live another way.
The wise live in the lake, sway in the tall grass,
Light up the universe in the prairie storm.
I listen,

And eventually
The voices penetrate my thick skull
Where my heart attempts
To understand.

These little frogs. Big ones too.
One sat in the folds of blankets
Its large eyes blocked our entrance
To the sweat lodge.
Why would it choose to wrap itself
At the door in this prairie sweltering?
Then I remember the large bullfrog
At our Elder's lodge, it would hop in
When the flaps were open
And hop out when the sweat began.

Sweet wet babies, brown, green
I hold them, release them to the slough.
These two, the one who yearns to return to you.
It just wants to go home.
And this one whose jump to heaven
In mid-death
it teaches me.

WHITE ISLAND

Rolling Head took me for a stroll.
My foot slipped on lichen and wedged
Between rocks. My boots and pants
Soaked from last night's rain.
Rolling Head guided me to a coyote's den

That later became my lair.
There, she said, you will exhume
Your lover, dig him out of your skin.

For years I dug through that coyote's tunnel.
The watership of childhood dreams
Emerged as I struggled to surface.
When my head peered through
My mother's hole
I felt the heat of bullets
The rolling thunder of wheels
I slipped back into that muddy hole.

I had not yet heard
About the battles my ancestors fought
Yet
Through my youth
I followed your green eyes
You carried my grandfather's stature
Though you leaned
Against the land.

Rolling Head swallowed us
In her cavity
We made love
Sweating to tear our skins apart.
I have a white island
On my left hip
You share with my beloved
Foreigners on my brown flesh.

Emiko Miyashita

HAIKU

the rumble of waterfalls
becomes distant –
I worry about my car keys

she unfolds
a new linen –
Tablelands covered with snow

winter sunset
a door opens
inside the mirror

with a handful of snow
I pat the snowman
dusk

city dusk –
to a still-lit shop window
a mime's perpendicular pause

John Steffler

COOK'S LINE

I cut into Cook's pen's
line at latitude 48° 57', longitude 57° 58',
just below his much vandalized
monument
on the edge of Corner Brook.

I lift the section of line extending west
along Humber Arm's south shore.
At first it is no thicker than a thread,
but I flatten it between my palms, I shake it
like a ribbon, sending
waves down its length.

I tug it from side to side, get it limber
and loose.

The pigment he used was remarkably
dense;
it somehow muffled everything on both sides,
like the Great Wall of China,
kept the smell of the sea out of the land and smell
of the land out of the sea.

I dip the severed line in the salt water
and make it soft,
knead it, stretch it wide like black
dough.

I hold the bottom edge down with my feet spread
wide apart. I stretch
the top corners out with my hands,
making a tunnel, a kind of nighttime road
of Cook's line.

The pigment thins and separates,
you can walk along inside Cook's line
like a long grey cloud.

Listen.
There are French voices inside the line
and voices that might be Micmac
or even Beothuk, men singing in something
like Spanish or Portugese, you can hear
birds and waves among beach stones,
taste the kelpy sound of the surf, clear
serum of mussel juice, clams' fine
squirts.

I take my cassette recording of Alfred saying:
"There's nar fish be d' wharf clar of a sculpin."
and throw that down inside Cook's line.

I take the photos I took of all the groc and confs
and take-outs between Corner Brook
and Lark Harbour and throw them down inside
Cook's Line,
                    then I throw in the C & E Takeout
itself and the John's Beach church that used to be
in my grade three geography book,
                                        and I pick up all
the kids hitchhiking in Mount Moriah
and drive them to the side of Cook's line
and let them out and watch them go
running out of sight in the ink mist,

and I pick up a ball that comes bouncing toward me
in the street in Curling and pitch it
down inside the line, and the ball-hockey players
go chasing after it,
                    and the car

that's rocking up and down on its springs
in the bushes just off the Cook's Brook Park
parking lot, I push it slowly into Cook's line
and give it a shove – two startled flushed faces
in the rear window –
                              and I throw in
Woods Island and Pissing Horse Falls
and the solar orgasm rock and Mad Dog Lake
and Lisa and me at the top of Blomidon Head
(Is that a caribou in the pond below? Yes,
it's moving, No, it isn't. Yes it is.)
and Walt LeMessurier napping in the sun
on the rim of Simms Gorge,
                              and I drag
the line over to the start of the Clark's Brook
road, and a row of skidoos, the riders all
in zipped suits and helmets, roars
down inside Cook's line,

                    and the line
is stretched to bursting now, the inside
spilling back out to the outside, birds'
calls, crinkled light on the bay,
Lorraine with her radio and barbecue – people
in trouble will find her and her help –
Randy and me coming down the scree slope
on the face of the Blomidons, long moonwalk
strides,
              and I know Cook is away down there
somewhere, bent to his table with pen and dividers,
still leaving his fine black trail.

What will he think when his line
spreads and explodes at his pen's
tip and the first of the ball-hockey kids
and skidoos come tumbling in front of him?

CEDAR COVE

If your wharf is washed away
it will come to Cedar Cove –
Wild Cove on the maps or
Capelin Cove. If your boat

goes down it will sail to Cedar
Cove piece by piece.
And your uncle, should he not come back
from his walk on Cape St. George,

will be found grinning among
the glitter of barkless roots
laths struts stays
stringers and frayed rope

in Cedar Cove, where no
cedars have ever grown,
but that's what the local people
call it. The water horizon

topples straight down
on Cedar Cove over
and over, box cars
falling, loads of TNT.

And the wind will not let you speak
in Cedar Cove, which could
be called Deaf Cove
or Lobotomy Cove, will not

let you think or stand straight;
the shrunk trees writhe
and have the wrong kinds
of leaves, but their roots spread

wide in Cedar Cove,
whose gravel is soft compared
to its air. We have come to Cedar
Cove overland, my love

and I, having been lost
at sea in another way.
All day we scatter
ourselves through the noise

and whiteness, learning the thousand
ways things can be taken
apart and reassigned –
the boot sole impaled on the shattered

trunk, the rust flakes,
the bone flakes encrusting a bracelet
of kelp – losing our pictures
of home, stick by stick.

After Cedar Cove,
how will we look?

Matthew Hollett

POEM FOR A FOUND PAPER CRANE

"i do not know what it is about you that closes
and opens; only something in me understands..."
    – E. E. Cummings, somewhere i have never travelled, gladly beyond

did the same small hands
that unfold dandelions,
tend abandoned gardens,
and rake ponds on windy days

fold you from castaway candybar wrapper
or discarded cigarette carton

deliberately, delicately,
as one would fold a frail and valuable map,
crown a cardhouse with the king of spades,
or spread the wings of a pinned insect?

were you marooned
on this low stone wall

like a compass rose
placed in the loneliest space on a map,
your four paper petals
pointing in all cardinal directions
at once, as if resolutely lost?

and isn't it true
that though you cannot fly
nor fold yourself into a paper plane

if i return tomorrow
you will probably be gone,

your lifting-off
implied but unseen,
like the wind's thin fingers
or the sun's soft thumb,

or as a question lifts gently
the end of a sentence?

Mark Callanan

TURK'S GUT WOLF

They chased that three-legged sunuvabitch –
he'd lost his fourth in a trap
while prowling the pen for sheep –
all the way to Turk's Gut, Brigus,
blood and tracks
marking the direction of his flight.

The loss of blood never tamed him.
His eyes were fire and brimstone,
his coat dark as the devil,
and that one stump
weaving in the air like a hand
casting incantations.

He reached the edge of the cliff,
might have sprung
bat wings and flown down over the ocean
but for the bullet that pierced his chest,
smoke from the hunter's gun rising,
an angel of god into the night.

WHEELBARROW
for Allison

Roll on down this muddy road, the handles
guiding me like two prongs of a divining rod,
only on the slope, it's gravity that pulls
and not water. I'm carrying serious-looking junks,
wood for the fire that will burn hotter
than hell, hopefully, or at the very least,
heat the living room through the winter's cold.

I've got a tuneless song on my lips and the whole
morbid weight of December on my mind, but I don't care.
I'm just rolling this wheelbarrow, catching some kind
of a rhythm as the wheel digs in and releases, digs
in and turns up earth, marking its lone tire track
along the path I travel – drawn by something stronger,
more urgent than the presence of buried water.

Carmelita McGrath

As Persephone

When she was young, she dreamed of herself as Persephone.
She might have been lovely if she hadn't such a cranky look
that without his chest shot full of the BB pellets of love,
even Lord Pluto might have avoided her.

But that day on the banks of the singing waters,
her face buried in wild violets and the spotty throats of ditch lilies,
she might have been transformed or he
confused enough to be fascinated.

Let go my hair, she shrieked, as he pulled her under,
I can fall on my own two legs; in his deep, ridiculous
valleys and labyrinths, she questioned him on the composition of
    magma
to show she was merely curious and not impressed.

She taunted him with his one-sided love;
did he expect a girl would make him live?
Pretended to find comfort in the brute subterranean architecture
even as the dawn and stars called her name.

When, tormented enough, he released her
she tore his purply fruit between her teeth,
knew she was tricked and gave him a look
that said same time next year, and you'll be regretting it.

She could hardly stand it at home. Demeter rising
out of her black funk and multiple therapies,
the loud ringing voices of the determinedly happy
who would dance in bright garments in the face of her winters.

She had given them something more complex than they were used to,
too subtle for them. She walked and felt the grass sharp on her legs;
at night she left their fires to sleep under the sky, careless whether
    it was
starred or starless, knew she'd always been half-wedded to the dark.

WATERING AT DAWN

Yes, it is the perfect time of day,
the silence and the stars thinning out,
the moon's shade fading in the bringing light,
the hidden birds of night meeting in song
the chorus of day, contrapuntally
and far off to the east over the sea
Apollo's stable boys sleepily working.
The best time, this, oh yes, before
the day's heat arrives to burn the leaves,
let them drink the dew delivered by my hands,
let it sink, let it seep to the deepest roots,
white filaments clinging to the earth
and eating of its riches; the mind's eye
imagines them stirring, sated. Now
the tremble of leaves, the gleam
of pearls and opals, drops collected in leaves
whorled or fan-shaped, in panicles,
in umbels and racemes. Of course,
I am rarely, if ever, up for this,
more prone to dreaming than to doing;
the mind's eye at times is all there is,
the days escaping east to west,
the garden going on as best it can.

MY FATHER'S GHOST

My father's ghost, while my father still lived
haunted a corner of Bond and Bannerman,
and each time I walked by I bit my tongue
to not ask him
"Now what are you doing in town, you never called me?"
Instead as the figure
tipped his peaked cap
and waved a hand that always
held a cigarette, I smiled
"Good day, sir," as I'd been taught
in childhood's other lifetime.
And he responded with comments on the weather.
My father was falling off the slippery slope of earth;
each day the summoning phone call
hung like a phantom in the air,
already there but waiting to manifest itself.
I imagined conversations with the man
in the peaked cap
that would recall summers of boats laden
with fish and sunlight,
and all the busy men in peaked caps
muscled and brown from splitting cod
and hauling hayloads. He was the last of them,
exhaling the past, all the failing memories
I wanted to draw from him
and carry to my father's body
in a gift of language.
My father's ghost, while my father still lived,
haunted a corner of Bond and Bannerman
and held the better part of a century inside him.
But he was frail and I fearful too long,
returned in grief for the elixir of his memories
to find him gone.

HEARTS OF PALM

Afternoon, desultory in the aisles
the way one moves distracted in a dream
I spy her sculpted in the white-green light,
a tiny woman in a camel coat, the years worn off it
here and there. Gloved hand outstretched
to roam among the wares
of this attenuated aisle of imports
where not much from anywhere's filtered in.
Tea? I think as wool-clad fingers flit,
a pale five-winged moth over blackcurrant jam;
a picnic's conjured by the lemon biscuits
until she alights on hearts of palm. A dust-
furred tin. Who knows what possible dinners
she dreams up, or what is caught in some synaptic clasp,
those night-long dinner parties of the past,
seeing the guests off down ice-slick roads
and lying there in the snowplow-thickened night,
a blue light beating through bare trees
and all the ambient noises of the night
astir in her, birds of wakefulness.
Did she value his body most at times like this
when lost in sculpted sleep he seemed more whole
in his nakedness, more than himself?
Her fingers nesting on his chest,
his captured heart beating through her palm.

Alan Garvey

No Longer New

Weather-beaten, pock-marked,
chipped like teeth that are tea-stained,
the lip of a cup round-bodied,
smothered by December and framed
by damp sand, the pale hue

of something no longer new.
Flung from fishing boats' sides
broken dishes beyond repair
flew through the simmering air.
There they turned and dived

across foreign waters and lands
to end as pieces in my hands.
Their designs never stray too far
from where their owners' hearts are:
seedpods burst over blue streams

by houses built with blue beams.
We see the familiar in trees,
sycamore and beech, a reprise
of ivy choking a blue bough,
now the hand at tiller or plough

as it weaves garlands of bows
to fit the breath of a blue rose
carried on an angel's wings,
and the blue patterned cross
as a bird flies to paradise lost,

the lost and found of things.

NEVER MIND

I can do no wrong here. My fiancé
is at work ten miles away. Colm's
in school; he clock-watches thinking
of play. Bach mellows my mind.
I imagine a small sandpit
lined with black plastic,

child-size spades and trowels,
castle battlements crumbling
beneath pebbles and shells.
I linger and test the weight
of a mother's bones buried on a beach
for thirty years. I see a TV screen,

her grown children dressed against
the weather, their tears of hope
for release, that longed-for peace
of knowing. Never mind the lies.
Truth is autopsy, caught under
fingernails, stained on our clothes,

the earth stuck to our shoes' soles.
We're certain when we see a strand
of hair, we know how it blows,
its colour, the dye we helped to apply.
We massaged that collarbone at night,
nuzzled next to that cheek, always believed

it would be right beside ours in grief.
The CD stops, cigarette burns to a close.
Is this the last we have of a loved one,
a wave goodbye, *do you want anything
in the shops?* They are too precious
to let go of when with us. Take hold.

Susan Gillis

LOVE AS STONE

That silver thread in the cleft in the hill?
Falling water, like a weighted line.
Plunges down the rockface into the stream.
Up ahead we'll cross it and I'll show you
something of my heart. At the top
the water pools in a kind of stone bowl
worn by eons of swirl, a pool so tranquil
you hardly believe it comes from the same spring.
After the climb I rested there, floating
chin-deep in its chill, looking out
over the caribou fields above the cloud
line, and down, at the string-like road trimming
the shore, the miniscule stream, this bridge
across it like a caught twig – I felt
a warmth kindle in me then, and became
aware of a steady pounding, as though heard
from great distance – the cascade, and
my blood. You have to remember the lull at the edge
becomes a punishing force as it descends,
that shimmer we love veiling the gouge it forms.

KITCHEN FLOOR

These past six days have been equatorial, transplendent.
We eat outside. Tonight it seemed the sun
bugled across the sky, draping Crow Hill
and the Blomidons in satin, rimming the inlets and coves
of Humber Arm with brass and scarlet, gold
at the day's last call and the sly falling in
of the humdrum. Creatures slide away to their night
hide-outs and watchtowers; we come in reluctantly,
dragging plates and cutlery and leftover potatoes,
to the fridge grinding on, and on the floor a dark
shock where a wind has come in and blown over
the vase of peonies, the wet petals wine-dark
in the gloam before you turn on the light; weather
gathering over the hills where we'd hoped for stars.

LOVE AS PURE DESIRE

His skills:
1. whets the knife whipping the blade toward his belt
2. while watching something else
3. usually the people coming and going on the other side of the counter
4. who are coming and going to and from their tables in his restaurant
5. where they hover hushed and reverent over his food

His person:
quick thin and sharp his long torso
dark his eyes which look long at the produce
wide-tipped his fingers which press at cuts of meat
ready his mouth lips poised to taste
in general, all appetite

he feeds from one spring, looking,
looking.

It chanced one day while he was weighing
a small yellow tomato in his hand, his look
landed on me, rippled through and opened my mouth.
"Taste this," he whispered, and eased it in.
My husband one step behind me.
One yellow tomato.
That was all.
But I can say to you, happy is she
who may dine nightly at his table.

Carol Hobbs

STEADY GOODS

Cabbage pickles
with bright mustard and black beads of pepper.
Considering also the beets, I stand in the pantry
while something famous happens outside.
My brother has climbed the ladder one story to the roof.
His running gait shakes the shelves and jars.
He leaps and flies, following the geese, south.
And in the brief silence
before the groan, I take
a silver rod of herring from its brine.

Everyone pities our mother,
commends her longsuffering and good sense
and speed in brushing him off –
      Stand up! Walk!
Mothers speak in this biblical way.

And in the known world, I am
lost among steady goods, the labelled bottles –
the preserved *moose, seal* (oily and black as loam),
jams in amber and garnet *bakeapple partridgeberry damson* –
a white rabbit in its perfect cardigan of fur,
hanged by the wire snare.

ICEBERG

There is an iceberg so big I have to drive my car
to different vantage points along the shore
to understand something of its perimeter.
It is high, a flat plateau, pristine.
If I lie in the middle of that ice island, I am
a new nation and the edge of it
is a long journey I might prepare for.
Or ignorant of edge, I live
all shining at the crystal center,
not seeing those others from the city
line the shore, empty shadowless people
who drive cars around the outside rim of my perfect world.
Their headlights are the bowl of stars.
This is a paradise. I have a perfect love,
life without any idea of what it is
to fall.

LATE AT BANNERMAN PARK

Certain girls can walk without seeming
to touch the ground.

Their shoes
never scuff, their skin
is blameless as moons.

Once we were this –
hyacinths blooming,

Colt cigarillos and wine,
the bottle smashed
in the hollow of the swimming pool.

While Iris squatted and peed against a tree,
Medina and I fanned our skirts
around her in a laughing wall.

And we, too long wrapped up
in boys we'd shrugged like scarves
all winter,

let our bare arms grow dusty
with stolen flowers.

Walking back,
I don't recall footsteps,
just drift

like silk slipping,
like that.

Lisa Moore

FRANK

As soon as Frank realized all of his money was gone, he put on the kettle and got out the plastic coffee cone and put a paper filter in it. He got the sugar bowl he'd bought at the Sally Ann out of the cupboard. It still had the piece of masking tape with 25¢ written in ballpoint pen. The day he bought the sugar bowl, there was a woman trying on a wedding dress.

She was scrawny and bucktoothed and the bones in her face were so misaligned that she appeared deformed. The two women who work at the Sally Ann on Waldegrave were excited about the wedding and they seemed to know the groom-to-be, whom they called Johnny and who seemed to be mentally retarded.

Frank found the sugar bowl in a bin of kitchen junk, spoons with enamel thumbnail pictures of P.E.I. and rusty ladles and a plastic spaghetti strainer that someone had put too close to the heat and had melted the side out of it.

The sugar bowl was pinwheel crystal, which his mother had had four wineglasses of, the same pattern; some client she cleaned for had given them to her as a Christmas present.

He picked at the tape with his finger now, and peeled it off and there was left a little skim of gritty dirt in the shape of the piece of tape that he rubbed with his thumb and it balled up there and he flicked his hand. Something about this flicking made it real to him how absolutely alone in the world he was, because he looked absurd doing it but there was no one to see.

At the Salvation Army that day in January he had filtered through a cardboard box of junk for a lid to the sugar bowl, he knew it should have a lid, and was surprised by how much he wanted a lid. He did not want to be someone without the lids to things. He wanted whole sets of whatever he had, or nothing at all.

He wanted, when he went to the paint store, to get the trim they suggested went with the burnt sand colour he had chosen. He wanted, when he looked into the eyes of the idiot they had working there, who said he couldn't mix that colour but he could mix one pretty damn close, to grab him by the front of the shirt and shout in his face that he didn't want close.

He never wanted close again. He had been living with close his whole life.

He wanted to communicate how this acceptance of second best infuriated him and the guy better find a way to mix the right colour.

One of the women at the Salvation Army was named Gert, and the other was Shirley, according to their nametags. Frank could tell by looking at them they were seriously religious women, and he saw they kept a stern eye out for shoplifters and they stood in the late-afternoon light with their arms crossed under their chests and watched the weather come in over the harbour.

Frank had been coming to the Salvation Army on Waldegrave with his mother ever since he was born, but he wasn't sure that they put him together with the baby and small kid he had been, or if they thought about his mother and wondered what had happened to her.

On the January day when Frank got the sugar bowl, Gert had pulled a chair across the floor and was leaning with a long pole to unhook a wedding dress from the ceiling. The dress was swathed in plastic and the plastic was covered in dust and Gert had to lean out too far and had lifted one foot in the air like a ballerina and Johnny, the groom-to-be, took her hand.

Frank saw how firmly he held her hand, saying, Hold on to me, Gert girl, before you break your neck. Everyone in the store was watching the hook sway slightly here and there around the wedding dress hanger, which was hooked over a waterpipe hanging just below the ceiling.

Gert lowered the wedding dress and shook off the plastic, clawing at it, and without the dusty plastic, the wedding dress, they all saw, was covered in sequins and it crackled with light and the girl with the misaligned face had covered her mouth with both her hands.

This dress was never worn, Gert whispered. She had fished a pricetag out of the froth and it said the dress was worth $1,500.

The girl gathered the dress up in her arms and went into the tiny dressing room and Gert and Shirley turned at once and started clucking and waving their arms at Johnny, telling him to turn around for the love of God and close his eyes.

After a few moments Shirley called out, Does it fit?

The door of the dressing room creaked open and the bride came out, and she was a scalded red with embarrassment and pride. She ducked her head into her shoulder and the beauty of the dress seemed more than she could bear. The red in her face made her eyes a dark, dark brown. Her misaligned face was lit up by her blushing and for a minute she looked weirdly beautiful.

Frank thought that maybe in the future this Johnny guy would beat the shit out of her, or they'd just live on welfare for the rest of their lives, or they wouldn't know about Canada's four food groups and the kids would be eating cake with blue icing blocked with sugar and chemicals and chips and cola and they'd be saucy and out of control all the time, and the parents would get something like cancer or they'd be alcoholics or have gambling addictions, but for now, in the middle of a snowstorm with the dress on, the girl, Frank saw, was ecstatic.

Frank saw her shoulders and neck were covered in deep brown freckles but below her neck the skin looked creamy and her body was pretty nice. Then he found the lid to the sugar bowl, his fingers had just brushed against it. It wasn't chipped and there was a small dip to fit a spoon in.

This sugar bowl, now in the cupboard in front of him, on the yellow mactac is shimmering, struck as it is by the light from the window and he takes it down and puts it on the counter and is humiliated as he remembers that he thought he would marry Colleen after a one-night stand.

He thought he would marry her.

From one night of making love he thought they were going to get married and everything he gathered together from that night on would be for her too. If he found a sugar bowl, it would be for her. If he bought an exercise bike or took cooking lessons or if they got into yoga or signed a mortgage, it would be for her.

He had allowed himself to be duped on such a grand scale that it made him light-headed.

He looked at the sugar bowl and this is what he thought: And I still love her. Because he thought of taking the strawberries from the fridge that were very cold and he had squashed one in his fist and tried to get the juice that ran over his knuckles to drip into her mouth but instead it ran down her chin and onto her neck and the smell of it on her skin when he licked it, and she liked what he was doing, which amazed him.

She licked his knuckles that were sticky with juice and she took his finger in her mouth and sucked it and he thought he was having the love tugged out of him. Tugging every single drop of love and loss and sexual-wanting-to-fuck and aloneness up out of his body through his finger with her gorgeous hot wet mouth, the way a magician tugs an unending line of knotted silk scarves from a gloved fist. Her mouth was a fist and he wanted it elsewhere. Her eyelashes were sooty and thick and her cheekbones and the strawberry smell was full of summer and when he lifted her up against the wall was she ever light.

And when she came, which he had never made a girl come before, he saw her eyes fly open and how startled she was, and that look was love he was pretty sure.

Even if she did take the goddamn money, which he knew she didn't need for anything, she just took it.

He took down the coffee jar and scooped out five spoonfuls. Then he tore back the bedsheets to check for a note.

For a minute he thought she might have left a note. He opened the door to the fire escape, half expecting to find the girl there.

When she wasn't there he felt the room behind him beat like a heart, thumpthump, thumpthump, and it was a very empty room and he realized that no matter how much it was clear she had duped him, he couldn't get it through his head.

Michael Winter

THE POINT DAVID MADE EARLIER

I had flown home for the summer and there was a party at David Twombly's house. A parmeham from Genoa with its pink hock in tinfoil. Bourbon and squares of chocolate in the alcove. West African music. That feeling when the lights dampen, David Twombly shouted. He was grave and flighty. Before you realize it's the light that is giving you that feeling.

David had his arm around a woman visiting form Boston. Some men walk around as if they are nude.

Your wife is looking for you, the woman said to David Twombly.

I'm in Toronto most of the year, I said.

She was married, her name was Julie Hazel. She was in St. John's collecting sound for a documentary on war. The groans men make dying on the battlefield. It is the same utterance in the throat during orgasm.

She touched her chest, as if her hand held a soldier's larynx.

We talked for three hours and then the walk to her house. A bowl of oranges, a ceramic deer lamp. Above her stove that night a painting she did of her husband, Walt. Walter Petey. We laughed a lot, she said, when I painted that.

It's like an icon.

A name tells you something.

Are you wearing underwear.

I'm wearing undies on my ovaries.

Three weeks later Julie Hazel said this: It seems opinion is divided on you.

Have we been seen together.

David Twombly said to me, if I were single like Gabe.

That's unfair, I said.

I wanted to tell him.
But you're married.

David Twombly was purchasing a socket wrench at Canadian Tire.
David a giant masculine cub. He cast out the usual male line on
desire: sexy, young, smart, funny. Those are the four things men like
to snag as they let their wet flies drift past an overhanging bough.

But David Twombly's second wife, a woman who had dieted
too much, so that her eyes bulged, a woman whose eyes were too
big for her face, her face too big for her shoulders (the first thing I
had seen of Carol Trask was her dress billowing out of a payphone
booth), she was teaching second year English at the campus in
Corner Brook and it was generally noted that both were open to
having affairs.

David: There's something vulgar about Julie Hazel. She
mentioned the condition of Albert Carter.

That he vomited on his shirt and wiped it off with your drapes?

Oh you know that story.

She's told it to me. I think it's hilarious.

Are you guys fucking each other?

He bought the wrench with a fifty dollar bill.

There was a fine scar in the hair above her temple.

It's surgical, Julie said.

You're familiar with sutures.

I've had an operation or two.

She described lying on a table covered with white noisy paper,
the wet antiseptic, the sound of a scalpel tearing the skin, the cords
of muscle. Three tense clamps prying the incision open. The carving
out of a cyst. It feels, she said to the surgeon, like my skull is being
scraped.

I am looking at your skull right now.

What colour is it.

White.

This thought, of a man seeing her skull, the thought was
behind the very plate of bone he was scraping.

Me: Jesus.
I'm in remission.

Julie Hazel had moved from Montreal to study at Cambridge,
met Walt and then found herself near hospitals for three years. I'm
ambitious, she said, to make it.
You're happy doing sound.
I'm talented.
And marriage.
When we're away let's play.
Thing is, I feel like I'm finding love. Whereas you feel like you
could be with every thirtieth man alive.
She was sprinkling icing sugar on a pound cake.
Torch songs, she said, are victim songs.
Well what's the difference between us?
You are without guile.

The summer went by like this. One morning she called from the
bath: What if I was in Toronto?
What about your husband.
Walter Petey and I are great friends.
He's okay with that.
He's encouraging it.

She bought a yellow bicycle. She found tubs of kimchi, fresh tuna,
a flowering hibiscus, a diorama. We toured the botanical gardens
and swam in a pond on the Southside Hills. She recorded men
throwing sewing machines out of a second storey window. I brought
lunch as she worked with Albert Carter in an editing studio on King's
Road. We sat on the roof and ate. She was an expert in something.
As long as you are disciplined in a field, you can be lazy with all else.
The patience in her neck. She forgot, while she was working, that I
was there.
Okay, I said. Come to Toronto.

But in August a lump was found on her backbone. She had gone in for a pap smear.

You will be single again, she said, and in your thirties.

Don't say that.

We made a date. We met at the Duckworth Lunch, beside the War Memorial. It's called something else now, but it is hard to call things by their new names. She was sitting in a booth where she could see the door.

I chose the trout. I prefer variety in plates.

I want to write a children's book, she said, and call it Big Fat and Wet.

I disengaged the backbone from my pale trout. It was like an old key.

You were born, I said, in 1972.

All summer we'd been having dates like this, pretending we were meeting for the first time. It allowed different selves to poke up. You like women, she said, and after this summer you're going to be alone.

Do you want me to saw my head off?

You're a man who has always had a girlfriend.

Ever since I was old enough to have one.

We walked up King's Road, to the independent film office where she was working. Albert Carter, shirtless, crouched by his dog, smoking a cigarette. Okay, I said. My shoulders strained with torment.

Remember when they tore that down, Albert said.

He was pointing his cigarette at the government building on Duckworth Street.

When they gutted it, I said.

All they left were I-beams. You could stand right here, Julie, and see all the harbour and the Southside Hills. Then they went and smacked her up again.

I had a little blue car. During my Toronto winters I left it in a snowbank in David Twombly's back yard. I drove Julie down to Kingman's Cove.

Your catalytic converter is rattling.

That's a resettled community.

We walked into the valley that sheltered a blue island. Plum trees grew loose around the foundations of pulled-down houses. There were gooseberries and when you walked over the old gardens you could feel with your feet the potato drills that had been planted for the last time forty years ago.

We kissed on the long grass and horsed around in the sun. She was game. Julie Hazel liked that I wasn't serious about her. I kept my serious side, the side that was blown apart, tucked into a shoulder blade. We did not have enough time for grief. What she was serious about was enjoying herself. It must have been two in the afternoon and we decided to pull off our clothes and wade in. She was like a piece of furniture that should be pushed against a wall. I was not going to fall in love with her any more. She didn't look like she was falling for me, either. We were both relieved about that. We were just enjoying ourselves. We kissed and sometimes we did not close our eyes.

There was an operation on the nub of a vertebra which left a coarse range of sutures. She was checking herself out in the mirror. Looks like a hasty repair, she said, on a mail bag.

There was another scheduled operation to explore a fatty tissue in her armpit.

Go to Boston, I said. Go home. Get the fuck out of here.

She was peering at me, as if I were far away. We got in bed and she told me cavalierly, as if she had told numerous people, as though it were a childhood illness and we were walking home after school – a part of a sentence had been said in the Health Sciences Centre – it was about a tumour on the aorta and when that eats through.

She wasn't gauging how I might consider this. It was selfish of her to tell it like that. But then I realized she was astute. If I'd been in love, she would not have said it like that. She was actually very kind. Motives are often different from what one assumes.

She came home delirious with news. There were noisy packages of cheese and dry sausage, a crisp baguette from the new bakery. I'm refusing radiation, she said. So I'm healthy and I have ninety days my God this bread is delicious.

Please go to Boston. Or fetch your parents.

Let's look at your horse calendar, she said.

We peeled off three months and that marched us deep into November.

I'm in Toronto then.

Let's stay here, she said.

I did not say anything because I knew I'd do the same thing. The zest it took to dare the wide open closet of darkness.

She made excuses for not sleeping together. I reminded her we had an understanding. She was not alarmed by this – some nights she did not come home.

I heard a rumour about Albert Carter. Then one day she said can we go to bed. I want to tell you something in bed.

The temperature and weight of her leg on mine, the scent of the dryer on the pale blue pillows. She was often pounding out heat. I tried to get interested and there must have been something of that effort in my face. She said, I know it might be hard for you to have sex with me. What I'd like you to consider is this, my one favour.

She said she'd love to get pregnant.

I want you to think about that. It's a selfish thing and very wrong of me, but.

She pushed me away so that she could see my face better. I have a big face. I want, she said, to know my body could have a child.

She slept beside me and I thought about it. So matter of fact. Julie Hazel was a generous person. She did not get along with her parents. Her father, she said, had never grown a beard. He had once told her not to walk with her hands in her pockets.

I was a man with no religion, with morals surely forged by society, yet I thought this was not a subjective position. I did not consider myself wise or a man with any solid integrity. I did not know what to do.

I called David Twombly. David's advice would not be absolute, it would be male, but I knew in talking with David Twombly he'd come to a conclusion of his own. There were worse things than being David Twombly.

David pulled one tire over the wet curb to pick me up, then plunged us down Prescott Street towards the harbour. It was raining hard, the defogger on. He listened to the story and said Gabe. He yanked up the handbrake outside the India Gate – it made that clicking traction. Gabe it's both wrong and right but in the end if ever there was goodness in a bad deed.

He rubbed his face hard with his hands, as if waking up. Now let's eat.

The rain made our inventiveness damp. We were both comfortable with this and we had nine drinks at the Grapevine. A sick woman, he said, youre bringing a new thing to someone sick.

He did not convince me.

We were flat on the carpet in my rented living room. That's all right, she said. She understood she'd never get a good deal. Being alive for twenty-nine years was the blessing and who was she to whine.

She said, Do this.

She was stretching her mouth open with her fingers.

The mirror.

Our floating bony jaws, our empty red teeth. Then her eyes, bulging with the frenzy of what death is.

She left while I was playing squash with David Twombly. It was a set-up. I heard from Carol Trask that Julie was staying with David. This pushed a quart of blood into my throat. I drove past the Twombly house and saw David's wife in one window. Carol was home from Corner Brook on a long weekend and looked insane. Their house, rich and bountiful, needed painting. For three days I heard nothing substantial. Than David phoned and said she was taken away to a cancer clinic paid for by her parents. It was in Boston, he thinks, where Walter Petey could attend her. Or perhaps technically some borough outside of Boston. She had been upset and forced him not to say anything until she'd left.

She stayed with you.

She was here for four nights, David said. Her stuff was here. Then added, Carol was here.

Your wife arrived from Corner Brook on the Saturday morning flight.

Listen, he said.

It was nights, I thought, David Twombly did not say days.

Okay look, I took her down to the Grapevine. His voice had a long piece of wood attached to the sentence, keeping it straight. I tried to find someone for her.

You found someone.

She found Albert Carter.

I flew back to Toronto in October. It was on the plane, sitting next to an old man wearing an emphysema mask. Below us the vast bridge securing Prince Edward Island. It made my own breathing erratic. I massaged my skull. I thought about how David Twombly told me, years ago, how Albert Carter loved anal sex. Loved it. I was thirty-six thousand feet in the air thinking about Albert Carter and the back of a woman I did not know. This moan. I turned, thinking the man beside me is about to die. But he was alert and patient, the clear hose feeding gas from a steel cylinder beneath his feet. It was my own chest, I could hear a sound leaking out from my ribs. Where did that come from? Feeling comes before the event is understood. It was the point that David had made earlier. I felt ruined. I was ruined.

Michael Redhill

MY GRANDFATHER'S EMPIRE

When I ring he's drying his fingers
on the flour-caked apron, rough
dough-webbed hands, he checks
the street, retreats into the dark hall.
The smell of bread puffs out of the ovens.
For lunch he lays out mandalas of petits fours,
wedges of soft cheese, roasted vegetables.
He's had sun, his face is sheened gold.
The pilot light moves against his glasses
as he takes the herbed bread from the oven.
When he speaks, fire is in the space
behind his mouth, orange
with a pale blue heart. He pours
white unkosher wine, tells me
to lay off stocks and bonds, buy gold,
only gold keeps. I can't believe
his good taste, the massive dogs
stretching their shanks by the fire.
He keeps looking at me, then
glances around the high adobe walls, a
conspiracy between us. He's even
lost his accent. He rests his hands
in his aproned lap, legs out,
the wineglass tilting
into the room. Such
a life, this! The pallor of happiness.
He says, don't tell anyone you saw me – I
didn't like being dead. It's our secret, then:
the tall rooms, the silky grey
Weimaraners. He waves from the door,

See how good it is to leave home! He is finally
a man self-rendered. And from the car,
I see how the house is spreading,
growing like a crystal into the nearby woods.
Wings and cupolas unfold over the street –
gardens, glassed-in front rooms, alcoves and buttresses.
The way becomes obscured by ash.
I pick human skin out of my teeth, smell
the sugar burning. By nightfall,
I can't leave the place he's in,
the seed of his life bursting open.
It was not too late for him, after all.

VIEWING DETROIT

We park the car across from the Cadillac Hotel, with its burgundy
awning sprawled on the sidewalk, a dog's tongue on a hot day. The
secret of America hangs in the air.

She straps on her sandals and stands beside the car. Nothing else
moves. Downtown Detroit. Four o'clock Saturday afternoon.

There is nobody here. An occasional person emerging from a
parking lot. A McDonald's nearby seems open.

We ask directions at the Journey's End. It's the hotel beside the
thirty-storey Cadillac. I ask about it: closed for eight years. The
mall across the road (two downtown city blocks) is now a small
town of coiled fixtures hanging out of walls. A giant exploded
clock. An entire downtown core, empty. Every day. Always.

We drive. She's staring out of the window, searching for life. Miles and miles of closed shops mark us. Suddenly, a flare of movement – *down there*, she says.

An open-air market. A mirage. There's no parking. People are shopping. No one lives near here. There's a frenzy for fresh corn. In the middle of a nightmare, this long dreaming road off to the side. We jump out and buy tomatoes, fresh water.

Why are we permitted to see this? We drive to the bridge (get lost twice). I know I am meant to dream of the Cadillac Hotel, its arid rooms, the windows I was afraid to look up to.

We cross the border. Sentimental moment. We try to find the CBC on the radio. Somewhere outside of Windsor, it crackles to life. A Sousa march. For a woman in Lloydminster.

(Looking up to the windows. There is a person at each one, standing, arms at their side, saying nothing, doing nothing, standing there, standing there.)

Stephen Reid

There Are No Children's Books in Prison

At 9:45 every morning the main doors to A27 open and a crowd emerges. Most of the men are already rolling cigarettes from their green MacDonald tobacco pouches, not wanting to miss a puff from their fifteen minute smoke break.

I wander off in another direction, down another corridor. I go to the library, not for a reading break, but just to be amongst books. Prison, in its simplest terms, is about not giving up, and not giving up requires respite.

The library here, fittingly, used to be the chapel. Taped to the double glass doors is a 'Take One' folder filled with photocopies of the daily crossword. I don't take one, but a friend of mine, an avid puzzler, wrote to tell me I was last week's answer to '17 Down'. Another high point, my life reduced to a clue in a crossword.

I feel safe in the library, away from the grind of the joint, away from those who invent crossword puzzles for the outside world. In here, between the green metal shelves stacked seven feet high, are my touchstones, the rows upon rows of books.

In the old days a prison library was more likely to look like a second-hand bookstore after a crowd of shoplifters had passed through. Now with yearly budgets to buy the books, and a television in every cell to ensure no one is interested in checking any out, the library remains well stocked.

I move through the familiar territory, my fingers tracing the lines of books, their titles, their authors, their publishing houses. I can almost feel the whole and complete world that is inside each. For most men, serving time kindles a more singular construct, for them the world is the thing they stand on. But between these shelves, amongst living books, the shape of your world can shift a thousand times, once for each title, or be changed forever in a single page. In its own way, the prison library is more dangerous than the big yard.

At the end of the row, I almost bump into a biker with a ponytail. His right hand, the one with the letters for LOVE tattooed across the knuckles, is wrapped around a slim volume of poetry. I want to ask who is he reading? I want to ask about his left hand which has only two letters across the knuckles – HA. Is it a zen riddle, or a tattoo interrupted? But the guy goes two and change without the ponytail; he leaves with his poetry and my questions untendered.

Alone, I roam some more. The arrangement of this library oddly reflects the prevalent social order. Brown leather bound law books, imposing by size and nature, sit all statesmen-like along one wall as if they were a private men's club. They even have their own sign, 'Do Not Remove,' as if someone is afraid we might take the law into our own hands. The adjacent wall houses the business section, beginning with a large gray tome on bank mergers which towers above all the rest. Then management books run in descending order all the way down to small entrepreneurs. The business section breaks nicely into vacation and recreation, books on golfing, skiing, and yachting. Then we enter the trade person's section with titles on plumbing, welding, auto mechanics, and carpentry. There are no children's books in prison.

The fiction wall has the most titles, lies and escapes being popular pastimes in here. Fiction begins with hardcovers – the classics, the new releases – but soon gives way to the gritty, the hard-boiled, the dog-eared detective paperbacks. It is in this seedier neighbourhood, the haunt of characters of Crumley and Chandler, Burke, Vacchs, and Bunker, where I am most at home.

But today I gravitate towards what the booksellers in the free world would refer to as 'The Woo Woo Section.' In a bookstore this section would be chock-a-block, thousands of books on crystals, and candles, and angels; guides for the twelve different stairways to heaven, recipes for dharma cookies, and chicken soup for everyone, even the chickens. You could find forgiveness, fight forgetfulness, or sue for false memory syndrome; learn to better raise your kids, your dogs, or your self-esteem. Recover your inner child, your authentic self, your femininity, your masculinity, your creativity, your sexuality, or even your virginity. But back in this library, the budget for spirituality seems thinner than a ghost. There are one hundred books, from Dewey Decimal 200.01 to 299.05, and fifty of them have Jesus in the title. Nowhere is innocence more lost than in the lives of those who reside here, yet the regional librarian must believe the only road to recovery is lit by the Star of Bethlehem.

A friend sent me a book, 'When Things Fall Apart', written by a Buddhist nun named Pema Chodron. Although Jesus and Buddha teach the same lesson – to learn to live with compassion for all things, I am compelled toward the Buddhist approach. Which is why I am standing here in 'The Woo Woo Section' looking for more of Pema Chodron. But what I find, placed there I'm sure without a trace of irony, are titles like 'Break Out' or 'Should I Leave?'. The title of 'Life, How to Survive It' takes on new meaning if you're doing it, as does 'Lethal Lovers' or 'Death in the Family' if perhaps you are the cause of such books to be written. I pick out one book called 'I Don't Want to Be Alone' and on my way out place it on the cart that goes down to the solitary confinement unit.

My fifteen minutes of sane is up. Time to return to work, tutoring South American drug lords in ESL. I'm thinking of getting LOVE tattooed across the knuckles of one hand and the words Ha Ha on the other. Or maybe I'll put '17 Down' on my butt, and if there's any ink left over, I'll tattoo some teardrops at the corner of my eye, one for every book I'll never read.

DAVID ELLIOT
NELD POET
THE HARE & HARE

12/18

*"like a hunter mapping
his path in the dark"*

FOUR

Leanne O'Sullivan

THE FISHERMAN

Between the water-sharded stones
and the whispering banks
I knelt watching you, my body
like a dark sun over the groping roots.
I knew the river by the nuzzle of marsh
at my thighs, the myriad eyes
of frog spawn floating softly
in their soaked nests, and the cavings
of my weight heaving in the damp earth.

I knelt there, watching you
on the borders of sight,
your legs and waist disappearing
in the stream as though you were half
woven from water, lifting your nets
like a creature with its scales
when the sun comes sifting down.
I had never so much trespassed, I thought,
as you bent into the crushing water,
the taut coolness of your skin
shining with the crystal salt.

I was yours, I was the waiting,
the mouthing space, the absence of language.
I had thought the first thing between us
would be a look or a word,
not that I would be watching you turn
through the shimmering coils of light
and feel between my lips the tongues
of those first hunters who wrapped
themselves in these wordless

rivers, peeled from their waists
a swaddle of knives and at once both
destroyed and devoured.

ABOUT MIDNIGHT

In among these wet, melon skins
I sit with my back to the bar,

cross-legged, smiling my red mouth.
I've painted myself black and leather.

My eyes move quickly, circling
the high, loud limbs of the night.

In the centre of the dance floor
a lioness shrieks in her own bath.

Like red pearls, dry lips pucker
to the eager glass. I drink and blaze.

An animal going mad for the garland
of a woman rolls over to the end

of the bar like a devil's tongue, red
and greasy, stoned on his own poison

and licking his lips. A man in love
spreads a flock of fingers on my thigh.

I undo them until he hates me
and raise a finger to his back.

The room is flooding, people float
as if on water and music. I stumble

onto my heels and drown with a wrong boy
while the moon turns onto her white belly

and is fed secrets by crippled mouths;
a boyfriend passed out, a glass shattered,

a woman tasted, a child coming to seed
with her legs wrapped around a man,

the night moistening the darkness
with its many breaths.

RIVER

You were the first thought the world had
when it dipped its palms and made rivers,
the grass banks sweetened and sealed
with dew, wells of healing, uneven
chanting of stones, let be, let come.

Your birth stepping quietly into light,
light wiping back the declining night.
I knew you then, restful, unknowing,
ebony in the fleshing sea, love humming
a syllable I would know you by.

Turn again. Carry your sweetness.
Bending my face to the river's lap
I can feel you, clearly, reaching up,
braiding my hair, speaking my name,
everything suddenly, beautifully, touchable.

THE LIGHTS OF NEW YORK

His funeral was six years ago. We wore black coats
and black gloves and stood at the lip of his grave,
waiting for him to disappear. The night before,

I heard that when he was a boy he sat on the hillside
near his house, and imagined the lights of New York
fluttering like candles on the miles deep horizon.

I walked out of his home, monument of his life,
to the same patch of grass where he crossed
his perfect limbs in meditation. I squinted to see his face.

The horizon burned into the night, as if the borders
of the earth came down, and I dreamed that his body
leaned forward, like a hunter mapping his path in the dark.

The last time I touched him his skin was soft,
like a spirit felt through flesh. I reach out my hand.
Eyes closed, I entered with him into that solitude,

the world of the mind, a room naked as the darkness.
It had taken all my strength to do this, to take the face
of the beloved back to the human night.

He sat calm and quiet, carpentering his city of lights.
I heard the slow preparations in the house, the life
in the town, the wind lining the sky with unutterable thoughts.

Gently, I pressed my hands into the earth.
Dark against the pale crop, in the shadow of a mountain,
the eve of his burial, at twilight, there I saw him.

Randall Maggs

BERBERS

With the plow enters dishonour.
– old tribal proverb

The way like tombs or death itself these
walls say in-here, out-there.
How they work their subtle way
when you're tired of wind and emptiness,
the numbing looking for what? water? grass?
That's when you'd think of the horses that pushed hard,
cities let back to the mountains' hush, small faces
wiped from pools. Were we after something?
Or running away? There was talk, always
explanations, none of which satisfied.
Best not to wonder at all in the end.
Still, sometimes we wanted a safe place,
rocks to crouch against, a chance to rest and
see if there was someone following behind.

But goat-hide's best. Or camel.
Haul it down when the grass
is gone. Walls like these don't breathe.
Touch them when the wind blows, you won't feel
God's whisper. And worse, they make us fat
and dull and slow to act. Enemies with
any brains at all would wait and joke
about us by their fires – what sort
of fools to trap themselves like this? –
And only when we stop we start
to wear the world away: the path from
door to door, the path to the pens
where horses wait.

For what? What need for
horses now?

And how to deal with the dead?
At night you hear them in the passes,
up in the melting snow.

With horses we make these foolish
games, bump each other fiercely at the goals,
curse our mounts when they swerve to
avoid the sweet collision.

But what about the dead?

These carpets that hide the walls, half-
moons and mountains and palms – they only
remind me of what we've
become. And my son a
mason's apprentice. He wants to go
down from the mountains to work in a city of
stone. My only son.

Another of God's great jokes.

Always I thought it was Him
behind us, chasing us into the glory
of His world. In motion is grace, I thought,
the way the spirit swells when the wind
turns and the horses, restless,
smell perfect places.

NARROW GAUGE

Stopped in a silent white country, not far
from Gallants they said, struck a moose or snow
on the tracks. A caustic rum went around, *central heating*,
said one of the locals and dealt another hand. Up ahead,
the locomotive, muffled in the trees and silent snow,
the falling snow recalling another time and frozen ponds,
skating in the dark by feel or ankling over to fetch
an errant puck, the crackle of ice in the reeds.

Step by step, he moves away from the train.
Something offers itself in the quiet. An invitation of ridges.
An odour of pitch and endlessness, of moose and bear.
But *n'ar wolf* was what he'd heard them say.

Seemed the perfect world for wolves to him.

The snow's hip deep if the crust gives away.
He used to know the way to walk like this, willing himself
to weightlessness. His eyes adjust. He sees a canopy
of trees. A hillside. Ice on a rock face.

The cars call him back to their warmth and light,
little cars on a narrow track, a train to take the kids to ride,
a loop in the park. *The Bullet*, they call her, watching to see
what you say, *takes her own time on the grades, a train for here.*

Inside, he sees Stasiuk thrashing about
trying to sleep in his too-narrow seat. Further back,
three faces pressed against the glass wondering what he was
up to, guys in the game he'd interrupted needing some air. He knew
that look that passed between them. *Goalies. What the hell.*
And two in the link for a smoke, eyeing the dark
padding closer over the snow. *Jesus Ukie, what are you
doing, a guy could disappear forever out there.*

Better than he deserves is what he thinks.

GAME DAYS

Woke to an unwelcome darkness at the window,
the clock unset, no singsong call through the locked door,
the silence out there too familiar.

What woke me? – Those kittens she got to get rid of
the golf course mice. Nervy little buggers they gallop over the bed.
Who let them in? The door locked as I said.

Must have slept on my bad side again, the elbow aches
and disintegrates. Slowly I come to the surface and there they are.
Locked in a fierce embrace, they rip at each other and bump together
over the floor. One disengages, distracted by a toppled shoe.
The other creeps closer, ready to leap, that moving
not-moving cat's trick with motion. I think of bloody Backstrom –
Lucky I call him, he can't figure why. He looks at me and lifts
his stick. *Hey Lucky, how do you feel tonight?*

God there's moments you love the game.

There's the telephone. That'll be Lefty
out in the corridor having a heart-attack. I dress and come
down to the kitchen's gaping silence. There's where my plate
hit the wall. Goaltender's theatre. A woman and children
taken to the road like refugees. I close my eyes.
I hear an unrepentant murmur from the living room,
some dreary talk show guest – *I'm not your girl next door
if you want to know.*

The sound left low as always game days.

I see their game is done. What's next
in the cat-world, I wonder. They look like glass cats
sitting on the bottom step, turning their heads together, watching
as I go. The eyes peer out at me from a world of well-timed
leaps and near-catastrophes, unexplained absences,
the skill that makes them cruel.

Stephen Brunt

from
SEARCHING FOR BOBBY ORR

On the river, he could skate forever. No barrier but the banks and the horizon, the ice stretching far out into the bay. Soon enough, the cold seemed to disappear, even for the boy who always insisted on lacing up barefoot – it just felt better, more natural, that way. Take the puck, and try to hold it. Keep away. Offer it up, then pull it back, tuck it behind the blade, make it disappear. Sleight of hand, sleight of feet. Learn to keep your head up, your eyes forward, feel the puck on your stick, don't look down. Speed up, change direction, the motion natural, deceptive, economical, graceful. No churning legs or laboured strides, even on beat-up, second-hand skates. He is smaller than the rest, a skinny kid, scrawny, no meat on his bones at all. But they can't get near him, even though it looks as if he isn't working hard, as if he is shifting through the gears in automatic – one speed, then another, then another. Size and muscle are of no use, without corners, without ends, without limits. There are no coaches standing by, waiting to impose their will. No parents shouting at the side. No drills, no repetition, but rather every rush is an improvisation, a jazz solo, a flight of the imagination. And when the boy is clear of them all, or alone by choice, when all he faces is open ice, the other sounds of his world disappear, the intermittent hum of small-town traffic, the rumble of distant factories, the angry shouts at home. Just the scrape and gouge of metal on ice, the rhythmic tap of rubber on wood, on, on forever. Pick a direction and keep on going, and eventually there's no one in the way.

* * *

This place and so many rural outposts like it are an essential element of the great national myth, the fantasy of one nation united around a puck. The truth is, most of us don't live out in the country, don't live in little towns, don't have homes within easy walking distance of a frozen river or bay or pond or slough where naturally, come winter, it's time to grab a stick and put on the skates and play the game of our ancestors. Most of us live in big cities not so distinct from big cities in the United States, in Western Europe, in Australia. Most of us would have to drive many miles on multi-lane highways through dense traffic to find a patch of natural ice (and that only if the winter was cold enough to sustain it). Many of us came from other places, far away, where hockey isn't bred in the bone. Many of us never play hockey at all. Most of us have little real experience of a place like Saskatchewan – the shinny Holy Land (at least in English Canada), birthplace of Max Bentley and Gordie Howe and Wendel Clark – which, for all its vast open spaces, is home to fewer than a million people, about a quarter of the population of Metropolitan Toronto.

Which is the real Canada? Well, that's not the point. The Canada of our imagination, the Canada that Canadians imagine while trying to pin down their elusive national identity, is somewhere just like Floral or Parry Sound or Brantford. When we look in the mirror, we want to see tough, decent people, honest workers, deferential, polite, grateful for what they have, willing to stand obediently in line, team players but unafraid to go into the corners, elbows high when it serves the collective good. We are hockey players the way Americans are, in their own very different mythology, Wild West gunslingers (independent and God-fearing and wary of authority, their individual rights held sacred above all).

The game of hockey, for Canadians, seems organic. It emerges out of the trees and rocks and ice, out of the long winter months, the rare, precious daylight, out of facing down nature, surviving and embracing whatever it can throw at us, enduring to spring. Hockey players, the best hockey players, those who go on to star in the National Hockey League – an American-based entertainment conglomerate, though Canadians can still pretend that it is their own, that it isn't just another business designed to sell tickets and beer and gasoline – come from all kinds of different places, here, the United States, Europe, the former Soviet Union. But so many of them, so many of the greatest stars of the game, seem to have come from a place just like Parry Sound. They seem to have emerged from a frozen river, from a backyard rink, to have found the source of their genius somehow in the landscape. Howie Morenz, Maurice Richard, Howe and Bobby Orr and Wayne Gretzky, spun out of the elements, out of the land.

***

It's a goddamn boring dangerous drive, Kingston to Sault Ste. Marie by bus, in the dead of winter, in a hockey league of faint hope, even without taking the scenic route, without crawling through the construction on Highway 69 and then stopping for dinner at a hotel in the middle of nowhere while the boss makes house calls. That's it. No more of this bullshit. Ask the old man what the hell's going on. You've been around. You know the ropes. You're the captain. It's your job. You tell the bastard. No more detours. No more house calls. Whatever he's getting on the side, he can get it on his own time.

The captain takes the lead, but with deference. These are hockey players who know their place, and this is 1961, before athletes in any sport dreamed that they had rights and privileges and power. The authority of the men at the top to prolong or end a career is absolute. In the Eastern Professional Hockey League, designed as a bridge between the juniors and the big time, far from the bright lights, far from the glamour (as it turns out, not far from extinction, destined to be shifted south soon enough and reborn in places where they've never seen the game), one false move and you're back home pumping gas, or worse. Still, there are a few dreamers among them. Some are young and fresh, and few will make it all the way to the National Hockey League – "Whitey" Stapleton's on the team, and so is J. P. Parise and Bruce Gamble. Mostly, though, they're guys who would rather do this than get on with their real lives, at least for now. The captain, Harry Sinden, stands out as a little bit different from his teammates, not a future star but still a hockey lifer in the making. Playing in the NHL was for him long ago out of the question. Only six teams there, only the best 120 players in the world (or at least in

North America, the known hockey world). Sinden was a decent journeyman defenceman, who had ridden his limited hockey talents and second-rate skating just about as far as they would go. He won an Allan Cup with the Whitby Dunlops back when that really meant something, the height of amateur hockey in Canada. The Dunnies were rewarded with a trip overseas, to Oslo, where they won a world championship for Canada in 1958. Two years later, Sinden was part of the Canadian team that won a silver medal in the Olympics in Squaw Valley, California. (The Americans won the gold. And how the heck did that happen?) But the pinnacle of his career, as measured in the only hierarchy that really mattered, was a single game in the American Hockey League, one big step below the NHL, and that had happened a while ago. Sinden had to be persuaded to finally turn full-time pro and move to Kingston. He was twenty-seven years old, had a wife and three kids and a good job with General Motors, but still here was the chance to make a buck playing hockey, maybe inching up the ladder, and wasn't that every kid's dream? Now he's the captain of the Kingston Frontenacs, a year away from becoming a player coach, stuck in the lowest reaches of the Boston Bruins organization – and the Boston Bruins were then stuck in the lowest reaches of the six-team league.

So there will be no boat-rocking here. Sinden knocks on Wren Blair's door a little sheepishly, even though he'd known him since they were both with the Dunnies, and it was Blair who had brought him here. Wren is a busy guy, the coach and general manager of the Frontenacs, running another team for the Bruins on the side, and he also considers himself a fine judge of hockey talent, though he feels as though he isn't getting quite the credit he deserves from his masters back in Boston.

It is evening, so he's surprised to see Sinden. Usually the boys are out having a few beers by now. When he first started coaching, Blair tried being a hardass, tried banning them from the bars and beverage rooms, but that didn't work, so he decided to take a new tack, to treat them like men. So far, so good. No one has been arrested yet. He hands Sinden a beer from his personal stash and grabs one for himself. It takes Sinden a while to summon up the courage to get to the point, to get past the hockey small talk. Then finally he steels himself sufficiently to do the captain's duty.

"Wren, the boys want me to ask you something. When we go to Sudbury, we used to drive through Smiths Falls and North Bay and then straight north. Now we're going back through Toronto and up Highway 69 and all over the goddamn place. We're eating at a hotel in Parry Sound, and then you disappear. The guys on the team are asking me to ask you what the hell is going on."

"I don't have to tell you nothing, Harry. It's none of your goddamn business."

Sinden makes his case, says he wants to learn how you run a hockey team, how you make decisions. He needs to know things about buses and highways and pit stops and the rest, as if all of that really mattered. It could come in handy someday.

"Okay," Blair relents, falling before dubious reason, and then begins his story. "There is a boy…"

He spins a tale that might as well be the Canadian hockey ur-myth, about a golden child, a genius, a prodigy, a shinny Mozart born of the rocks and the trees and the water of near-Northern Ontario, fully formed, original, perhaps the greatest player who has ever been born. And just maybe he'll ignore the Maple Leafs and the mighty Habs, he'll turn down the Wings and Hawks and Rangers, he'll sign over his playing life instead to the sad-sack Bruins and lead them, finally, to the Promised Land. He is up there in Parry Sound and Blair is courting him, buttering up the family, keeping in touch, trying to get the inside track. That's what the mysterious side trips, the detours, the dinners are all about.

"Shit," Harry says. "That's all? That's it? We thought you had a broad."

Ben Hynes

WE SPOKE ONLY WITH OUR FEET

"Each of them moving like a wedge into the blackness"

Shovels in hand we stand
at pond's edge. Step onto snow,
push powder back, expose
opaque surface, a flatness reaches
frozen to the invisible shore. Breathe

steam out. Wood-stove smoke
loans my hair its scent. Bent double,
lace chases rabbits to tie
silver blades to our feet. We carve
secret inscriptions in ice; blades

cut long hand calligraphic letters; toe
pick punches periods,
exclamation points, indents,
sprays chips into low
snow falls.

She skates a figure-eight.
I make myself the axis
of her infinity. She seals forever
with a hand in my back
pocket. The lines signed on water

stay only until spring thaw.

John Ennis

POOL ICE

Bare ash, beech and elm stood round like hopeless parents
  about the frozen pool

in thorn hedges at right angles, whose diminishing crimson haws
blackened in the steady north-east wind with snow.
A knife plunged randomly round my fiery lungs.

How the freezing water rushed my kneecaps!
I saw the world tilt on me out on the ice.
Fear gutted me in that forge-field hollow.

The pool ice groaned beneath my eyes,
my depth and more to the bottom.
Breath burned in my windpipe.

Found the adrenalin to spring toward the edge of the pool,
studs digging in the lower-tiered ice cracking, too, fell flat
with flailing hands feet kicking out froglike. Bellied
  to the first grass tuft,

pulled clear with the aid of a withered dock,
saw at my back the centre ice beyond repair;
no matter what frosts, snows now might stay with us

fun evenings, ice fit no more for skating on.

Boy Amongst Sparrows

i

He recalls Tony's hay benchknife that carved halfmoons
and a white-beamed sun over wintry boughs
on a hurley Sunday his cousin Michael did not come.

They were the days of family and grain farms,
of oats tall in the stem lodged by a rogue shower,
the end of August when the first gale blew,
when crows and pigeons glided down in flocks.

We children were dispersed to scatter them.

Each midland house with its own tilled ripe cornfields,
grain scattered freely in yards of rhode island red and sparrow,
grain fed to pigs and calves and ground in a barn where the new
electric grinder spread a fine white flour dust even out the door.

Contesting the troughs with turkeys, ducks and geese
untameable, domestic, close and yet distant, the birds
held assemblage over him, as a child in the yard, up in the great elm.

Sparrows battling with wyandottes for the evening victuals.

Their cheeky skulls are long fallen into nettles, mosses of the dyke,
covered in the ground like fathers, mothers,
freckled cousins let loose in the back meadow
where sparrows of the air rose up for them in flocks.

Sparrows no strangers then in blue changeable skies.

ii

...and the young calf dying.
I do not recall what malady left him prostrate kicking,
made him bawl so. It happened all the time.

Half a century before, children fell down in swathes

from diphtheria. Staring at us, through us, we cradled
his head with an armful of fresh straw.

Whether fattened animal or old man,
Westmeath was a county where death
  called like the postman.

iii

And after supper, they'd bury you
sorrowing one to the other, for you never bothered sheep.

All the late sunlit afternoon you lay, my brothers' collie
by the garden hedge, but out on the south-facing riverfield,
your white teeth bared in little ivories for your tongue,
glossy bluebottles tinkling one open almond eye,

late August or so for sweet pippins with magpies
up in the old tall apple trees ripened red and unseen
the orchard side of the hedge with the bitter crab,
your bushy tail rigid, your thin legs, too.

Corn was on the noisy mind of reaper and binder.
Gold barley bearded me like an older brother.

And I who loved to raise up my two arms,
cross them round your ruff neck, rub your slender nose
  that tapered,
touch the black-tipped ears that looked forward
hurried past you in the hot sun. Bluebottles lit all over me;
magpies in the apples cackled for your other eye,
and I was so afraid in my heart of the dead.

iv

No bawling as the nose ring gripped. Orgy of kicking of a
sudden went numb. The sawing of horns started in dusk, and my
mother thought mist was mist falling or midges grasped vainly
in the bloody fist (hot water to wash she left on a shed window
sill for fear the beast lunged). Sawing through horns sounded
poor, like sawing a hempen sack, or sacks together as the bullock
peed. Crows cawed eternally towards Lynch's and the pine
plantation. Water splashed as she lashed milky water on sliced flesh.
Head runny with blood to be dry before morning, and the flies,
the bullock unchained staggered off shaking his hornless skull all
down the long garden. Then the next bullock, and the next, eyeing
us through torn galvanized. Outside, below the elm tree, thin
bracelets of hair adorned horns piled in a heap at the gate post into
the long garden. In the kitchen as men sat down to a meal, a faint
odour of blood on overcoats hung in the porch.

v

Always on the dusty summer roads
after mealtimes when the men had left,
they'd call at the kitchen door. Males in flight,
they knew the short-cuts parish to parish,
said little. Sometimes word travelled (de-frocked
and priest, another lost his farm in poker).

Sussed out the sheds for a doss
as they sat at table for a bite of bread.
Once sawed a whole panloaf for one
till our eyes met over first names.

Something wrapped for them,
a little pep then in their step,

their stained windy greatcoats filling out like Suibne's wings
they hit the road to put down some other house miles away
where they might expect the same

no questions asked.

vi

...that whirr-whirr-whirr of wing
...that high-pitched honking in the sky
passing over, mostly sideways wild geese
like a correct tick on a copy at school
from the north west south south-east
across November trees gone bare.

In their long necks a virility of ice-ridden times,
a promise of snow for us in their grown-up plaints.

Their wings like the arms of ballet dancers grown dancers' wings
in the now musicless heavens, but we heard them on their skies to
the green sloblands, no nuisance to cattle or sheep-intense acres
to peck and peck long intervals within ease of flight and the sea.
At school, history caned our arms and legs in short pants with
dates old finger-gnarled Mammy Burke said were important and
she breathless in her chair by the fire.

Neighbour met neighbour stopped on the road,
their legs crooked over the bars of bikes

looking up too late to the empty heavens.

As kids, we wished them like foreign cousins back
till they were specks lost on the sun's horizon.

Look at them, look at them, we cried

vii

You, high up, stretching to each fruited twig
a rising October moon east of our damson tree

a nip, then, in the freshening east wind from Murtagh's
you, shirt-sleeved, up the branches after the tartiest

your fingers nimble as talons
closing on the velvet harvest

gathering the last of the damsons
the indigo sky at your back.

Balanced on a hook
from a trusty bough

the galvanized pail filled,
or nearly so, with tangy fruit

goodly-sized and wild;

you reached out to whet your tongue,
Tony, spit out the stone.

A pale and placid midland moon
rose higher with a blackbird cry.

With ease of limb
you lay horizontal on the boughs you loved,

on branches you could depend on
to gather your knees round,

lowered a full bucket
to a boy in corduroy.

Adrian Fowler

THE RUSSIANS ARE COMING

That winter we trudged
through snow-laden woods
at twilight
slowly and in single file
picking our way among the landmines.

In spring, we gathered on a hill
and awaited the order to charge
the valley below
across an oil-surfaced, pot-holed road
and a brook locally known
as the sewer river.

At times, life was more mundane.
Wielding pickaxe and shovel
we cleared drains of ice and snow
against the sudden spring melt.
We were said to be good at that
having laboured outdoors
in all kinds of weather
all our young lives.
Hadn't our grandfathers survived
the November storm in Gallipoli
when hundreds of others died,
though they occupied the trenches
struck with the worst floods?

But the air raid siren and the school drill
told us we were civilians after all
and the rockets carried weapons
our traditions could not comprehend.

With friends from the American base
whose fathers were charged to protect us
we scanned the clouds for bombers
and the darkening trees for spies.

Laura Lush

THE OTHER SIDE OF THE LAKE

Frank and Bea Donkersley lived on the other side,
the sandy part where their dock jutted
out in a long brown tongue.
Around their cottage were the birches
and the laugh lines of sun at dusk.
Our cottage was on the rocky side – a chocolate
melted into marble.
Every morning our father would throw us off the dock
emptying that two-room cottage
like you'd empty a fishbowl.
On the other side we could see Frank and Bea
sitting at the dock's edge sipping coffee,
Frank's hairy chest like a blanket of spiders.
In the afternoon we'd beg them to take us over,
our orange motor boat plotting through the water.
When we got there, Frank would stand up and salute us
with his tall gin, in his plaid bathing suit, the white
peaked cap. Then he'd walk over and say, "Fee, Fie, Fo, Fun,"
cup his giant hands over our pink-shell ears,
lift us up as if lifting us from the earth we'd been planted
in for a little while, the slender parsnips of our bodies
dangling so we could see his face –
those wonderful fuzz-covered ears creeping open.

How Trees Grow

Between bark and wood, the secret cambium
layers keep growing. Each dark ring adding a new
layer of wood to the older wood.
(As if what grows new will never have to suffer.)
But it's the darker interior portion, the heartwood
that deceives the most. Even the hollow trees, leafy impostors,
go on living year after year.
How do such things continue?
It's because, like all great survivors, the living is done
on the outside,
in the tenuous outer few inches of trunks
until they are found out, until some storm breaks them.
But for now, they are everywhere, dusting the hills
with their lush green tresses,
so tall and woman-thick, fruit-heavy
with plum and peach. Their hearts tucked
in dark spidery knolls.
In each of the seasons, trees are the only things
worth looking to.
Listen to the trees. They are never wrong.

WITNESS

My father at 61
clings to this farm
like blood to an accident.
How for thirteen years he's tried
to make it work.
I watch his geese bobbing behind him,
the water balloons of their bodies
splashing forward, their necks
loose white springs.
Watch him chase his heifers
across the fields, his legs
graceful as a hockey player's.
And I watch him drive the tractor back
to the barn at night, hunched over,
the porch blossoming with moths.
But mostly I watch him watch
other farmers falling.
Their big hands
fold over their faces while
the earth tightens.

Riverside Heights

It was as if some giant had landed there years before
and, from his pocket, placed the little blue house
down on the grass, fresh and shiny as an after dinner mint.
And the house sat there for a little while
until they came – these Irish – all seven of them,
dragging the tattered cloth of their own island behind them,
and stuffed their too-big bodies into those too-small rooms
with the too-small beds that shook every time a train rattled past.
They didn't know then that they were making local history,
that for years after their departure,
the neighbours would still be talking about *them*.
How their windows and balconies flowered with dirty laundry,
how their boxers sailed from the TV antennae regally as kites.
How on Friday nights – or sometimes even Tuesdays – they'd run
up and down the stairs banging pots – and still later,
home after the pub, they'd charge through each other's flats
with *kendo* sticks and boogie boards, mad as bulls.
It was presumed on many a night that they had killed one another,
squashed each other's bodies into wardrobes
and garbage bags, tossed them off the balcony
into the clear shimmering of rice paddies.
While their fortress slowly grew – the tall brown
beer bottles, toppling one after the other
like fallen soldiers.
Some nights
they still see them dancing.
The white-bellied pagans from another kind of island.

Gordon Rodgers

from
EMERGENCY ROADSIDE SERVICE

Okay he says I'll tell you what happened then but first we gotta get a couple more he whistles and the beers are on the way don't know if I can swallow another mouthful without...can I swallow another mouthful without throwing some of it up...I nod can't speak I focus on him so he becomes the center the full of my vision the bar lights left and right an unstable skirl....

All I wanted was something to keep me busy busy busy got this job with a shop and worked days did overtime and coulda worked through the night felt like it and one night when I was heading out to Mingles the phone rings and just for the hell of it I pick it up and there's this guy broke down on Mundy Pond Road and he's desperate to get his car out of there but all the shops are closed and all the tow trucks are out and the guy is practically crying there on the phone I ask him what happened well it sounds like he's lost transmission fluid which I tell him could be a big problem or no problem depending on where it's leaking from and I say and this is the beginning of it really I say look I've got to go that way anyway so I'll drive by and have a look at it for you and when I'm leaving the shop you know I take a length of rubber hose borrow some liters of fluid and I take my kit cause if it's the line that's broken I can fix that on the spot at least enough so's the guy can get to a garage and I get there and the guy's sitting white with fright and worry there in the dark locks all the doors when I pull up behind him and it's the line alright but fixing it was a bitch first of all I forgot to bring a light so I had to use this guy's penlight had to bite it between my teeth cause I needed my hands to work and the car was on this soft shoulder and kept shifting on me after I got it jacked up and this guy keeps saying watch out get out the jack's slipping but I didn't care I figured thanks to Lisa I was in too much pain to die death would've been too easy but I sure did learn the first thing you have to know about roadside service Neil is that you are always working in less than ideal conditions so when the job's done the guy gives me a hundred and I was going to give it to the garage but I paid them for the hose and the fluid and left it at that used what was left to go towards the GMC half-ton and I spent a coupla weekends building the box on back you know I figured I'd fix it up later but I'll guess you'll have to do that now Neil boy but that was the beginning of the Emergency Roadside Service got off to a slow start but when I got into the Yellow Pages business went boom you wouldn't believe the number of people out there and the kinds of trouble they get into and most of it a little care and maintenance could've prevented but it was perfect for me I was my own boss I had everything I needed in the truck I was ready and willing to go anytime as long's I could get a coffee and roll a smoke on the way and hell I wanted to be going all the time if you stop you have time to think hell I don't believe but for one night that I've slept eight straight hours in two maybe three years and I'll tell you that's a hell of a way to go brain dead and another thing is it's not a job where you're going to meet a lot of women not many are going to call and arrange to meet a man on some lonesome stretch of highway or back road where they're stranded I'll tell you it just don't happen they'll wait get their husband boyfriend or brother to call and meet you and another thing Neil don't work on anything foreign I learned that one the hard way the North American cars your alternator gives up the ghost you whip it out you might be able to pick one up rebuilt or you buy a new one and you stick it back in I mean it's so simple you could almost do it with chewing gum but anything foreign you'll spend hours trying to unwrap it from the engine and then you'll wait weeks for parts so Neil save yourself the aggravation and the heartache and do as I did first question I ask what kind of car are we talking about it keeps things uncomplicated...

As the waitress passes by he points to our glasses I hold up my hand but he's having none of that insists two....

Gotta be ready to go in any weather in the worst kind of weather because cars die in the wet in the cold the worst night I had wet and cold freezing fucking rain a car *kaput!* on the Arterial you remember that night coated everything in a foot of ice knocked power out in some places for days and I swear to God my trusty GMC steed and I were the only things moving on the Avalon that night they even took off the salt trucks but we two shattered out of our ice mold and slipped and slid to the rescue and the guy had just flooded out I thought at first and I cleaned those plugs burned the crud off so they could spark reaching down into the guts of that engine into that freezing metal to pull them out the cold running down my neck man it was one miserable miserable time and it wasn't the plugs anyway I ended up under the engine trying to twist this rusted nut I was soaked through and through I knew I could give it up come back the next day but I got it in me that I was not going to give it up so I took off my gloves wrapped both hands around that wrench and pulled and I was not going to give up until it sprung free and that was how it went all night I mean I worked on that shitbox the whole night through in the morning the guy started up and drove away and my hands were raw meat for a week where they'd been cut and frostbitten where I'd torn skin off infected but that night you know I discovered I wasn't completely brain dead after all I kept having this thought you know this particle of light at the base of the brain somewhere that someday I'd live in a warm place and things were different after that cause warmth was the first thing I wanted in a long time Jeez this beer is a-loosenin me *up!* More *More!* now don't you ago fading on me Neil there you go straighten up and let me tell you how it ends why I sold it all to you you see I got this call this day from a woman broke down said I should come right away guess I was so surprised forgot to ask what make and sure enough when I get there it's Japanese-make and I'm planning to tell this woman that I don't do foreign jobs but this woman is something else is a sight to behold the kind you see in shampoo commercials the interior of that car was white and that car was made for a woman like her for people like her not for a grease monkey like me for sure she had gold rings and bracelets she was the first woman I'd seen in a couple of years that I was attracted to right off the same way I was with Lisa but no way did I have to worry about this chick improving my life so I did the job and she was on her way and

162

things proceed as usual but this car's giving her a lot of trouble which I gotta admit is unusual for those foreign jobbies so I see her again and again I guess you know like it was meant to be and this one night she calls and the car's dead in the driveway and I'm there in a flash because you know like by then we have this professional relationship because I know what I'm doing under that hood and I don't fuck around with her billing because you know it turns out she's a lawyer you met her earlier Neil the lawyer Neil she's my woman and I'm her man but what happened that first night is like romance and that's nobody's business but our own but you know the first time we bedded down you know I'm hard like the fucking wrench and clean too you know you know she made me shower and *Goddam'* it's over just like that I almost cried I mean she was the first since the other one...you alright Neil...maybe skip this round, eh? – so anyway one thing's led to another so we've decided to go where it's warm – *ooooh!* watch out there Neil boy...cause whatever else this place is you know it is some kind of a place to dream out of...we traded in her car on a Chevy by the way I'm just an old-fashioned kind of guy I guess...O-*kay* party's over, no no you ain't driving lad you'll only get yourself all kinds of grief...c'mon Neil I'm driving you home.

Joel Hynes

HOMECOMING

They crouched underground for all time and grew too close.
Each crumbling descent to the front door
became late night and hazy, confused
somewhere between a homecoming and a life sentence.
An arrangement with a double bed,
week-old sheets and a stab at some form of living.
Then came talk of a real home,
and with that talk her heart stopped giving in.
The dishes piled up, the floors changed texture
and forces lined up against them.
Their separate histories went to war,
refusing to blend or bend or even negotiation.
He left her there and reawakened groggy in foreign bedrooms
with foreign arms wrapped around him.

Later that same life he waits,
shuffling on her dainty new doorstep smoking
and hoping she will approve of the latest change that had come
    over him.
Fingernails chewed down to the quick and bleeding.
But she arrives tornado fashion, distant with anticipation
and with the willful abandon of a lost child drawn away by a
    stranger
from all things familiar and warm, he follows her inside.

The walls and floors and ceilings of the house are made of wood.
The windows are glass. There are pipes and wires concealed.
And because we come closer to death with each passing breath,
he labels it an adequate place to hunker down in the final hours,
confessing and healing and burying hatchets.
But it might take him two or three years to fix an omelet with a
    clear conscience.

She could always rig 'em up so quick.
Even the mice in the crawl space will rest easier
to hear her footsteps on the hardwood floors above.
And watching her fill those hollow rooms with new used furniture,
tits and tats and brick-a-brack,
he smells no coffee in the mornings to follow.
There will be no poems shared over new glass tables here.
No long nights to come staying up too late to get things done.
The place will never feel anything for him.
Yet she will find camouflage amongst old press-back chairs,
the fisherman's couch her eye's been on since Christmas.
That drawer in the kitchen will never get on his nerves.
This floorboard needs to be replaced
but she wouldn't think to ask him
and he wouldn't think to offer.
Later that same night they found blankets, musty and gray
and lay down fumbling,
in a futile attempt to rekindle a spark that had winked out long ago.
She slept feeling safe and he lay beside her listening,
the empty old house creaking and alien, leaning with the wind.
The first of the rain came
and with it a steady drip through a rustic stain in the ceiling.
He placed an ancient tobacco tin beneath the leak
and he willed his feet to do what feet are meant to do.
There was an oilskin on a hook and he left the house with it,
thinking it all he would need.

Later still there came a hammering, biblical downpour
that arrested and consumed the speck of him, the dot that he was,
stumbling and stung out on the old highway.
And despite the ferocious and prophetic anger to this rain,
it followed only him for miles, blackened the untreated oilskin
he'd stolen from a hook in a house that would never know him.
And since the rest of the world was bone-dry and filled with
    certainty

he threw his head back to scream at the onslaught,
unable to empathize with workers out on the water.
He waded through to his final hours and set himself waiting.

Who to hunker down with in the closing moments.
Which face from the past would track him down to pass judgment
or clear up some delicate matter of conscience.
Who loves you enough to place themselves beside you in the end.

The oilskin clung to his dark frame and he knew the frozen panic
of confused and trapped animals at night on slick black asphalt,
yearning for the cubby holes they've long ago outgrown.

Ruth Lawrence

FIRST PRIZE

I have scribbled so much
savoured so little
in my search to win you.

If I scrounge together
all the most perfect words
and place them in the correct order
will you then be mine?

What if I devour dictionaries
diet on grammar and binge upon
Plath and Pittman
Neruda and Agnes Walsh
Yeats, Heaney and Kavanagh

And still you leave me to my picking and pecking
attempting to reorder language in a fitting
tribute to my love,
to outwit,
outdo outright, a poet?

THE SCAVENGER
for Helen Gregory

This room is filled with remnants.
Exoskeletons of beetles and bees
interred on your shelves
find their way into conversations
between a broken girlfriend
and a hand-picked beach rock.

Across the room, atop your breastbone
the skull of some fortunate crow
rests, eternally engulfed in oil
and your brush strokes, its white sockets
peering through your contented sternum
the same way you peruse my aching heart.
You are the seabird,
home amongst the wave-blasted builder's bricks
and forsaken floats of last year's fishermen,
collector of devil's purses and whore's eggs.

Perhaps one day you could
salvage my life,
paint me with a comfortable skin?

Christopher Pratt

I HAD ALREADY WRITTEN POETRY FOR YOU

I had already written poetry for you.
I had said, rhetorically,
you were a symphony of pink and gold,
a song of white and blue.

Forgive me my small jealousies.
I could not bear to think of you
in someone else's arms
for all you shielded me from that reality
I feared the silent evidence
the echo of a foreign substance on your lips,
a different rhythm on your breath.

Did I tell you that one night I dreamed
about a perfect meadow, shining, square,
polished by the sharp salt air
filled everywhere with flowers and waving grass –
it didn't seem that anyone had trodden there.

You brought me petals every morning,
fresh, until I held them angled to the light
where I could see that something
had passed over them at night.

Homecoming to the End

That way he had of looking over his glasses at me
when I tried to say something matter-of-fact,
but knew I wasn't pulling it off.
He wouldn't say anything, would never answer right away,
just go back to his paper
and say it to the print, matter-of-fact.

I told him I was going to marry a sailor
and go away. He said: "Go away?
To where you know no one?"
That stopped me, made me lonely
before I'd made the steady plans.
"It's your life, and you can always change
your mind," he said.
He made it difficult to rebel.

Years later, he rowed us across Southeast Arm.
With the sail up, the air felt softer on the skin,
the mind relaxed into a carefree sinking.
The open canvas flapped in the wind,
billowing out like a blossoming magnolia.
As he coasted us in, I trailed my hand through the water.
Then the *plunk, plunk* of each oar
hauled over, and placed inside the boat.

Dad cut off a thumb-size slice of tobacco.
"You can row back," he said, "if the tide is right.
If not, I'll take her, or we can wait til the tide turns."
I thought, how odd for him, his daughter gone away
and come back with a southern accent.
I remembered that line from *Gone With the Wind*,

where the black servant says, "I don't know nothin'
bout birthin' no babies, Miss Charlotte."
I'd change that around to, "I don't know nothin'
bout rowin' no dory, Daddy."
But he wouldn't get the joke, besides, we never joked.
Joke was an American word, like cookie, and divorce.

I sat transcribing ballads from cassette tape to page.
He leaned into the doorjamb of my bedroom,
listening to the songs about people he knew
who had died in gales, or sly youths
who had gotten away with something.

I'd say, "What's that, Dad? What's he saying?"
He'd look over his glasses at the machine,
"Clamped ahold to" he'd say, or "Two-buckle spring in your knee,"
a grin spreading into silent memory.
I'd imagine him leaning on a wall at a dance,
waiting to make sure he'd pick the right girl to ask.
Mom said, "Your father would wait til the end of the night
to ask for a dance, right when you'd thought
he never cared for you. A hard man to figure out."

But he was never hard. No. His curse word was "Judas."
His temperament even, his pace full and steady.
At his wake, a man took my hand and said,
"Your father wasn't a man you prayed for, but prayed to."
I turned away. I didn't want him made into a saint,
a man unreachable. I wanted his prejudices, his blind
church-going to meet my sinful life of drinking and manizing.
I wouldn't let him get away from me that easy.
He wouldn't rise at the right hand of anyone.

So I lay in his bed the night he was buried,
remembering his hand in mine, us going for ice cream.
Mom banged on the door, "Come out, you'll drive your nerves bad.

Come out and join the party for your father."
But I lay there surrounded by his few clothes hanging,
the smell of Beaver plug, the crucifix,
the blurred and moving Blessed Virgin dissolving into the
    Bleeding Heart.
I lay there with his words and stories, ships hove into rocks,
St. Pierre wine in wooden casks, the whaling factory in Rose
    au Rue,
words I clung to, knowing his passing took away a world.

In the morning, before dawn, a light touch on my head,
a blur of white mist in the room, the faraway words trailing off:
"Get up, now, and let me rest. Go on and help your mother, now."
I threw back the blanket and stumbled into the grey light of day.

THE COWS WERE THERE
Bere Island, West Cork, Ireland Nov. 2003

In the kitchen with just a low light on
I watched the sky break open into the day
and I heard the cows rustle through the brittle leaves
before I saw them. They came out of the old orchard
into the day and stood and stared at me,
seven of them. I said What? And they blinked.

Once a great grey heron dropped out of the sky
into Bere Haven inlet just as the sun was opening
orange right behind it. The heron looked like he was
called in to report to the sun.
When those cows realized I had nothing to offer,
they looked disappointed and moved
away from the window to the other side of the house.

Simone stands at the half-door with the top
half opened and latched back. Her arms are folded over
her chest and it is half dark behind her. "Don't you
love the cows, Mommy, how they're just there?" I'm
in the kitchen with the heron in case it flies off,

for it is there still, only shifting from leg to leg now,
and the cows there, there all day for one whole week.
We are in their pasture.

The lane we walk up has hidden ditches covered in gorse
and hawthorn, deep ditches well hidden which is why we have to walk.
I ran the car into the ditch grinding the rim, so here we are in the
half-dark walking so she can wait with Silvana's children
for the bus to the ferry.

The walk back is full of cows and the sun really coming up
over the inlet and spraying out over the barren hills of West Cork.
Across the harbor I see the house Neil Jordan bought for his mother
after he did good with *The Crying Game*. Old ascendency homes dot

the shore and there's the heron again, ascending himself, toes
    delicately
reaching for the rounded rocks on the shore.

My hands are in my pocket but I'm not cold.
It is more the need to place my whole self
squarely, straight up and down into what is new,
never mind the need to connect again with what is old,
with what could have been me.

FOR ANITA

There was a soft rain there on the balcony in Porto.
All of us were happy there, happy with expectation,
that beautiful country, so open for us, so full of us already.
Take me back to this beautiful country, oh my heart.

You and me Anita, at the table with the senhora so severe,
with the chicken and the perfumed white wine, the bread,
the ghost-white cheese. That was enough, that was us in an
    afternoon,
a lifetime of history behind us, on the heels of ourselves,

knowing we trailed after ghosts, that they lay in vaults
like bottles of old port hauled up to the light.
We sat, expecting nothing and anything, and the ghosts spoke
because we cannot live unless they whisper, unless they shout,

and echo on the stone squares, and bang into our hearts.

Wayne Johnston

from
THE STORY OF BOBBY O'MALLEY

I was eight when we moved from Little Annie's to Duley's. On the settled shore of a small lake, Duley's was the summer home of a St. John's businessman.

We moved into Duley's the first of September, knowing all the while we would have to move out by the middle of June. "Our days are numbered," my mother said. "Our days are always numbered," my father said, "it's just that this time we know what the number is." The number was 289.

But Duley's was a great house, if only *because* our days were numbered. It had wonderful hardwood floors, so waxed and polished you could slide across them on stockinged feet. My father and I had contests to see which of us could slide the farthest. We polished one side of the living-room at least twice a week to keep it in prime condition. In the evenings, my mother would sit and read, or watch television, pretending not to notice as my father and I slid to and fro along the opposite wall, arms outstretched like surfers. Sometimes we slipped. I had sense enough, when slipping, to let myself fall, but my father would fight it until the end. A look of sheer terror on his face, propelling himself backwards with a mad flurry of feet and waving his arms for balance, he sometimes skated halfway across the room before finally encountering the furniture. On these occasions, my mother, as soon as she saw that he was slipping, would get up from the chesterfield and stand safely off to one side. It became a routine inconvenience, one she would perform without in the least interrupting what she was doing; uninterested, as if standing at the movies to let some stranger by, she would not even look up from her book, as my father, like an errant pinball, careered about the room.

There was a chandelier at Duley's, suspended like a great cluster of tear-drops from the ceiling.

There was a bunk-bed, with drawers large enough for an eight-year old to crawl into.

And there was an attic, not the kind in which you had to go round on all fours, taking care you didn't plunge between the support beams, through the ceiling, but the kind you could live in if your mother let you. Of course mine didn't. In fact, after the first day, I was not allowed up there. But it was enough to have seen it once. It was dark and damp and smelled of old wood. At the far end, there was a small round window you could look out of. Except for the big boxes, piled in the blackest corner, it was empty. There was the kind of space that only a mind can fill.

I saw it only once, but I remembered everything: the constant droning whistle of wind; the way the walls were cracked and creased with daylight; that, by sitting to one side of the window, you could look out onto an unsuspecting world. Always, I imagined I was in it, and when we moved, I took it with me. It became the setting for all the books I read, for I read only those with twilit covers, covers that promised cold wind and grey skies, gloomy northern gods and heroes fated for hardship and misery. I loved every minute of it. I was up inside my head, up in the attic where no-one could see me; and what came through that window was dim and dismal, filtered so, through dust and glass, even the sunlight made me cry.

There was the weather. At Duley's, the verandah was enclosed in a lattice-work of wood and glass. It was there I would go on grey or stormy days, and at night. I loved to watch the weather from that verandah. We did not spend a summer at Duley's, so it seems, that year, there was none. There was only fall and winter for me, and me with my face to the glass. Before I was ten, I knew all about weather. I knew how, in winter, with a storm coming, to tell if it would snow or rain, or if the snow would change to rain. I knew the colour of pavement was important; and I saw how, with rain on the way, the hard clean edges of snowdrifts soften, and the texture of old snow changes. I could tell a storm-blue sky, and the difference between cold and the rawness of wind.

My father found my fascination with weather strange. He abhorred my passion for snowstorms. Winter storms have been all things for me. Back then, they brought people together and would not let them go away. They had my mother and father, for a while, live life as I lived it – within walls, safe inside the storm. I loved it when a storm closed in, when the world got smaller and smaller, until it seemed our house was all there was.

My father could not bear to watch the weather, because it was constantly doing things he hadn't predicted. He had me watch it for him. "Snowin' yet, Bobby?" he'd say; or, late at night, pacing the floor: "Jesus Bobby, where *is* that storm?"

In the mornings, my mother was always out of bed before him, and the first thing he would say when she woke him was, "Okay, Agnes, give me the bad news." A synopsis of the weather would follow, punctuated at intervals by my father shouting, "Aha, I told you so," or, more often, "How can that be?"

He was not the "I don't write 'em, I just read 'em" sort of weatherman. He wanted to be, but people would not let him. In our town, my father was both shaman and scapegoat. The first few years, he tried to explain to people that he was not responsible for forecasting the weather: meteorologists did that. Of course this convinced no-one. "Meteorologist" was a word just big enough to be resented, just strange enough to suggest that my father had made it up. In fact, people seemed to believe that my father not only forecast the weather, but somehow controlled it – either consciously, in straight-forward witch-doctor style; or unconsciously, in that the weather somehow took on his personality. Whatever way you looked at it, he was an enemy of the people. It got to the point that, when the accusation of rain, drizzle and fog was brought against him, he would, with a shrug and a grimace, goodnaturedly admit his shortcomings – and give promise of better days ahead.

In the telling, a life should open slowly, but it doesn't, because memory accelerates the early years to make sense of them. There is, however, a point where this acceleration stops and real memory begins. This happens at Duley's.

There, my mother and father have faces that I know are not borrowed from later years, so it is a kind of birth for them. Here are my parents, newborn, middle-aged. I find my father in the living-room, with his back to the window. Once I touch him, I will not see him like this again. I will only, through the years, from time to time, almost remember. I will watch him from across a room and almost remember the way he was before he became a part of me. I will not, but almost, remember how to step back and see him, strange and real. Perhaps I should wait. I should walk about him now for as long as it takes and memorize everything. And yet I know that, no matter what I do, the world, when I touch him, will come between us, and I will never see him again. Arms about his neck, I hug him hard and kiss his cheek; and, as I do so, he speaks my name.

I find my mother in her room, at her desk, writing, looking like a woman on the cover of a handwriting primer: feet on the floor and slightly apart; posture perfect; pen-hand, free hand and paper each in its right relation of angle and space. She has stopped, pen poised above the paper. I have caught her in the middle of a sentence already written. There are words on either side, but those to come she cannot see. If I could tell her, now, before I touch her, I would tell her she need not write. I'd say, "put your pen down, please. Stop. Stay here." But I can't. So neither will I remember that, slow as sorrow, I cross the room and, stretching forth my hand, touch my finger to her cheek. There is a fine, tinkling sound, as of sleep falling from her eyes.

They have faces. My mother, 35 years old, whenever she was accused of being beautiful, put on more lipstick, the thick, deep harlot-red kind which, back then, looked unnatural without a wrinkled face behind it. She powdered her face all over, except where there was a redeeming pimple or blackhead – these she would highlight with eyebrow pencil. She wore what my father called a "construction bra," which was, he swore, applied to the body very much like a plaster cast. She also wore a girdle, giving her what he called "that steel-belted look."

More than my mother's body, I remember the things she put on it. What she was like underneath I hardly know. There was her perfume. She always reeked of perfume. She was a woman under siege, behind a fortress of fragrance. She was like a planet, with an atmosphere all her own.

Her hair, which I know from old photographs to have hung, Godiva-like, down her back, she had cut the day before she married my father. According to him, she had, till then, gone all her life without having it cut. Growing up, she was the envy of the other girls. Imagine, to have a mother that would let you grow your hair, they said. But to everyone's horror, the day before her wedding she went to town and had her long brown hair cut, and brought it home in a box. And those who came to the wedding were given cake and a lock of her hair. Afterwards, she kept what was left of her hair short, rolled it with spiked curlers and kept it, all of it, on top of her head. As for the box of hair, not all of it was given away at her wedding. My mother kept more than half, and by "kept" I mean she never did destroy it. She kept the box under her half of the bed, and moved it with us from house to house. She told me once that she cut it so that, in later years, she would have something by which to remember her childhood – a part of life, lopped off, preserved. Talking of her childhood, she would gesture, almost imperceptibly, toward the bedroom.

One day at Duley's, I went into her room without knocking and saw her at the bureau, with the box unopened on her lap. She was absorbed before the mirror, watching herself in the glass. I was in the mirror behind her, but she did not see me. She folded her arms the way the arms of the dead are folded and began, with her hands, to caress the air, as if there was a kitten on each of her breasts. That was the first time I'd seen the box and I didn't know what was in it. Confused and frightened, I backed out slowly and closed the door.

The 13th Annual March Hare
an evening of words and music

"rocks over rocks tumbling /
towards Ireland"

FIVE

Michelle Dwyer

OLIVER'S COVE, 29 SEPTEMBER

The waning voice of a hurricane
unstuck from the throat
of the ocean
here.

Gale winds blow white capped waves
gulls and gannets,
to shore
seeking shelter from storm surge.

Underfoot –
stones
the smoothed teeth of the old world,
glass shards made docile by turbulence,
driftwood,
secret bones twisted among kelp.

All scattered jewels
for children to covet on windowpanes.

The growl of oncoming October
subdued
by rocks over rocks tumbling
towards Ireland

Michael Crummey

WOMEN'S WORK

Sit down, my son, sit down, she won't stir now till dark. Gives me an hour's peace of an evening to smoke. Never had no use for cigarettes but I'd as soon take a pipe as a feed of salt beef. And you can tell by the look of me I don't mind eating.

She always said what she loved about me was my appetite, that I was an easy man to keep happy. I take that to mean she got nothing complimentary to say about my looks but I never held it against her. Ate whatever was put in front of me and fell into flesh. Sat with a pipe after supper to watch her clear the table and put the house to rights.

All that women's work and the looking out for her I does now, she won't abide anyone else in her kitchen so I learned to cook after a fashion. Spoons soup to her and washes her arms and legs with a cloth and a pan of warm water before we settles for the night. She keeps a hand to my belly while we lies there, pinches it like a youngster's cheek – proud of it she is, as if it was some prize creature she raised from a pup.

Her dirtiest days she'll say Hubert, some young thing will put the gaff on you before the first spade of gravel hits my casket. I tells her I got my doubts about that notion, a man can't help his face after all.

No, that's just a gull out the harbour you're after hearing, she's sound up there a while yet.

That's a lovely evening out there now, that is.

PATIENCE

This is my kitchen, mine and Gasker's. Him with the two hands on his knees like he's just about to help himself to his feet. Even set still he always seems on his way to some bit of work or other. But that's only show these days. Can't get out of his own way most of the time, spends his nights turning like a spindle on a lathe, some ache working at him. He got old of a sudden and I never saw it coming.

There's people claim the second sight and I count myself lucky to have the first. Twenty-seven when my sister died. Gasker left with two young ones and I never saw it coming all the same, him proposing. Not the marrying kind was what people said, and me along with them. Aunt Annie set me on Mother's stomach when I was born and said Put a pair of boots on that one, Sarah, she's ready for the woods.

That one over there is my daughter Patience. First child of my own. I had no time for youngsters in those days and I thought it would be a nice reminder. It's hard to stand in the middle of a room yelling Patience! without feeling like a fool.
    It didn't always work. But nothing ever does.
    She still got the look of it about her. Like the firmament could fall into the ocean and her with the hands folded in her lap like that, calm as you please.

Don't mind the dress and the apron on me, I was never happier than in the backcountry hauling wood or setting snares or picking berries in over the barrens. Can't be at that sort of business now though, Gasker the way he is. And sitting don't bother me like it used to. Had near enough of life to do me, I guess. In my mind I'm still knocking around in the woods most of the time I sit by this window, washing out in the light.

This is the kitchen, like I said. First time I ever set for a photograph. Some American stopping in on the coastal boat.

I thought the man was simple is the truth of it, ducking in behind that box of his, waving at us to hold still. Let him go about his business and then told Patience to see to the kettle. If I'd known it would mean being gawked at by you crowd I'd have told the man to put the machine away, sit to a cup of tea like a sensible person.

Saved myself all this gabbing.

BIRDING, CAPE ST. MARY'S

The last keeper at Cape St. Mary's before the light was
automated. His people all from Red Head Cove and he once
had the burnished copper hair to prove it. Not much above a
youngster when he tended his first light on Baccalieu, just him
and the wife out there, women and their ways another remote
island he'd chosen to strand himself on. A privacy he was learning
to love the strangeness of. The first child born to them in a storm
and when Agnes told him to cut the cord he snipped too near the
navel to knot it, had to tie the umbilicus off with a shoelace.
Family the only company they had most of their lives together,
keeping one isolated lighthouse after another along the coast.
Carried that shoelace in a pocket all his days.

  There was an empty keeper's house next his own at the
Cape and birders camped out there in latter years, scientists and
students and eccentrics drawn by the colonies of migratory birds
on the cliffs. Two or three burrowing in for the season, scores
arriving for weekend counts under the weight of binoculars and
field guides and forty-ouncers. He drank the nights dry in their
company, laughter loose in his chest, carcinogenic, a flooded
engine turning over. His light endlessly stirring the darkness out
over the water. Agnes rocking sober and silent in a corner as the
room pitched on its ear, slipping off to bed unnoticed in the rack-
et. When the guitar made its rounds Vince would pass it off shyly.
He'd demur a second time without touching the instrument, like
a man refusing a drink too tempting to look upon. Third time
round he cradled and kept it, trawling through a repertoire of
folk songs and shanties, old country tunes fished from the
background static on a lonely radio. He had one eyetooth
missing, a gap where he'd snug his cigarette butt so he could play
and smoke and sing at the one time. Never slept until all hands
were down and maybe it was the years spent in small company he
was making up for. Drank preserving alcohol one night when the
songs outlasted the booze, cups of ethanol kept in a back room
for pickling specimens passed around, the stink of it cut with coca

cola. Never so in all my life, sir. Hey diddle-diddle-die, diddle-
die-doe.

And up the double-helix staircase spiralling the walls of
the tower next morning, polishing the flash of mirrors and brass
to a sheen.

Talk always comes round to Vince when the birders gather at the
Cape now. How he strung a rope thick as a man's wrist from his
back door to the tower, let it lead him blind through the fog and
the black, clung to it in wind that could strip the shoes from your
feet. How a storm surge once doused the light with granite stones
thrown a hundred yards up the cliff-face, Vince gathering scat-
tered shards of the prism for months afterward, passing them to
friends as a keepsake.

In their cups they stumble through his favourite songs, the
tight knots he made of them coming loose in their mouths,
verses out of order, lines misplaced or forgotten. Fall back on
the language of field notes finally, as if they were comparing
sightings of some rare creature glimpsed seasons ago. Bald crown
of his head mantled with white tufts, tawny median stripe of
nicotine staining the white beard. The one missing eyetooth.
That gap.

Tom Dawe

ELSEWHERE: A POEM TO EMILY

Somebody wise once said
that if you had not existed,
we would have to invent you.

Perhaps you have not.
Perhaps we have to.

I retreat again into dreamscape,
follow dark soul-maps
down secret paths
to the old parsonage
and you, wrapped in a shawl,
still writing.

Am I the body moving
between you and candle
when wick sputters
momentarily, and flame spurts back?

Am I eligible
to be counted somehow
in the old superstition
of the stranger coming?

Elsewhere, as always,
you never look up.
The answer to my question
left for another day:

Another day. Another setting.
And you, in overcast,
escaping the company

of young men in the parlour.
The kitchen, your garrison,
your tall frame leaning
over loaves of bread.
Moved by the demiurge,
you laugh defiantly:
Scorning parish superstition,
you toss crumbs on the fire
to feed the devil.

Along the moors, signs
of an ice-age,
and hints of the great chill
inching back.
And you chasing your dogs
across a furze-brushed sky.

In barren, wide spaces,
face raised to parting clouds,
you wave your arms,
call out gleefully
as a crow sails by.
Mist billows
low on bracken.
And far off somewhere,
fractured by the wind,
a curlew's cry.

Back down in the world
of parishioners,
"caught by the cold"
is what they understand,
whispering about you,
the pale one,
out one last time

to feed the dogs,
and a December wind
almost carrying you away.

Alone on your last day
you sit, grooming yourself,
waiting in firelight.
The comb rattling
to the floor
and you not bothering
to pick it up.

Elsewhere. The stranger coming,
and you, most unlikely
Rapunzel,
letting
your
dark
locks
down.

SLIPS

"Slips" he always called them,
he moving away from us
in woodsy October sunshine,
rabbit snares coiled
and bulging in his pockets.

This is a memory of years ago.
Mother is spreading a picnic blanket.
I cry after Father.
But Mother comforts me,

explaining he won't be long.
Waiting, I toss chuckley-pears
into a swift brook,
watching them
swirl away.

He returns in a scent of turf,
squashberries and pipe tobacco,
sitting on the blanket
to tell me things:
I learn that rabbits
turn white for winter,
their feet are lucky,
and a brace is two.

Now, all those years later,
just the two of us
in a hospital room:
He in his final dementia,
babbling in snowy afternoon,
a Lear of sorts
in his own
great storm...

And I, crying inside,
wanting to follow him,
playing the fool
again...

"A great place for slips," he says,
indicating the white walls
and the long, fluorescent corridor.
"Rabbit paths all over the place."

"Do the doctors catch any?"
I ask, playing along.

And then, surfacing...
just for a second or two,
the old hunter arrogance,
the planter's entrenched resentment
of all authority:

"They wouldn't catch shit,"
he snarls.

FROG-PRINCE

Resplendent in the ranks of mud,
Unmindful of the race of man,
I bloomed with water-lily bud,
Lolled blissful in the pools of Pan.

Cavorting in a classless ooze,
Oblivious to all amiss,
My life one lovely, swampy snooze
Before that metamorphic kiss.

Now as a prince I pace bright halls
And palace floors are prickly dry;
I plop from ornamental walls
To catch the odd bug on the sly.

Weighed down by crown my mother sits
A-counting out her kingdom's woes;
My princess screams and threatens fits:
She's found a blemish on her nose.

I keep a swamp tune in my head
Against the stress of courtly knack;
I crave the id of watershed
Caressing moonshine on my back.

XANTIPPE

They said Xantippe was a shrew,
But what else could the woman do?
Her husband was completely free
To teach young males philosophy;
And, most amazing to the masses,
He took no money for his classes.

So she was left with child, to spin
And worry when the bills came in;
While he sought meaningful debate,
She grumbled to an empty plate;
While he defined the common good,
She combed the hills for firewood.

His robes were torn, his eyes looked odd,
He bore a message from a god;
While people joked at her demise,
Some oracle declared him wise.
They etched his likeness on a frieze:

There, by himself,
Was Socrates.

Nellie Strowbridge

EMERALD ISLAND 2003

The sun's orange tongue pokes out over
home, pub and castle,
stretches itself into a golden lick across
Donegal Bay,
slips over pools and lakes
in a brush of sunset
and is gone.

A lone rook in black silhouette
on a leafless tree
titters to music
rising through dark nights.

Towers mark the sky,
castle walls tell of invaders, conquerors
when cracker fire sounded above
blood smeared stones,
glistening ponds and rushing water.
Women wept and children's eyes
were pools that violent winds
swept over,
leaving silence.

The ravished Irish body is rebuilt:
the Irish soul, itself a fort,
                    a castle.

The Emerald Island is a cut stone
on the finger of a god
who tips his hand to the pale horse:
the fire of the emerald in his eyes.

THE FISHERMAN'S WIFE

Middle-aged,
she'd had more expectation of life
than laying dead fish head to tail
like some unspoken rite:
lifting them one by one,
limp and cold,
from the icy waters
of rusty-hooped puncheons
while underneath her barbel –
underneath her heart
her eighth child stirred.
And while fish bulks
got higher and higher
in the dark
skeleton-like stage
and her tired hands
threw sprinklings
of salt crystals
down on the fish,
she wondered
if next year
things would be the same...
Then when she slipped
and fell –
her black rubbers losing grip
with the briny slime
beneath her feet,
they carried her home to bed.
She didn't speak
at first –
feeling gutted and cold,
and when she whispered:
"Where is my baby?"
their silence was too harsh an answer.

She lay in bed for the first months
of that cold, stark winter,
and wondered often
why life chides so cruelly,
leaving her
with a dead, empty womb
and bearing the guilt
of her lost child.
She had followed
the expectations of her man;
now, try as she would,
though she searched
deep inside herself,
there was no sign
that she'd ever wanted
more out of life than what she had.
Her dreams, her hopes
had become
as lifeless
as the fish
housed in
the darkness
of the stage.

Carl Leggo

WEST COAST PRAIRIE

Last Saturday, biking the dike around Lulu Island, a sweeping
sand sculpture in the mouth of the Fraser River, Norm asked why
I had moved to Richmond, and I confessed

economic necessity, and Norm said he chose Richmond because it
is flat and has farms like Saskatchewan, and how when he first
moved here, years ago, the Coast Mountains

around English Bay held only threats, the world written in the
geography of our growing up, and I told him about Corner
Brook curled in the Humber Arm, the world's biggest

paper mill belching sulphite steam smoke ceaselessly, except
Christmas and Labour Day, and how I always thought the world
had come to Corner Brook with Hollywood,

Eaton's catalogues, and visits by famous people like Pierre and
Margaret Trudeau, Gordon Lightfoot, Ian and Sylvia, Gordie
Howe and the Queen, until at 15,

I visited Montreal and couldn't believe how big the world was,
and after growing up perpendicular on the side of a hill like a
robust Merlot kissed by wild autumn,

spring ice, summer heat, and winter light with long shadows on
the retina of the heart, I now live in Richmond's long wet season,
flat like Saskatchewan, reminiscing about

Jigg's dinner, dark rum, cod tongues, stewed moose, fish and
brewis, Celtic rhythms, Al Pittman's poetry, Skipper's rants,
Stripping the Willow with Eddy Ezekiel on accordion,

always going back in my poems, knowing that I never really left,
knowing that we can never really go back to the world written in
the geography of our growing up.

COME-BY-CHANCE

From Corner Brook, I drive the Trans-Canada
across Newfoundland on a bare black highway
under a blue March sky.

I am surprised how little has changed,
how well I remember the land's writing.

The sun falls as I drive through the late afternoon:
I chant with the sun's ancient blood rhythms.

In an ESSO overlooking Random Sound
I eat fish cakes and later drink a Black Horse
at the Tanker Inn near Come-By-Chance.

The whole world is at rest like anything could happen,
like nothing's going to happen,

perhaps the world has simply stopped on a Wednesday night
in this vast vacant island where an eternal flame

burns in the night sky over a moth-balled oil refinery,
a steady sign that Joey Smallwood had less sense and more dreams
than a narcoleptic on valium.

Having nothing else to do, we watch CBC with gulls' weary eyes,
another documentary on Barbara Ann Scott,
still skating with a frozen smile,

and Mel tells me the roads are slippery
and complains about politicians
who won't provide enough salt trucks for the highway.

    I nod.

Boyd Chubbs

FOR THE CREATURE
WHERE HE WEARS THE FLOOR THIN

Is it empty or full, this cup
I look and there's only a deep, brown season
I lift it to my mouth and a river flows out
slips into the throat
a curve of weather down and through
to the nerve and creek of bone

And rain drains the window
chapters and history of places and time, draining,
holding briefly the pattern of a bird
It's the marked black of a saddleback
with a raggedness where his wings break
and one, stone stare before he's drained from there

A being lives in many places
and many faces are shown
between the rise and fall; between hours and days
ways to bring the heart through its wall
I can stumble from corner to corner and not see
or brave the pushed masses with bright intensity;
talk in shops of Rome or Nepal
by the lazy stream of cake and tea
while the street repeats its rage; age
pass the towers, alleys and grins
and suffer the promise of ships piloted in
All I have is a frame that moves
takes me here and there and lays me down, mercifully
when I've found a warmth or two

I've wept pass every reflection, every action
made in mirrors, waters and dreams, and every sight
of light on a salted face
tastes of memory in the throat. And the names
strange all around, tumble, the wild nouns
trumpet and tremble clear:
Brigus, Burin, Cape Broyle, La Scie;
Badger, Buchans, St. Mary's, Fleur de Lys;
Bonne Bay, Brule, Cape Chidley, Western Bay;
Bonavista, Broad Cove, St. Brendan's, Cape Ray;
Forteau, Battle Harbour, Nain, Old Mokami;
Hopedale, Rigolet, Makkovik, Sheshatshit

I speak them with love, each love; each tone
and turn through the longing
to the saddleback ragged from the thunder he'd flown
And I know it, I grieve it
It was in his one, stone stare
'You are here, but your soul, your soul is home'

Ottawa, 1995

I MET A SAINT

I met a saint on Coronation Street
against snow, blackened in April
the remains of salt, smoke and rain
He said, there against all the stuff and sun,
sizing the day against the porch:

> There are several arctics
> and several americas;

several neighbourhoods and several ways
to gods and puzzles of all sorts

Among blackened snow, the street cat,
a Labrador and early crow, he said:

> Can't find a church
> to record my miracles
> Can't find a friend
> who's heard of oracles

The crow found a half-loaf;
the cat scratched and groomed the Labrador
I pressed one hand upon the membrane
between night and day
and stared at the man by his door:

> Don't make a city
> where brooks run dry
> and don't go without leaving
> love where it dies

Light enlarges and the crow has flown
The cat purrs on. The Labrador licks his parts.
I turn to leave this stunning reprieve
and hear before I depart:

> Sir, I'm a saint with saintly ways
> But no one records my miracles these days
> After the melt I'll lie with gulls, lichens and locks
> in the passed-by mansion of the sea rocks

At that, I pause but there's no more
Just a slow and rattled closing of his door

Enos Watts

ROCKY MOUNTAIN BIGHORN

Watching one bend
to the dawn grass
or motionless stand on a ledge alone
in twilight,
or two rams
rearing in combat
is like seeing
some ancient frieze unfrozen,
beasts that might range
the perfect dreams of a god

What shaped
those proud heads,
drew out the great spirals,
laid down two layers of skull?

Something we struggle to name
and can never define,
forming, transforming
through time –
part impulse, part memory,
a design and a striving

There's peace on the high ground
in summer; then late October
brings them down to the ewes
Ask any rancher
and he'll give you experience

uncomplicated by awe:
"They move out at first snow"
But in the season of their descent,
imagine a flint struck
deep in the brain,
or old rhythms
roused in the blood

A century of men,
and sage has taken the alpine meadows
the bighorn have fallen
under the guns, the lungworm's bite,
the stroke of too many early winters,
the hard, slow hunger...
A remnant still
follows the ridgelines,
the old migrations
Some flame that a man might
call *memory*
flares, courses the brain paths
So they batter each other
to beat the odds

There's something we struggle to name,
might never define:
You will find it
in scarred flesh
and blunted horn,
in the *crack*
of collision
you can hear
a mile away

and a big ram swaying
bloody and dazed,
his thin legs trembling

FOR ONE WHO DIED ALONE IN THE NIGHT

It was the way she passed
from sleep to sleep
that grieved me
                    She
who had known too long
the ache of solitude, knew
in the night
pain's own loneliness,
a ruined heart's
last shudder

            Now
I'm condemned forever
to dream her face
in clouds
as some sad oval moon
for a moment caught
in pale bewilderment:
her sudden startled
waking into dying

MARGARET LAURENCE'S *MANAWAKA*

At the edge of Manawaka
I challenge a pathless hill
to seek
a garden of old graves,
the disordered habitation
of a citizenry long dead
Living, they knew their places
kept them
till they died
and were remembered
for a while

Beyond this hill
few names survive:
here and there
a storefront, street, inscriptions
on church things –
though men of money and power
dreamed dynasty

The huge-headed peonies gone,
cowslips and couch grass
hold sway
in death's democracy;
for if time has favoured anything here
it is the lowly:
scattered about a fenceless field
three slanted slabs
still stand,
while the few proud angels
have crumbled
and, grain by grain,
taken to the air

Eiléan Ní Chuilleanáin

ON LACKING THE KILLER INSTINCT

One hare, absorbed, sitting still,
Right in the grassy middle of the track,
I saw when I fled up into the hills, that time
My father was dying in a hospital –
I see her suddenly again, carried back
By the morning paper's prize photograph:
Two greyhounds tumbling over, absurdly gross,
While the hare shoots off to the left, her bright eye
Full not only of speed and fear
But surely in the moment a glad power,
Like my father's, running from a lorry-load of soldiers
In nineteen twenty-one, nineteen years old, never
Such gladness, he said, cornering in the narrow road
Between high hedges, in summer dusk. The hare
Like him should never have been coursed, but clever
She'll fool the stupid dogs, double back
On her own scent, downhill, and choose her time
To spring away out of the frame, all while
The pack is labouring up. The lorry was gaining
And he was clever, he saw a house
And risked an open kitchen door. The soldiers
Found six people in a family kitchen, one
Drying his face, dazed looking, the towel
Half-covering his face. The lorry went off,
The people let him sleep the night, and he came out
Into a blissful dawn. Should he have gone there?
If the sheltering house had been burned down, what good
Could all his bright running have done

For those kind people? And I should not
Have run away, but I went back to the city
Next morning, washed in well water, and
I thought about the hare, in her hour of ease.

THE SISTER

i

How on earth did she manage
That journey on her own?
When she was a young woman
They had plenty to keep them busy,
They were small, they felt queasy,
They gripped a pillar in the shade
And held on,

And as for leaving home –
Still, the trains have never changed,
They thunder up the valleys,
Built for strapping fellows
Flinging their big bundles
Easily on to high shelves –
Real men.

She turned up at the station,
Small, her clothes, once elegant,
All black. Past the train window
Slid the suburbs, a fast river.
She saw a white-haired man, waist-deep,
Ducking under and rising again –
A cormorant.

ii

A lump of a lad handed her bag down to her.
Lopsided she walked as far as the convent door.
They greeted her with a leathery kiss, they told her
Where to find her bed and the hour of dinner.

They knew the silent meal would be no surprise,
No more than the hard bread, tougher at every slice,

Nor the dead silence of night until the first train
Troubled the valley. She would know, lying there,
Others were sitting up, working in pairs,
To finish the stitching, tacking the last of the lace.

But the cold woke her, and a subtle mist, as thin
As lawn, hung on the glass. In the freezing dawn,
She dragged a web just as fine across her skin,
Veiling herself for good, and she slept on.

Bernard O'Donoghue

A Nun Takes the Veil

That morning early I ran through briars
To catch the calves that were bound for market.
I stopped the once, to watch the sun
Rising over Doolin across the water.

The calves were tethered outside the house
While I had my breakfast: the last one at home
For forty years. I had what I wanted (they said
I could), so we'd loaf bread and Marie biscuits.

We strung the calves behind the boat,
Me keeping clear to protect my style:
Confirmation suit and my patent sandals.
But I trailed my fingers in the cool green water,

Watching the puffins driving homeward
To their nests on Aran. On the Galway mainland
I tiptoed clear of the cow-dunged slipway
And watched my brothers heaving the calves

As they lost their footing. We went in a trap,
Myself and my mother, and I said goodbye
To my father then. The last I saw of him
Was a hat and jacket and a salley stick,

Driving cattle to Ballyvaughan.
He died (they told me) in the county home,
Asking to see me. But that was later:
As we trotted on through the morning-mist,

I saw a car for the first time ever,
Hardly seeing it before it vanished.

I couldn't believe it, and I stood up looking
To where I could hear its noise departing

But it was only a glimpse. That night in the convent
The sisters fussed me, but I couldn't forget
The morning's vision, and I fell asleep
With the engine humming through the open window.

ANAMNESIS
for John and Prue Fuller

Each January you learn anew
How little cold it needs to be
For the raindrops slanting past
The window-pane to turn to snow;
And whether by preference you'd remember
From year to year, or settle for
This dreamer's pattern of forgetting
There is no call to know.

In budding-time you rediscover
The willow-warbler's shapely song
And the scent of resurrection in
The dried-out dust revived by rain.
In such games of Blind Man's Buff
Whoever stood behind your back,
Clasping their hands around your eyes,
Will always stop. You'll see again.

'STAY, YOU IMPERFECT SPEAKERS'

My dreams now increasingly move along
the unmetalled roads of childhood: sometimes
I'm already on them before I fall fully asleep,
watching the camber edging round the corner.

But often too I dream of a wrecked room,
unreclaimed when the old house was done up.
There's mould on everything, and grass
invading from the broken chutes outside.

My clear duty is every time the same:
to clean it out, ready for the nextcomers.
But then something intervenes to mean
I don't need to prepare it after all.

And then I am back out on the roads again,
at the turn by Julia's well, or further down
by Dan Jims' boreen, by the primrose stream
that Dominic dammed to make pools for his cows:

where I once really met a tinker couple
trudging through the rain ahead of me.
No matter how slow I walked, I couldn't fail
to overtake them, when they stood and watched

a donkey grazing by the verge, a ravelled rope
around his neck. The woman drew her shawl aside,
showing her face, and questioned me directly:
'Do you know is anyone the own of him?'

THE STARLING'S LAMENT

Life, they say, 's a battlefield, and I for one don't doubt it.
From every garden in the land my kind and I are routed,
Even by ornithologists who lower their field-glasses
When we come into focus. Crowd of solemn, lunch-packed asses!

There are birds that people write about and birds that they throw
    sand at:
Just like the Manichean split between the vole and land-rat.
It's fashion simply; that is all. That's simply all there's to it,
Like cultivating liking for a toadstool or a blewit.

Look in the book: my wing's magentaish – *cf.* the pigeon.
My feather is as ink-black as the blackbird's. Yet the widgeon-
Watcher growls when I approach, and then goes mad about a peewit.
What's so great about the nightingale? I'm sorry, I can't see it.

It's like writing on *Piers Plowman* or on Hoccleve or Duns Scotus,
Or translating medieval verse and signing it *Ignotus*,
Which should surely win us standing or acceptance with the best of
    them.
Yet all we get is ostracised and sneered at by the rest of them.

Once I tried my hand at writing goliardic measure.
I thought that such formality might give some kick or pleasure
To those who write of throstle or of cuckoo or of linnet.
I might as well have saved myself the bother. For the minute

That they saw my name (like 'Kerry', 'Bush' or 'Nader')
They were off! They wouldn't read it! – though they'd simper, I
    would wager,
Over Ashbery or Olds or some other favoured Thyrsis.
If they'd only give me half a chance I'd show them what a verse is.

The way they're so sure that this year's garb (this is what pisses me off)
Is the very best conceivable, so they all start saying 'Be off
With you!' in their poncy bloody upper-middle voices!
As if you couldn't drive without defining what Rolls-Royce is.

So how about a break? It would be more fair and bolder.
Even the crow's apologist gives starlings the cold shoulder.
Yet we don't destroy the wheatfields; we don't defecate on Wembley.
So how about a higher place in the avian assembly?

Thanks a bunch for listening! Yeah, sure! Beholden to you, brother!
For, unless I've got you wrong, it's in one ear and out the other.
So sod off back to your elite, to Paul Muldoon and Seamus Heaney,
And I'll hop back up on my perch, like Heaney's loony Sweeney.

Barbara Helfgott Hyett

IN THE RING OF TWENTY SIGNS

The third ring is the future scraping
the present: what is next enters, closes
itself to the past. The fifth ring is
observation. The sixth, satisfaction
of what is known. The fourth ring
is worry, but that is naïve, short-lived,
a waste of time, which is the tenth ring,
the middle. The eleventh ring is pleasure;
feeding, but not gluttony, sex but not
depletion. The twelfth ring: love.
The thirteenth, love undone, unleashed
attachment. Rings six through nine are
marriage. The fourteenth ring is silence.
The fifteenth, desire. The sixteenth
ring, mercy. The sixteenth ring is true.
At seventeen you stand alone on the stairway.
The seventeenth ring is achievement.
The eighteenth gives it all away. Not
generously. Not regretfully. Just given.
The nineteenth ring is loneliness suffered
despite oneself. The twentieth ring is the moon
and all its shadows. Rings one and two –
these are the human, delicate and susceptible.
The first two rings are the eyes.

THE KEEPER OF THE LIGHT

When he dreams, all sound is the voice of water.
Like a man in the drag of sleep, he listens
to the crash on the shoals, waves, the lost
Powhatan, the *Frankfort*, the schooner *Nile*.
The keeper of the light has no secrets.
He has closed the logbooks of ships,
accounted for cargo and the passengers who
drowned. In his room he studies clouds.

He has engineered nothing.
His house was built by someone else:
Two hundred steps that fan and spiral,
ten thousand bricks. Ten thousand storms,
the sea as hard as chrysolite.
The keeper of the light is marooned.

Sand rebuilds itself. A city grows
Around him. The coast is driftwood,
Rancor and spume. The keeper
doesn't notice. Every morning
he gathers baskets full of birds –
wild ducks, geese, sandhill cranes,
stunned or dead at the base of his tower.

At dusk, birds slam against the white
And banded side, blind, maddened
By the light twirling
In the heartache, the din of wings.

THE LIGHTKEEPER'S DAUGHTER
Cape Bonavista, Newfoundland

Windows so encrusted with salt
they couldn't see through.
Sent the daughter out
into it, back to the wind.
Hand to the window, her
rag soaked in vinegar,
her pail hefted while the tumult
of brothers under the stairwell,
played. The catwalk held
and she began to turn, as
the light turned in its nest –
like clockwork, her whole
world a semaphore of sound.
Her heart was a chapel
in that dark. Cold she was
and her hair was iced by sea,
wild and fiery and full
of the spit of life. She leaned
on herself out there. The light
sent out its own raw warning:
in red, in red, in white.

IN THE WOODS NEAR MUNICH
April 1945

This soldier, this boy
Who moves through the innocent
Trees, does he regret the man
He half pushes half carries?

The Rhine – simply another
Battle, a collage of mines,
The human spasm: hands, hearts
Lost to maggots in the undergrowth.

He marches on a thin gravel road,
His footfall, meagre. A dung beetle
Clings to the eyelet of his boot.
Every afternoon is tenuous, balanced

As the helmet floating just above
His brain. He knows April by the pods,
The ripening ochers, the mating
Feathers of a strutting grouse.

Through an alley of pines,
A railyard, the unexpected
Stink and gray, in boxcars,
A thousand astounded corpses.

Shoot out the one slat window.
Murder all the green and budding
Leaves, Call on God, the outstretched
Hand of the Virgin Mary,

The *Pieta* he saw in Rome,
How her marble fingers sink
Into the flesh of Jesus
Under his armpit,

Where she presses his wound
With the willowy hem of her skirt.
How quickly human flesh,
Like mud, gives way.

from
LANDSCAPE

One day before Jack left, I went across to the beach on the other side of the island with Eloise and Sarah and followed them into the sea. The saltwater was warm and clear as glass and suspended my body as gently as music. I imagined myself cast inside a glass marble, a swirling sea of blues and greens from which only my head emerged.

It was then I realized that I had been changed by this landscape. I thought, surely there is a landscape somewhere in the world for everyone. Landscape with the power to peel you away, strip of flesh by strip of flesh, until you understand nothing. Landscape like blind love.

* * *

Thomas comes down the path wearing yellow shorts with a blue seashell design I have never seen before and says, 'Billy, I think it's going to rain. Know why? I felt a raindrop.'

I look at Billy just as his hands drop to his sides. Wind moves through the undergrowth like an invisible hand.

The rain lashes, sideways. Inside the house, the shutters closed, I fold laundry in the kitchen in the half-light in air like a sauna, though I know that Eloise and Sarah will later refold theirs, rolling them into tight cylinders to keep out insects before packing them into their bureau drawers.

At nightfall Billy brings us candles. His feet are muddy with white sand. He puts the candles down then stands inspecting the room. My children are silent, watching him.

'I was renting this place for good money,' he says. 'Five hundred a week in the good months.'

'What do you need money for?' I ask. I watch his mouth, waiting for it to move again, to expose his white teeth. I picture him eating those foods I know only by smell, that I have never seen or tasted.

'By the way, I'm going back up north. To talk to Jack,' I say. 'Miss Kitty will stay with the children and get them across to school each morning. But don't worry, I'll be back.'

He sighs, as though this is the last straw, and looks past me to the outside, but the shutters are closed. I figure he doesn't want Miss Kitty around the place, hauling over her second-hand clothing and baked goods, then visiting him twice a day just to get a peek at his lifestyle.

There is a cold fog hanging over Ottawa. Jack is there with the car. He kisses me lightly, then suddenly holds me.

'We've had a miserable spring,' he says into my hair. 'How's it been down there?'

'Better than this.'

But once we're in the car Jack seems to recover and says, 'You can't stay there. It wasn't our matrimonial home and you've only been living there six months. Besides, Billy wants you out. I have to respect that. You don't have a leg to stand on, Natasha.'

After a while I realize the sky is white here, and Jack is crying. The heater in the car isn't on, but I don't ask why. I rub my hands together then shove them between my knees.

When I return a week later the orchids are in bloom: violet, tangerine, ashen-white flowers suspended high in the trees. The house is empty, and I hesitate, then make my way to Billy's. He's sitting in a beach chair among the stumps of his casuarinas facing the sea.

'There's no divorce,' I announce. Then I realize, of course, he already knows.

'Does this mean Jack will be around too?'

I am surprised by this, but he has not turned to look at me once and I wonder whether I have only imagined him speaking. On the flat stumps of the trees someone has placed a collection of rocks, feathers and shells. My children have been here. Suddenly I am sorry to have taken so much from him.

I turn, just as Miss Kitty emerges from the interior of Billy's house and stands there in his doorway in her green dress exposing her trunk-like legs, her eyes on mine. It's then I understand the folly of words here, and the order that reigns.

Billy shifts in his chair to face me. His collar is caught, turned under on one side of his neck: a second-hand orange shirt, new to him. Suddenly he laughs, a sound I have not heard before, with his mouth open. I see him lying over Miss Kitty, his ankles criss-crossing hers as though they have grown there.

That night I lift Thomas, despite his protests, out of my bed and lay him on the mat on the floor in his sisters' room. I have not seen my daughters all day, but I can hear them now, breathing in their sleep. I return to my bed and cover myself with a sheet.

Now that summer is here it is hotter than it ever was. Harmless grey spiders the size of a child's hand possess the top corners of all the rooms. Insects knock at the trees. Night herons thump the outside of houses up and down the island.

I hear him enter the house. He approaches without hesitating or asking, without lifting the sheet or undressing, and lies over me.

I shut my eyes, aware that the secret pleasure of this landscape is that it denies my mind access to both my past and future. But in the distance beyond my closed eyes I see myself and the immense place of craziness where I have crept, and know I am fortunate not to remember what it is I have lost.

Stephanie McKenzie

CUTTING MY MOTHER'S HAIR

i

At sixty, my mother goes blonde
with highlights. Grey at sixteen,
she now joins the cover girls.

This dresser is no newcomer to her trade,
gets migraines, has a bad upper back,
stutters the same dirty joke in her sleep.

She fingers the straight blondeness,
stops longer to think. She needs this cut
to be perfect, kneads fibers;

her hands twitch like willow for oil,
come up dry. My mother has found a divine wig
at the market. She bears hair

into the salon under her good right arm,
demands to be cut. Radical,
surgeon now,

she commands sutures to sew an extreme blonde bob.

ii

Ran a hospice on Hastings, thinks
she's seen it all. Rings $10.50, as always,
washes her hands in the back of the shop.

The blind faith of breastplates tucks cells behind ears,
    trims bangs just so.

iii

When she tries her haircut on
for her daughter come home,
we strip

stories from musings. Our distant
minds rest. I want to leave her
something on the coffee table

like words, or little soaps,
wounds
healing with nutmeg and chocolate.

But that morning she Endusts old cherry wood,
    stubborn stubble staring back at her.

iv

Scissoring glossy
mags, I cut. Hair
falls from airport

models. Pretty they are
and so free. In a second, eyes
shift. Breasts droop,

burn the hair, cut,
falls to the floor.
I want to tell her:

look, until they separate from the bold relief of body,
    breasts can never be free, anyway.

THE FRUITPICKER

i

She is thirteen, pregnant, her town
a farmer's field. She knows every blade,
every man's chest sticking

out of the ground. She make-believes
with huckleberries come staining
her tongue. Inside her belly, a plum almost bursts

its seams. She hates ripeness,
some days loads her wagon
with fruit, hauls it in front of the old wood stove,

bottles and bags their dried skins,
hides them in the basement. She lives
whole lives down there,

wizened faces staring at her. She prowls
through cool grass, flicks for four-leaf clovers,
presses their dewy bodies in the covers of Nancy Drew.

Not even the best Okanagan farmer keeps peaches alive
   like her.

ii

She falls asleep nursing
paper dolls, wakes
to a handful of sog.

Some nights the moon's belly
breaks; her endy scabs
stick out past stars. She washes dishes

behind the ears, cautions willows
to mind their manners: *it's not polite*
to whisper.

One night, she takes a kleenex to the river's
mouth, gently wipes its shores
till dawn. She sleeps past noon.

Beach stones in her belly, she dares them come within
    her reach of claws.

iii

Thirty years later
she plays the bars of Medicine
Hat. Twelve hours a day

she lines up lottery's
fruit. The boys
are impressed.

She can track maraschino cherries in a cloud of smoky sweat.

THE MARCH HARE
(1998 Programme)

 Friday, March 13 @ 8:06 p.m.

Casual Jack's Roadhouse
presents
"WEST TO WEST"
a prelude to The March Hare
featuring internationally renowned artists
Lorna Crozier, Patrick Lane, Susan Musgrave and Stephen Reid
with Al Pittman, Kenya Plitman
and hosts, Ron Brown

Saturday, March 14 @ 7:45 p.m.

THE 11TH ANNUAL MARCH HARE

 (an evening of words and music)

featuring
Rex Brown, Martin Ware, Nick Avis, Al Pittman, Susan Musgrave, Adrian Fowler,
Emile, Susan & Friend, Patrick Lane, Clyde Rose, Nellie Strowbridge, Des Walsh,
David Freeman, Randall Maggs, Kevin Piersson, John Ashton, Larry Small, Stephen Reid,
Lloyd Bartlett, Gerald Squires, Lorna Crozier and The Fountain Creek Band

The Columbus Club Ballroom

Bar service available

Admission $6.00 per person, $3.00 for students with I.D.
Price includes Intermission Soup, etc.

Sunday, March 15 @ 2:00 p.m.

A SUNDAY SESSION
in celebration of The March Hare
featuring
Fergus O'Byrne and Jim Payne
with their gifted and not so gifted guests

King Henry's Pub, The Glynmill Inn

bar snacks and happy hour prices from then to when

 Saturday, March 14 @ 2:00 p.m.

THE MAD HATTER'S MATINEE FOR CHILDREN
featuring words and music with
Elinor Benjamin, Vicki Pike, Sarah Pike, Lloyd Bartlett, Anne Ferencze,
Fergus O'Byrne and Fergus Edward O'Byrne
The Columbus Club Ballroom, Reid Street

Liam Murphy

ME MAM

Me Mam

    Is a stooped figure
    Shovelling coal from the shed
    Worrying the world

Me Mam

    Smacks me bum
    And laughs and gurgles with me
    At me

Me Mam

    Prays a rosary for me
    Seems to threaten me
    With prayer and forgiveness

Me Mam

    Knows the child in me
    Knows the child I am

Me Mam

    Admonishes me with a look
    Looks right through me
    Purges me with
    Californian syrup of figs
    Scourges me with unspoken words

Me Mam

Reads to me
Feeds me comics
Words from the Beezer
The Dandy and the Hotspur
Words for the making of me

Me Mam

Watches over me shoulder
When I am faraway
And I'd thought I'd forgotten her

Me Mam

Sentinel and sentient
Praying for me
And me brother and sister
And ours
And the poor souls
And all who know me

Me Mam

Worrying God with her vigilance
Her persistence
Shovelling coal from the shed

Me Mam

LITTLE HURLER OR EVEN SMALLER BALLERINA

miscarriage

        out of the ordinary
        of tea and saturday night
        death of a life
        leaking away
        phones and doctors not working
        rain falling
        ebb and flow
        losing losing
        lost generation
        little one
        warm of our womb
        too soon too soon

never mind
sure you are young enough still
it could be worse
god's holy will

        child of our dreams
        gone
        hearseless priestless
        heartless
        disappointed eyes
        angry at death
        sterile instruments
        sluiced out
        incinerated
        obliterated

throb of memory
silent thurles terraces

        sweat and smell of oranges
        game stopped
        our little hurler
        stretchered off
        too soon too soon

why us

        our time child
        ballerina
        never got to the musical box
        why us

obliterated.

Pamela Ollerhead

ONE NOVEMBER IN MEXICO

Our first cockroach motel
Sex above the sheets
Sleepy confusion in stifling heat
Spun into dreams about bargaining, Mexican fiestas, and cheap beer.
We forgot to dream about the meaning of free trade,
Why we couldn't eat Mexican cuisine,
Why Coronas were less than a dollar.

Hostelling in Cancun
T.D and sunstroke
You comforting me
Making plans to swim naked in the Caribbean,
Take glass-bottom boat rides in Playa Del Carma,
See some real Mexican culture.
You forgot to mention the outbreak of cholera,
Wal-Mart and KFC,
The truth that always lay on the other side of town.

Ahhh Tulum
Sun warmed bare breasts
Experienced stomachs welcomed
Mollettos and agua purificada for breakfast
Tangled in a hammock beside the green-blue sea
The mosquito net in our candle lit cabana
Turned to Egyptian cotton with the darkness.

Hustled on a third-class bus
Bound for Mexico City
Laughter over pre-conceived notions
Changed to tears over revelations

Heading home after two weeks
Broke.

232

Clyde Rose

MORNING IN BOLOGNA
for Al

On this Spring afternoon
the Piazza Maggiora sings
with life: young men romp
in the square: old men rant
and shout at one another wildly
proclaiming each other's right to be right.

A cathedral sits solid and silent
on one end; while on the other
brisk with business and in glorious sunshine
a cluster of cafés pours forth
cappuccino, espresso, beer and vino
to lovers, travellers and the curious.

Long legged olive skinned women
strut their youthful way
through torrid glances
across the square;
Italy comes alive.
Pigeons flutter in exultation;
old men octave their voices
to a higher pitch in argument
young men flex their limbs
and play poetry with a pig's bladder
bouncing the ball on head, knee and toe
while their eyes, like shafts of fire,
fix on the moving madrigals
that slide their sultry, directionless
ways through the crowd.

My mind winds its way
back in time
to a little room
on the Via Independenza
in the Majestic Bagliona
where my friend, a poet, and I
sat all night long
reading verses to one another.
At dawn an old man came
down the street:
he was the first alive that morning
and we watched him stretch and yawn
glance up at the old cathedral
then bending
unlocked
the door of his shop
ready for the day's business.
Above him in our room
across the street
we felt like two gods
watching, smiling on the man below.

Our day-long night
rolled into one
come too soon to an end
while his long day
had just begun.

Glen Sorestad

MID-MARCH RIOT IN BEACON HILL PARK

Randy rhododendrons are mounting
an insurgence for the viewer's eye,
flaunting pompoms flushed with spring.
Daffy in a dazzle of sun, daffodils
nod and nudge the over-scented
heady hyacinths to the sidelines,
toss brazen yellow like lamplight coquettes.
Camelias jostle for prime time,
heaving pungent sighs; antsy azaleas
shimmer like sequinned dancers.
Off by itself the magnolia bares all,
its limbs lurid as over-sexed orchids.

In the annual beds primulas primp
and pansies perk in bluesy purpleness,
winking shamelessly at passersby.
Tulips, fresh from their upward tunnelling,
thrust their stalks and wave their buds,
frantic to overshadow their usurper neighbours.
Blumen, blumen, blumen – a floral riot
rolls through Beacon Hill Park, look
where you will – bursts of bloom leap
from behind gnarled trunks, petals
poke their faces from rocks and grass.
March and the park is crazed with spring.

THE LADY WHO LOVED SHRIMP

She said she loved shrimp and she told no lie.

I sizzled them briefly in a hot skillet
with butter and chopped garlic, lots of both,
a minute on each side, then transferred them,
lightly salted and liberally sprinkled
with freshly ground black Madagascar peppercorns,
with just a faint suggestion of cayenne,
and a healthy squeeze of fresh-cut lemon,
to a serving dish, then rushed
them to the table where her eyes
glowed with tiger light, pounce-ready
as they surveyed the dozen-and-a-half
large and pink and succulent prawns,
redolent with lemon and garlic.
The predatory way those eyes encompassed them
while the tip of her tongue flicked
the edges of her delicate lips with just a hint
of lasciviousness, I could see I had seriously
underestimated the depths of her prawny passion.

As one shrimp after another
made the quick journey from her fork
to her eager mouth I was torn between
delight at the growing glow that spread
across her face, a kind of gastronomic orgasm,
and alarm at the rapidity with which
the heaping dish of prawns diminished.
But no one exudes more pride and joy
than the chef who witnesses first-hand
the throes of supreme gourmandish bliss
glistening on the buttery lips of the sated
and like the perfect lover must remain
content with tell-tale outward signs.

And when she'd forked the final prawn
across her now slick garlicky lips
and heaved the sigh of the spent lover
I knew this was to be my reward –
at least until the next course.

DEAR KYRAN

I have been happily reliving
moments of my affection for your father
in the pages of *An Island in the Sky*.
The volume itself is so handsome.
Wherever Al may be, if he's holding
a copy of the book I have in my hands,
his smile is broad as the Humber.
I say this knowing full well
that in literary matters and especially
having to do with his own poems
he was one not easily satisfied.

Right now I'm in a hotel room,
but if I were at home I think I
would be waiting for the phone to ring
and when I answered I would hear
his familiar O-so-unmistakable,
slow, tentative opener, as if
not convinced he'd dialed
the right number. Then, "Glen??
This is A-a-a-al." He'd ask
how I was doing and then
"How's Sahhhnia?"
The opening never varied,

not simply words to conform
to anyone's expectation
but a reflection of who he was –
someone who cared about others,
deeply, sometimes too deeply.

Your father would always phone
in response to my infrequent letters
because, as he was quick to confess
with perfect, if understated accuracy,
he wasn't a very good correspondent.
His phone call, sooner or later,
usually in the early morning hours –
was predictable as the tides.

But all the same, he responded
in the way he felt he must
and though I listened, groggy
with sleep and did my best to hold
my end of the conversation
the late-night calls were mostly Al,
in the only way he knew how
telling people what they meant
in his life. So how could anyone
not listen and when the call
had run its course, wish him
good night and hold him tightly
across those impossible miles?

All this comes back to me,
as I read your father's poems,
how his love encompassed
you and me and so many others.
I just wanted you to know.

Kyran Pittman

LAUNCH

I was six the summer I learned to swim
in a lake, in Maine
face to face with my father.
His beard is as black as the water
and when he smiles his small teeth
glisten like a flash of trout
mid-leap against the lowering sun.

He is just within, and out of my reach:
thirty-six years old,
as I am now thirty-six.
We circle each other, like Pisces.

I remember thunderheads gathering
at the edge of the sky, time
pressing us both forward.
The water was cool and dark
like the river near our home
where he canoed and fished and where
I poured out by the fistful
the ash of his teeth and bones.
How it glinted like mica as it ran
through my fingers to drift
across the sun-studded surface of the river
rain falling
on a lake in Maine
my father's face
like God moving
over the face of the waters.
I believed in it
and pushed off.

Goh Poh Seng

SUMMER IN LARK HARBOUR

Past April, the hill sides turn leafy again,
starlings and robins, white-winged crossbills
return to pick at the green earth,
while the warbler warbles, doing just what
it knew best, and that, very well indeed.

Butterflies flutter their wings of such
splendiferous colours, they are paeans
to the bright glory of summer,
the very ones that old Chuang Tze
dreamed were men dreaming

they were butterflies, or else were
butterflies dreaming they were men;
for me, it somehow gets lost here,
and soon, they are all gone levitating
to other trees, to more salubrious patches.

We do not doubt these birds and butterflies
so delightful to us in the summer
enter straight into paradise when they die,
while we're so fearful, so tormented.
O why can't we have the same privileges?

VIETNAM 1967

Beginning another vigil
he regards the tentative sun
through a fragmented sky;
otherwise there is only greenness.
In the still quiet dawn
he downs a mug of tea,
leans his rifle against a tree
and now and then recalls his home
unearths another day.
He is far from his hamlet.

It was an unquestioning life,
tilling the stubborn land that defies
the controlling hand of man.
There was consolation, now he knows
the laughter of his child,
the softness of his wife
who yields to him at night.
So what if kingdoms topple?

His dream shakes the silent air.

He sees his home gutted in the sun,
he sees his wife, head blown off,
the body of his child strewn
among young stubble of padi.

For days he prowled that waste
unable to quell his hate.
How to mobilize that precise pain?

Time passes.
Now and then a recall of home:
she chants at night to their child
who smiles, remembering small mischiefs.

After losing them,
their absence remains.

He makes his fists into a power
fierce as one whose sinews
could manage the sun.

In the glare of the sun
the planes beautiful
like silver spears
come in an eddy of air.

Amongst battered tree trunks
his blood splatters
into uncanny flowers.

Over the gentle contour of hills
and the sea,
the happy young crew from afar
returns to the air.

CEMETERY BY THE SEA

In life,
we're subject to vagrancies
and vicissitudes of fate,
our hearts many times exiled,
flung onto distant shores
but we all tread the footprints
of our ancestors
        home to our final rest.

I see visions of the headstones
up on the hill
above the village and the sweet bay,
white as white can be
in the daily outpour of light,
alive with shifting shadows thrown by clouds,
on land green,
on swags and relays of wild flowers,
buttercup and dandelion,
iris and lupin.
We can then all forget
our own private histories,
unfurl our wings
        and walk joyous on the air.

Susan Musgrave

MAGNOLIA

Another Valentine's Day behind bars
and I bring you light from the stars
that you might find your way back to us
out of darkness. I bring you memories
of me – naked, happy, nine months pregnant
tasting applesauce in the kitchen.

I bring you the wind, the way
our house creaked as you rocked
our newborn daughter who couldn't sleep.

I bring a handful of rain
that you may remember the sound of it,
and the smell of the earth
when you turn it in your hands.
I don't know why our life took
the turn it did, but now the smell
of earth reminds you – the magnolia
tree you planted the day
our daughter was born: did it live?

I bring you tears, the ones you wept
mixed with the milky scent of those I kept
locked up in me as I sang our daughter
to sleep those first merciful years –
if I could I would give you wings
to carry you up to the sky.

When I kiss your eyes, your sudden cry
startles the magnolia to a deeper white.

NO HABLO INGLES

What I want to say to His Honour
who sentenced the father of my children
to eighteen years for armed robbery
is let's just let bygones be bygones
be bye bye bye he'll be gone so long
but it doesn't come out that way, instead I say
it's not like he knocked off a Food Bank
Your Honour; nobody's going to bed hungry.
The first time this parole officer
comes to my house to see if I'm the kind
of woman suitable to be visiting her better half
in the bucket, he won't shake hands due to it
being flu season, a titch touchy. Your Honour,
having a parole officer in your house
is like going through airport security
without leaving home, jokes bomb
as mightily as the U.S. Forces
in Afghanistan. Last week leaving Deer Lake,
Newfoundland, the security guards
made me gulp down my bottled
Evian water to prove it wasn't a controlled
substance, my fault for pointing out
Evian is Naive spelled backwards: like the sign
says *joking is a criminal offense punishable*
by whatever it takes to make a person think
twice before being a comedian. This encourages me,
I say *heard any good jokes lately* to the comedian
in front of me who looks seriously like the dead
poet Al Pittman, and he cracks to me it is taking
so long to get through security he is afraid
his forged passport is going to expire
after which the drug-and-bomb-squad pit bulls
are onto him taking formidable bites
out of his right to remain
silent; Al confesses he returned from the dead

without remembering to warn anyone
and is flying back to Kandahar under the alias
bin Pittman, which is why he wears the T-shirt
with the many faces of bin Laden on it,
inside out. I try to diffuse the situation,
saying Al joined Al-Qaeda and all he got
was this lousy T-shirt but then when
it is my turn to be interrogated I err
on the side of terror and swallow the one bag
I haven't packed myself, a small bag
of white powder a criminal
lawyer in St. John's has given me
as a going-away gift. The false-sense-of-security
guards start sniffing around, and suddenly
I feel a new solidarity with Al
going away for good
to the jug in Corner Brook
so I get all Joan Baezy pro-active singing BAN
THE BOMB BOMB BOMB he'll be gone so long
until I cough up the gift bag of white powder
a sodden bath BOMB with Souvenir of The Rock
written on it for the love of Allah, so arrest me
why don't you, these are desperate times.
If you want my opinion they should detain
all passengers who *don't* board the aircraft joking:
a sense of humour should be a prerequisite
for *anyone* flying Air Canada these days.
Your Honour, when I offer this parole officer
coffee, he says I don't *use* caffeine
as if I've just suggested we inject heroin
with a turkey baster. Then he goes *you ever
considered therapy?* like I must be
some kind of case to stand by a man who steals
honest money from an ATM to make ends meet.
I don't miss a beat. I spent twenty years

in analysis until my therapist finally said
three words that would forever change
my life, he said *no hablo ingles.*
An old joke, Your Honour, but a good one,
ever noticed when you cut *therapist*
in two you get *the* and *rapist*, how half of *anal-*
ysis is *anal?* When you analyze it that way
I don't need some bad-ass parole officer
repeating how my better half is bad, badder
and baddest, why couldn't he try putting
my kids' Dad in some kind of positive
historical context? I mean, he ain't bad like
Hitler was bad, not like Stalin-bad,
Attilla the Hun-bad, Jack-the-Ripper or
George-the-Bush-bad, not half as bad
as the Bader Meinhoff Gang. Furthermore I say
to him, when was the last time you went into
a bank feeling holy? That's when this excuse
for a parole officer pulls out his Corrections
Services Canada pen and writes that I am a minimizer
of my spousal equivalent's crimes, unsuited to visit
said spousal equivalent due to my non deferential
attitude and negative influencing factors.
Your Honour I had three words to say to said
parole officer after that:
no hablo ingles.

THE ROOM WHERE THEY FOUND YOU

smelled of Madagascar vanilla.
After touching you for the last time
I scrubbed the scent from my skin –I would try
to remember later what the water felt like
on my hands but it was like trying to remember
thirst when you are drowning. They say love
doesn't take much, you just have to be there
when it comes around. I'd been there
from the beginning, I've been here all along.

I believed in everything: the hope
in you, your brokenness, the way
you arranged cut flowers on a tray
beside my blue and white teacup, the cracked
cup I'd told you brought me luck, the note
you wrote, "These flowers are a little ragged
– like your husband." The day you died

of an overdose in Vancouver
I found a moonshell in the forest, far
from the sea; when I picked it up
and pressed it to my ear I could hear you
taking the last breath you had the sad luck

to breathe. Our daughter cupped her hands
over her ears, as if she could stop death
from entering the life she had believed in
up until now. Childhood, as she had
known it, was over: the slap
of the breakers, the wind bruising the sea
tells her she is no longer safe in this world –
it's you she needs. I see you pulling away
after shooting up in the car while we

stood crying on the road, begging
you to come home. The vast sky
does not stop wild clouds
from flying. This boundless grieving,
for whom is it carried on?

UNDERSTANDING THE SKY

*"Sometimes I go about in pity for myself, and all the
    while
A great wind is bearing me across the sky."*
        – *from the Anishinabi (Ojibwa)*

The ravens arrived before daybreak,
awakening me. I moved from my moonlit
bed to the window, my heartbeat the sound
a hammer makes striking emptiness, before
and after. How much easier to embrace
pain than the common miracles of freezing
rain, the fires of smudgy juniper
smouldering across the water
or the mist that stills its whispery music
in my mind. What sound does the wind make
if you don't name it? Oh my ancestors
you are like clouds with nothing
to keep you from flying, like the running-away
river with no one to depend on. I go outside
understanding the sky is
just as present beneath my feet as it is
up above, and so try to tread

lightly on the crust of this earth, knowing
it is thin. The ravens slope towards the stars,
the black night in their beaks, and I think
Be light, light, light, as I make my way
in darkness to the river's edge. And then,
from overhead, a branch drooping
with snow, the owl takes flight, swoops
and glides down beside me. Even though
the requiem birds had failed to roust him
from his place of refuge, it is my quiet
uneasiness that causes him to strike
out over the river, to the brighter side.
What brings tears, I do not know, nor grasp
the thieflike tendency of tears to disappear,
but I feel graced to have felt the snow
owl's breath upon my face, as if I no longer need
to go on breathing; I am being breathed.
Be light, I whisper to the wind
as I climb the bank back to my dreaming
bed, nodding at the green bamboo stalk
I used to stake an unruly chrysanthemum
clinging to life in the frozen garden. The going
doesn't get any easier, but by any name
I'd miss the wind too much to be
parted from this life for even one hard winter.

Des Walsh

TALAMH AN ÉISC (LAND OF THE FISH)
for Paddy Keenan

Across an ocean of salt-drenched myths
this is where we live now
this is where we belong,
our hearts lined with fragments,
and like the lichen-covered rock
unaffected by storm.
Our souls are in every boulder
that inches its way to the sea,
we rule the meadows they
have claimed and the
gulls that rest there.
We sing to the drowned
tear-soaked families and
cling to the broken truths that
made us call this home, our voices
crying out over the pounding waves
only to be blown back to a sparrow's throat,
to have the melody cradled
in the arms of spruce and wind.
We are the songs of weather.
Back then, when these harbours
showed themselves only to
St. Brendan and the Beothuck
we came for fish, their scales becoming ours,
their justice becoming ours.
Back then, when the echoes of a
single note would ring out and
caress our granite graves
we would sing ourselves from sleep,
women would kiss the ocean,

their mouths smoothing the water that has
called us all back, to this place,
to hear that note again, which
will sound in our hearts forever.

I KNEW YOU THEN

I knew you then
when the earth was fresh
and these harbours
were deserted and silent.
I knew you then
when the sun
had not fully ripened
and the horizons
were not quite defined:
I knew you there
in that unchartered wilderness
always you in front
with compass and directions
always me behind
with stale bread and ginger ale.

SHE IMAGINES HERSELF FORGETTING

She imagines herself forgetting
along that unforgiving shore
where the limited sunshine
escapes into her moistened mouth,
she is not concerned with this poem
this honour, this distance.

Down among the seaweed and sculptured bone
she will quickly discard these things
as memory or disease
never hearing the voices from the cliffs
excusing her for walking too close
to the burning sea
she believes cold and worthy
of her brave thighs.

PIUS POWER JR.
Caul's Funeral Home, June 1, 1996

My friend, a former United Church minister,
acknowledging the crosses on Caul's doors,
remarked that the Catholics get you
even before entering. Fair play I thought.
My first time seeing those crosses was 1968.
My mother, cold from hours of death,
surrendered and fell into character.
Not you Pius. Your eyes opened and
fell on mine, your too-often neglected
journey blinded me, me aware of my
place here, set against yours and
your father's before you. Your eyes, wide and awake,
were singing "Mowing Meadows Down," and I, like

the fool I am, thought I knew the words.
And when I heard the story of earlier,
how they had to glue your hands together to keep
them resting in the ordered way I thought,
good thing you're only singing in my heart,
for if you were to sit up and break into it,
your hands would swing, and Newfoundland,
knowing its loss, would hold them forever.

ANTIBIOTICS

I have black Irish crows
in my chest
I cough them up
on the road to Corifin,
splattering the faded
lime-washed stone walls
with black feathers and whiskey.
The doctor in Ennis
who chose the Bahamas over Newfoundland
tells me the infection is genetic,
my people coming from Cork,
and that my cure is with the pills
and not to kiss the bare rock of the Burren
and ignore any shrine to the Blessed Virgin.
That said, I press my dry mouth
to the history of stone and
light candles and say three Hail Marys
at every crossroad in Clare.
I may indeed swallow his medicine
but I'm no fool.

Arne Ruste

from
POST-IT NOTES, JUST IN CASE

On the bathroom mirror cabinet

If she (in all improbability, or because it suddenly
                              grew so quiet) were to find him in the bath
with an erection the like of which she has not seen
                              in all their life together, a real tower of Pisa
stooping over the surface of water, it wouldn't be such a big thing
                              to get worked up about:
She mustn't immediately imagine she's caught him in the act,
       or that he has his mind on something beneath the covers,
or that down there, in his sunken, soaked
                              and heated-up state,
he's dreaming of other dames of every hue
                              and size and age and build:
brown, ebony, cross-eyed,
                              squat and leggy, pencil-thin and plump,
mature and newly ripened –
       someone who perhaps wouldn't be out for the count all night –
but she can pretty much relax,
                              because in all likelihood
he's just dead –

So there's no need to hurry,
                              in due course they'll get this sorted –
if only she could let the bath water out
                              and rinse away what's going to be there
by way of muck and other things

But if she should start to wonder
                              why and how it can be
that the scalding hot water

the burning-damp mound
and the sudden omen of departure
are all pumping blood in the same direction:
the death cramps, the orgasm,
the indescribable lightness, the weightlessness,
the definitive heaviness, the creeping cold;
if there's a certain similarity, if somehow
it can all add up,
then unfortunately she'll just have to make enquiries
some place else

By the telephone

If someone or other,
in all improbability, should phone
from the pub at getting on for midnight,
without introducing themselves,
a woman, her voice a little flustered,
she should simply relax,
not think straight off he must be lying
head down over a tabletop
his face ground down into shattered glass,
spilled drink and stubbed-out cigarettes,
or already under the table
his arm around the ankles
of the former chairman designate
after a four-hour slanging match
over the nonsense of the community plan
and he has also, in turn, insulted
the fellow's wife, three waiters and the landlords,
all within range,
and they phone to tell her she has to come
and get the swine

before anything else happens, or else they'll have to . . .

but for heaven's sake, there's no need to come to hasty conclusions,
                         because in all likelihood he's dead,
peaceful as ever,
                  and they've drawn lots
                                  to ascertain who should phone
to say that he's been driven off,
                              so at least she should be spared
                                                           that
After all: that's part of the job

Under the apple tree

If the utterly improbable should happen that she comes home
                              early one day, and that she
doesn't find him right away anywhere in the house,
                              or in the shed or workshop,
and she does a round of the garden and sees a form against the trunk
                  of the largest apple tree, and glimpses a ladder
and notices rope between the branches,
                              she'll maybe hesitate half a minute
or so, possibly considering whom she should call first –
                              neighbours, friends, the surgery – but
most likely she'll go down, or even run,
                  and find that he, having tumbled with the clippings
in the far too cramped and tangled top, sat down
                              his back against the mossy trunk
the March sun in his face
                              and purely and simply dozed off
right in the middle of the morning . . .
                              and in sheer relief she'll shout
and scream a whole half hour, because of
         her mother-in-law, the kids from next door, the washing up
from yesterday and the final warning
                              last year

(Translation from Norwegian by Kenneth Steven completed by Clyde Rose)

Helen Fogwill Porter

HOT NIGHT IN JULY

In St. John's Centre on sultry nights like this we sit on our
door-steps and chat with our neighbours. One old man wanders
from house to house, trying to remember what he's looking for.
My old black tom cat wakes from a dream of his hedonistic prime;
he fixes his gaze on the young tabby across the street and slowly
saunters over.

"Beautiful night," I say to the man next door. "Fantastic,"
he replies, smiling. He looks good in his khaki shorts, firm and
strong and limber. He has no wife, I have no husband. Why are we
always so polite?

I stroll along the sidewalk with no destination. Rock music
blares from the open windows. Teenagers stride by, six-packs
cradled in their arms. They do not see me.

The sweet smell of mock orange mingles with fabric softner
from the Laundromat. Fat fries out of Leo's back window. In a
nearby doorway an old woman with wild white hair wheedles "The
Star of Logy Bay" from her mouth organ while her daughter
paints the window trim, paying no attention to the lowering light.
Through his open door the shopkeeper on the corner hands a
dripping popsicle to a passing child. She grabs it quickly and
hurries away, afraid he might change his mind.

On LeMarchant Road a taxi driver snuggles with his
sweetheart in the back seat of his Chevrolet while the intercom
transmits unheeded instructions. At Caul's Funeral Home there
are no cars in the parking lots.

When I wander reluctantly back to my house, my neighbour
is still sitting on his steps whistling at the moon. He interrupts
himself to bid me good-night.

In my bedroom I kneel at the window, an elderly Juliet.

Sunday Best

It's Sunday and I'm washing dishes
from my late lonely lunch.
The sharp tap on the door startles me.
Standing there is a young man
in Salvation Army uniform
with a bundle of *War Crys* under his arm.

"Mrs. Porter?" he asks, smiling,
and my heart sinks.
It's a visit then, not a drop-off.
I show him into the living room
conscious of my shabby jeans
and the blob of mustard on my blouse.

As he settles himself I remember
long-ago Sundays when wearing jeans
would seem a kind of sin.
I hunch my shoulders to hide
the mustard smear.

"I'm Cadet Carter," he says, still smiling.
His teeth gleam white, he has a small mustache.
"I've been asked to call on you now and then
along with others we don't see in church very often."

I know if I open my mouth
I'll make a fool of myself
but that doesn't stop me.
"Oh, I still go to church sometimes," I sputter.
"My daughter goes to Gower and I go with her."
I try hard to remember the last time
either of us was there.

He smiles wider and says
"Well, as long as you go somewhere."
I find myself nodding and smiling back,

Why can't I tell him I'm not a believer
that I don't think there's any heaven
or any hell either, except the one on earth,
and ask him why God's son had to die on a cross
to save us from sins we had not yet committed?

As if he sees into my mind
he turns in his Bible to Psalm 51
and reads in a clear persuasive voice
"Behold, I was shapen in iniquity
and in sin did my mother conceive me.
Purge me with hyssop, and I shall be clean.
Wash me, and I shall be whiter than snow."
As I listen I think of my grandchildren
Shaina and Dylan and Julia.
I cannot see them as such deep-dyed sinners.
Does this man really believe what he's reading?

He kneels on the floor to pray
and I bow my head.
He murmurs words about family and love and blood.
I'm no longer concerned about the stain
on my shirt.

Before he leaves he tells me
he might not get back to see me for a while.
I try not to show my relief.
He opens his notebook and points to a list of names.
My fellow sinners.
"I don't have a car," he says
"so I do one neighbourhood each Sunday."

When I close the door I want to weep
but I don't know why.

Is it because I've lost my faith?
Or because I'm remembering the Sundays
of long ago
when we all went to my mother's after church
and ate the kind of dinner only she could cook?
Or do I weep for this young man
so secure in his salvation that he gives his life
to the cause
and trudges from house to house on Sundays
bringing the good news of the gospel
to people like me?

Patrick Warner

MORMON

How will a Mormon boy get a wife, I wondered,
if he declines his mission to wander the world,
spreading the Mormon word as he goes:
no wife for a Mormon boy who refuses.

So I was kind to two young Mormon men
who came to my door last Saturday morning –
the point man in short-sleeved shirt and blue tie,
his back-up in short-sleeved and blue tie –

the former displaying a pulp magazine
which featured a story on the fashion industry
and its dangers, especially to young women:
anorexia, bulimia, and low self-esteem.

I listened until – as if at some prearranged signal –
the second flipped open a leather-bound book
he had held until then with a sloth-like grip.
It was my cue to say: I am not a Christian.

This had been true of my life for so long
that to say it out loud gives only a moderate high,
which in turn brings only a moderate low.
And so I did not take it too badly on coming back in

to hear my eight-year-old daughter say,
in her deepest voice: *I am not a Christian*;
though to hear her say it brought it home in a new way,
and I thought for a moment that this is serious

and that she should take it more seriously,
so I considered putting the fear into her, telling her
that if her grandfather heard her say such a thing
he would think us condemned to eternal damnation.

Instead, I sat back down on the couch beside her
where it so happened there was scheduled
an end-of-season *Fashion File* – the year's best show,
the year's best designer, the year's best newcomer.

And watching, I reserved my loudest cheers,
for headdresses of ostrich and emu feathers,
for models with bleached invisible eyebrows,
for models with slack, stew-bone thighs.

While she preferred the more womanly models –
though she did not care for naked breasts –
and reserved her loudest cheers for young Marc Jacobs
and for the ready-to-wear from Donna Karan.

What a world this is for a Mormon boy, I thought,
who declines his mission to wander the world,
spreading the Mormon word as he goes:
what a world for a Mormon boy who refuses.

GUMSHOE

Packed in pick-up trucks they arrive at dawn,
these small, overalled, dark-skinned men,
from countries south of the Rio Grande,
who tend to the trees and bushes and lawns

in this mature suburban neighbourhood
where month-by-month nothing changes
except the flags, I mean the flaps that flap
from slender dowels, that are set alongside

the tasselled poles that fly Old Glory,
silk flags set to mark a holiday or season,
pumpkins, shamrocks, hearts, and bunnies
signal the year-long consumer obsession,

in this neighbourhood where nobody walks,
where in places there are no sidewalks,
where no one seems to notice what I notice
when I walk, and there's no one to ask

about these inch-square zip-lock baggies
I find every morning, dew-fogged and stuck
to the pavement – what are these exactly,
sandwich bags for wee folk, for fairies?

Such folk myths belong to old countries,
to the Irish pubs down by the harbour,
to Germanytowns, Dutchlands, Little Italies.
New World folklore is of a different order.

Myths here are a poor man's collateral,
so new they don't seem like myths at all,
but swap stocks and bonds for gold and silver
and the city skyline for the magic kingdom,

and you'll understand why these lawns
are tended each day by Guatemalans,
Mexicans, El Salvadorians, Peruvians,
and you'll know why yesterday when I found

a sanitary napkin perched on the gutter
my first thought was of a magic slipper,
followed by thoughts of the ugly sisters,
and girls who will cut off their toes to fit in,

because that's the way it is in this place,
where the bloated frog is always the prince,
where there is blind belief in tomorrow
and in the wealth tomorrow will bring.

Today it brought a pair of black underwear,
women's black Moschino underwear,
dropped in the middle of an intersection
where I barely had time to examine them.

I thought, naturally, of Puss 'n Boots,
and maybe because I knew the ogre's fate
something a bit more sinister crept in,
and, as well, I was getting these looks

from a pair of Mexicans or Guatemalans,
both of whose faces barely topped
the four-foot hedge they were trimming,
faces right off a frieze in Tenochtitlán.

What's next, I wondered, a severed finger,
an arm, a ripped-out human heart,
a dead co-ed like Snow White on a lawn
surrounded by seven diminutive men?

Not that I'm saying it's all going to happen,
(as cases go it's not open and shut),
there are reasons the future is hidden,
but clues, too, if you know how to look.

Paul Durcan

MR AND MRS TALBOT

5 a.m. Tuesday May 29, 01
I am hearing voices under my dormer window
In the Foot of Slievemore House.

Realising that I am not dreaming,
I stumble out of bed and look down;
I see Mrs. Talbot in her pink dressing gown

Wrestling with a lamb, grappling to
Untangle it from the wire fence;
The lamb is mute, prone, vertical

Like a carcass hanging from a meat-hook.
'Come and give me a hand, Joe.'
'Wait till the morning, Louise.'

Joe's full tide of Dublin working-class vowels
Swirls in and around and out
The sand-castles of Louise's Dublin middle-class consonants.

Joe and Louise are Dubliners on Achill Island
Who have sold up their home in Dublin.
Although they have at least two great grandchildren

They are as youthful a married couple
As you could hope to meet.
Gleefully bickering; together forever.

'The lamb will die, Joe' Louise scolds him.
Joe lopes out with a pair of pliers.
Three snips and the lamb skips free.

Mr. and Mrs. Talbot would shame you,
Know-alls of the airwaves and the broadsheets.
While I sigh my way back into my single bed

They gambol across the gravel,
Bouncing back into their bedroom.
Spicy old Dubs of the mountain.

THE FAR SIDE OF THE ISLAND

Driving over the mountain to the far side of the island
I am brooding neither on what lies ahead of me
Nor on what lies behind me. Up here
On top of the mountain, in the palm of its plateau,
I am being contained by its wrist and its fingertips.

The middle of the journey is what is at stake –
Those twenty-five miles or so of in-betweenness
In which marrow of mortality hardens
In the bones of the nomad. From finite end
To finite end, the orthopaedics of mortality.

Up here on the plateau above the clouds,
Peering down on the clouds in the valleys,
There are no fences, only moorlands
With wildflowers as far as the eye can see;
The earth's unconscious in its own pathology.

Yet when I arrive at the far side of the island
And peer down at the out-port on the rocks below,
The Atlantic ocean rearing raw white knuckles,
Although I am globally sad I am locally glad
To be about to drive down that corkscrew road.

Climbing down the tree-line, past the first cottage,
Past the second cottage, behind every door
A neighbour. It is the company of his kind
Man was born for. Could I have known,
Had I not chanced the far side of the island?

THE 12 O'CLOCK MASS
Roundstone, County Galway

On Sunday the 28th of July 2002 –
The summer it rained almost every day –
In rain we strolled down the road
To the church on the hill overlooking the sea.
I had been told to expect 'a fast Mass'.
Twenty minutes. A piece of information
Which disconcerted me.

Out onto the altar hurried
A short, plump priest in middle age
With a horn of silver hair,
In green chasuble billowing
Like a poncho or a caftan over
White surplice and a pair
Of Raeboks – mammoth trainers.

He whizzed along
Saying the readings himself as well as the gospel;
Yet he spoke with conviction and with clarity;
His every action an action
Of what looked like effortless concentration;
Like Tiger Woods on top of his form.
His brief homily concluded with a solemn request.

To the congregation he gravely announced:
"I want each of you to pray for a special intention,
A very special intention.
I want each of you – in the sanctity of your own souls –
To pray that, in the All-Ireland
Championship hurling quarter-final this afternoon in Croke Park,
Clare will beat Galway."

The congregation splashed into laughter
And the church became a church of effortless prayer.
He whizzed through the Consecration
As if the Consecration was something
That occurs at every moment of the day and night;
As if betrayal and the overcoming of betrayal
Were an every-minute occurrence.

As if the Consecration was the 'now'
In the 'now' of the Hail Mary prayer:
"Pray for us *now*, and at the hour of our death."
At the Sign of Peace he again went sombre
As he instructed the congregation:
'I want each of you to turn around and say to each other:
"You are beautiful".'

The congregation was flabbergasted but everyone fluttered
And swung around and uttered that extraordinary phrase:
"You are beautiful."
I shook hands with at least five strangers,
Two men and three women, to each of them saying:
"You are beautiful." And they to me:
"You are beautiful."

At the end of Mass, exactly twenty-one minutes,
The priest advised: "Go now and enjoy yourselves
For that is what God made you to do –
To go out there and enjoy yourselves

And to pray that, in the All-Ireland
Championship hurling quarter-final between Clare and Galway
In Croke Park, Clare will win."

After Mass, the rain had drained away
Into a tide of sunlight on which we sailed out
To St Macdara's Island and dipped our sails –
Both of us smiling, radiant sinners.
In a game of pure delight, Clare beat Galway by one point:
Clare 1 goal and 17 points, Galway 19 points.
'Pray for us *now*, and at the hour of our death.'

Rosalie Elliott

I RAN SO FAST

I ran fast into the face of death
And refused to see it coming.
Certain, alone, steadfast, intractable,
With its eyes penetrating mine,
I thought I could run through it.

If needs be I could carry you.
I was healthy.
I was strong.

I ran so fast through death,
With blood on my face,
Parts of you missing,
Not to mention half my mind,
I called to you
"Hurry up!"

But you couldn't keep up with me.

I went back and back and back again.

There were flowers and blood on the trail.

But you had gone.

I ran so fast into the face of death,
I didn't see it coming.

It must have been hard for you
At the end
With me so many paces ahead.

THE HONOURABLE BIRD

"I am understanding honourable father.
I am understanding honourable son.
I am not understanding honourable bird."
     – Asian immigrant to Canada *(overheard on the radio)*

Worms crawling over beloved bones.
Maggots feeding on putrified flesh.
Blossoms fallen to dust.
Trees to rot.

But yet the honourable bird
Spreads his wings over all.

The dust
The ashes
The hideous glue
The gelatinous mire
Which we come from
And to which we go.

The stuff we won't put our hands in –

Out of that, our spirit comes,
Holy and fresh.

Water
Cows
Butter
Flies
Milk
Supper
Even (dare I say?)
Love

The honourable bird prevails
And spreads his diaphanous wings
Over all.

I too do not understand the
Honourable bird.

But I believe it flies
Somewhere between
Hello and goodbye
Before and afterwards

Holy and fresh.

Alistair MacLeod

from
NO GREAT MISCHIEF

Chapter 42

And now it is dusk turning towards darkness as my car moves deeper southward. Not far away, across the river the United States – that country born of revolution – sends its towers thrusting to the sky.

On Monday in my office I will offer solace and change and perhaps hopeful improvement to those who seek me out. We will talk about retrusion and occlusion and the problems caused by overbite. "Don't bite off more than you can chew," Grandma used to say.

When I first started practising dentistry, I sometimes saw myself in my white coat with my dentist's drill as an extension of my earlier self, with the jackleg drill. Leaning towards the surface that I drilled while the cooling water splashed back towards my face. Drilling deep but not too deep. Trying to get it right.

In the landscape around me, those who harvest the bounty of the earth are stilled for the day. Yet they are there in the near-darkness with their own hopes and dreams and disappointments. On the East Coast, the native peoples who move across the land, harvesting, are stilled also. Tomorrow they will cross back and forth across the borders, following the potato harvest and the blueberries, passing from New Brunswick into Maine and then back again. They are older than the borders and boundaries between countries and they pay them little mind.

In Kenya, at the base of Mount Kilimanjaro, the tall and arrogant Masai follow their herds. For strength they drink the blood of their cattle. They follow the cycle of the seasons and pay no heed to the boundaries of the parks and game preserves. They were there first, they reason. Unlike the Zulus, they have not yet been confined to certain "homelands" which are really not their homes at

274

all. Perhaps the Masai do not know that others are planning "to do something" with them. "Soon," perhaps.

In Kingston Penitentiary, Calum said, a disproportionate number of the prisoners were from the native population. In many cases they did not fully understand the language of those to whom they were entrusted or condemned. They would hang their woven dreamcatchers in the windows of their cells, he said. There were not many dreams in Kingston Penitentiary. It was the only thing he ever said about his years of incarceration.

In the language of the law, a life sentence is really twenty-five years and one is eligible for parole after ten. This is why I am able to visit him on these days. I try to do so faithfully.

In the waters near Glencoe perhaps the mythical "king of the herring" still swims. If he exists, perhaps he is as complicated as many other leaders. He is regarded as a friend to some, but those who follow him may do so at their peril. In any case there are no MacDonalds who wait for him and his bounty, and perhaps without their beliefs he is just another fish, who should be careful where he swims.

Ahead of me, at home, my wife and children wait. In the hell of eastern Europe an official visited my wife's home when she was just a little girl. The official had a list which contained the names of her father and her two older brothers. They were commanded, said the official, to be at the station the next morning. When the door closed, her father said that he and his two sons should leave during the night. They could be far away by morning, and later they could work something out. Her mother argued that they should follow the rules and regulations that were laid out for them. She said it was not good to break the law, even if you did not trust it. They argued deep into the night. In the end her father reluctantly agreed to take her mother's advice. In the morning she said goodbye to her husband and her sons and they left for the station. She never saw any of them again.

My wife is supportive of my journeys. "We never know what lies ahead of us," she says. "There is never time enough."

I turn off the cruise control and the air-conditioner as I enter the "estates" where I live. My wife is already dressed for our dinner engagement.

"How was your trip?" she asks.

"Oh, fine," I say.

"Did anything happen? You look tired and pale."

"No, nothing happened."

Grandma used to say, "Everyone's tired."

I shower and change my clothes. I go to the phone book to check the address of our dinner engagement. In the margin of one of its pages I see the words "*Le pays de Laurentides*" and a phone number. Underneath the notation, in my son's handwriting, is the message, "Tell Dad."

"What's this?" I ask my son. "When did this come?"

"Oh," he says in embarrassment, "a long time ago. I was going to tell you but I forgot. The man sounded French. He had a name that sounded like 'gingerale.' He made me spell out that '*Le pays*' stuff. He said you would understand."

I dial the number and a pleasant woman answers the phone. I make my inquires.

"Oh," she says. "This was their boarding house. They only stayed here for a little while. They said the money wasn't good enough so they went across the border to the States. I remember some of their names, Gingras, MacKenzie, Belanger. Do those names ring a bell?"

"Yes," I say. "Those names ring a bell. Thanks anyway."

Chapter 43

And now it's six months later and the phone rings. It is evening. Outside my window the blustery snow swirls. "March may come in like a lamb, but it goes out like a lion," Grandma used to say.

"Hello," I say.

"It's time," he says.

"What do you mean?"

"It's time," he says. "Time to go." He coughs into the receiver.

"You mean now?" I ask. "It's snowing outside. It's dark. It's March."

"I know all about March," he says, "and so do you."

"Are you sure?"

"Of course I'm sure," he says. "I was never one to fool around. Have I ever called you before?"

"No, you haven't."

"Well then."

The operator comes on, asking for the deposit of more coins. Of course he is at a pay phone.

"Hang up," I say, "and call collect."

"No need for that," he laughs. "Always look after your blood," he begins to say, but the line goes dead.

There is no way to call him back.

"Be careful," says my wife. "The road report is bad."

"I will do the best I can," I say. "Perhaps I should take some liquor?"

"Take all you want," she says, "but be careful."

I take a bottle of brandy. We embrace and say goodbye.

Highway 401 is not as bad as it is reported to be. Often the weather reports are exaggerated to keep unnecessary travellers off the road. Sometimes my car fishtails, but I am able to keep it at a steady pace. The snowploughs with their flashing lights come and go. The salt trucks spray their pellets on the white roadbed. There are not many cars out tonight.

In Toronto, he is sitting on his bed. His white hair is combed and rises in waves upon his head. He has had a haircut. He has a small club bag at his feet.

"Thanks for coming," he says. "Are you ready for this? I'll help with the driving."

We leave his door open so that the desperate may take whatever they wish.

"Do you want this brandy?" I ask.

"No," he says, "Leave it on the windowsill. It won't last long."

We go forward into the night.

He is quiet beside me in the car. Sometimes I think he is sleeping or dozing, but when I look at him, his eyes are open. He coughs again and again.

The night goes by as does the highway as we head north

and east. Sometimes there are snow squalls but then they clear. The leaden sky begins to lighten. Deep into Quebec we stop for breakfast. The breakfast special consists of eggs, toast, bacon or sausage, and beans.

The waitress brings us our order. She does not bring us the beans but instead an extra sausage. The French Canadians around us are having beans.

Calum laughs. "They think we make fun of them for having beans for breakfast," he says. "I suppose it's like us with our porridge."

We ask for the beans. The waitress looks at us. "You want beans?" she says. "Okay, I just looked at you and well, you know...."

She brings the beans in two dessert bowls.

"No extra charge," she says.

"*Merci*," we reply.

Highway 20 is flat and fast. We move beside the ice-caked St. Lawrence.

At Rivière du Loup we turn south towards New Brunswick. The road becomes two lanes and our progress is not so rapid. Still, we go forward. We drink coffee from Styrofoam cups and when we are finished Calum throws them out the window, where they blend with the whiteness of the snow.

When we approach Grand Falls, I raise my eyebrows in a question. "We will go through Plaster Rock," he says. "It will be shorter and there'll be no traffic. I'll drive through that section of the trees."

"Do you have a driver's licence?" I ask.

"No," he says. "I let it lapse a long time ago. I had no need for it."

He drives steadily and surely. There is no traffic. The signs warn us to be aware of moose. "This is a good road," he says. "I wonder when they paved it. It used to be just gravelled. It was that way the time we came from Timmins. With the compressor and the kitten."

We pass Renous, home of the penitentiary. We pass through all the small communities with their disused schools and abandoned halls. We come to Rogersville.

"This place always struck me," he says. "The graveyard is so big and the community so small. More people in the graveyard than in the village. When we worked in the shafts there were never any graveyards. People never lived in those places long enough to die."

"Although some of them did," I say.

"Yes," he says. "Some of them died. Died in different ways. Here, you drive for a while."

We approach Moncton. After Sackville we cross the border into Nova Scotia. There is no piper on hand to welcome us, as is the case in the summer. There are only wisps of blowing snow.

It is dark when we pass through Antigonish and the wind tries mightily to lift our car. The road signs warn us of blowing snow. The storm has increased. When we come to the base of the Havre Boucher hill, he says, "I'll drive now. I'm more experienced on hills and in snow than you are."

We begin the long ascent. It is a two-mile climb. There are no other vehicles on the road. The car slides and bucks, but he holds it to its course. The red light comes on to indicate that the engine is overheated. We make it to the top and begin the short descent. The mountain from which the Canso Causeway was built looms ahead of us and to our right.

"Do you know that song?" he says. "'Causeway Crossing' by Albert MacDonald?"

"Yes. I know it."

"Good song," he says.

The flashing lights of a police cruiser appear before us. The police officer waves us to the side.

"Where are you going?" he asks. "It's not often that we see an Ontario car around here at this time of year."

"To Cape Breton," we answer. "We're trying to get across."

"You can't get across," he says. "The waves are washing right over the road. The causeway's closed."

He speaks with an accent that is not local to the region.

"What are your names?" he asks.

"We're MacDonalds," we say.

"MacDonalds?" he says. "Are you the guys who make the hamburgers?"

"No," says Calum, "we're not the guys who make the hamburgers."

The snow increases and the wind blows so that officer has to hold on to his hat. He runs for the safety of his cruiser.

Calum starts the car.

"What are you doing?" I ask.

"We're going across," he says. "That's what we came for."

As we approach the entrance to the causeway we can see the waves breaking. There is a shroud of mist in the air and dirty balls of brown foam fly before us. "This end is the worst," says Calum. He takes the car to where he can assess the situation. The waves are coming from the left, breaking and then receding. When they break, the roadway is invisible, buried under foaming depths of water.

Calum begins to count the waves.

"After the third big wave," he says, "there will be a lull and then we'll go. If the motor gets too wet the car will quit. The third time is the charm. Above the roar of the gale he says, "Here we go!"

The car springs forward. The red engine light is on, the engine is roaring, and the water comes in at the bottom of the doors. The windshield wipers are thick with ice and stop dead. He rolls down the window and sticks his head out into the gale to see where he is going on the invisible road. We are hit by one wave and then another. The car rocks with the force of the blows. The causeway is littered with pieces of pulpwood and dead fish. He weaves around the obstacles. The wheels touch the other side.

"Here," he says, "you can do the driving now. We're almost home."

We exchange places. Away from the pounding of the waves it is relatively serene. We can see the lights of some of the houses. I begin to drive along the coast. He settles into the passenger seat. The road we travel now is not directly in the path of the storm. Gradually the windshield thaws and the red engine light goes off.

Grandpa used to say that when he was a young man he would get an erection as soon as his feet hit Cape Breton. That was in the time, he said, when men had buttons on the front of their trousers. We, his middle-aged grandchildren, do not manifest any such signs of hopeful enthusiasm. But we are nonetheless here.

Tomorrow when the day breaks we will see what is now invisible around us. It will not all be pretty. Near the open water the bald eagles will pounce with mighty talons upon the white-coated baby seals. They will scream in different voices as they rise above the blood-stained ice. "You've got to take the bitter with the sweet," Grandma used to say. "No one said life was going to be a bed of roses."

I recognize all the familiar landmarks, although it is dark and there are mountains of snow. Here is the place where Grandpa threw the top of his whisky bottle out the window the day we were returning from my graduation. The day the red-haired Alexander MacDonald was killed, although we did not know it then. The day his mother bought him the shirt.

I turn to Calum and he is still, though his eyes are wide open, looking at the road ahead. Once we sang to the pilot whales on a summer's day. Perhaps we lured the huge whale in beyond his safe depth. And he died, disembowelled by the sharp rocks he could not see. Later his body moved inland, but his great heart remained behind.

By the glow of the dashboard lights I can see the thin scar on Calum's lower lip beginning to whiten. This is the man whose tooth was pulled by a horse. This is the man who, in his youthful despair, went looking for a rainbow, while others thought he was just wasting gas.

The car crests a high hill and in the distance, across the white expanse of the ice, I can see the regulated blinking of the now-automated light. It is still miles away. Yet it sends forth its message from the island's highest point. A light of warning or, perhaps, encouragement.

I turn to Calum once again. I reach for his cooling hand which lies on the seat beside him. I touch the Celtic ring. This is the man who carried me on his shoulders when I was three. Carried me across the ice from the island, but could never carry me back again.

Out on the island the neglected fresh-water well pours forth its gift of sweetness into the whitened darkness of the night.

Ferry the dead. *Fois do t'anam.* Peace to his soul.

'All of us are better when we're loved.'

CONTRIBUTORS

Avis, Nick. Nick Avis was born in England. He moved to Newfoundland and Labrador in 1971 and now lives with his daughter in St. John's where he practices law. He has been writing most of his life and his poetry has been published nationally and internationally for nearly thirty years.

Blackmore, Isabel. Isabel Blackmore has been a resident of Gander for sixty years. Married with seven children, she is a housewife, writer and amateur painter. She has worked as a commentator for the CBC and an essayist with the St. John's *Evening Telegram* and *The Downhomer*.

Bonnell, Arch. Arch Bonnell was born in Grand Bank, Newfoundland, and educated at Memorial University of Newfoundland and Dalhousie University. A lawyer by profession, he has published one novel, *The Boys of Jubilee*, and has a number of others in various stages of completion. He is soon to retire with the aim of devoting himself full time to his writing.

Brunt, Stephen. Stephen Brunt has been sports columnist for *The Globe and Mail* since 1988. His most recent book, *Searching for Bobby Orr*, was published by Knopf Canada in October, 2006. *Facing Ali*, also published in the United States, the United Kingdom, Australia, Norway and Japan, was named one of the top ten books of 2004 by *Sports Illustrated* magazine. He splits his time between Hamilton, Ontario and Winterhouse Brook, Newfoundland.

Butt, Bill. Bill Butt was born in Gander in 1956 and is a Programme Specialist with Nova Central School District. His father's family came from Exploits Islands, Notre Dame Bay, which inspired a life-long interest in Newfoundland folklore – he holds a M.A. in folklore from MUN. He is a member of the band, *Final Approach*, with Sheldon McBreairty and Rex Kean. The group has released two CDs of original tunes.

Callanan, Mark. Mark Callanan was born and raised in St. John's, Newfoundland. *Scarecrow*, his first collection of poems, was short-listed for the E.J. Pratt provincial book award. A selection of his work appeared in *Breathing Fire 2: Canada's New Poets*. He lives in St. John's.

Chubbs, Boyd. Boyd Warren Chubbs was born and grew up in L'Anse au Clair, Labrador. His most recent poetry collection was *The Winter of Remarkable Oranges* (Breakwater, 2004). Poet, visual artist and guitarist, he currently resides in St. John's.

Clark, Joan. Joan Clark's latest novel is *An Audience of Chairs*, which won the Winterset Award and the Newfoundland and Labrador Fiction Award. She is the author of two short story collections, four novels and a stage play as well as eight children's books.

Coady, Lynn. Lynn Coady's latest novel is *Mean Boy*. She is also the author of *Strange Heaven*, *Play the Monster Blind*, and *Saints of Big Harbour*. She lives in Edmonton.

Collins, Tony. Tony Collins was born in St. John's in 1951 but moved to Gander in the early 1970s. He has remained there ever since, raising a family, working with several non-government organizations and writing a regular column for the St. John's *Evening Telegram*.

Creelman, Libby. Originally from Massachusetts, Libby Creelman has lived in Newfoundland since 1983. Her stories have been published in literary magazines across the country and have been included in *99: Best Canadian Stories* and *The Journey Prize Anthology*. Her collection, *Walking in Paradise*, was published by Porcupine's Quill in 2000. She is currently working on a novel.

Crozier, Lorna. Lorna Crozier was born in 1948 in Swift Current, Saskatchewan. Her first collection of poetry, *Inside in the Sky*, was published in 1976. Since then, she has authored fourteen books of poetry, including *Inventing the Hawk*, winner of the 1992 Governor-General's Award, and her most recent collection, *Whetstone*. She chairs the Writing Department at the University of Victoria. Her first selected poems will be published in the spring of 2007.

Crummey, Michael. Michael Crummey's latest novel is *The Wreckage*. He has also published the novel *River Thieves*, the story collection *Flesh & Blood*, and several books of poetry including *Salvage* and *Hard Light*. He lives in St. John's.

Cull, Kerri. Kerri Cull lives in St. John's where she works at Creative Book Publishing, *The Express* and Memorial University. In her free time she likes to read, write, and hang out with her family and friends.

Dalton, Mary. Mary Dalton lives in St. John's, where she teaches at Memorial University of Newfoundland. She is the author of four books of poetry; the most recent are *Merrybegot* (2003) and *Red Ledger* (2006). Among her awards are the TickleAce/Cabot Award for Poetry and the E. J. Pratt Poetry Award.

Dawe, Tom. Tom Dawe was born in Long Pond, Manuels, Conception Bay, and has been a professor of English at Memorial University, visual artist, editor, folklorist and writer for both children and adults. His last book of poetry, *In Hardy Country*, was published by Breakwater Books in 1993. Martina Seifert has written a critical study of his work, *Rewriting Newfoundland Mythology* (Galda + Wilch Verlag, 2002).

Dean, Paul. Paul Dean is a geologist who sometimes writes stories which he reads at the March Hare. Most of his stories are based in his birthplace, North Harbour, Placentia Bay, Newfoundland.

Downer, Don. Don Downer, born at Indian Islands, was resettled to Lewisporte in 1959. Don's experience ranges from inshore cod trap fisherman to writer, biologist, businessman, teacher, principal, university professor and research office administrator. He holds a masters degree in marine biology from Memorial University and a masters and PhD in educational administration from Ottawa University.

Dragland, Stan. Stan Dragland's most recent book is *Stormy Weather (Foursomes)*, from Pedlar Press. He is the author of several other books, including *Apocrypha: Further Journeys* in the NeWest Press Writer-as-Critic series. With Don McKay, he is publisher of Brick Books. He lives in St. John's.

Durcan, Paul. Paul Durcan was born in Dublin in 1944. The author of over seventeen books of poetry, he has read his work all over the world. In 2001, he received the Cholmondely Award for poetry. His most recent collection, *The Art of Life*, was published by The Harvill Press, London, in 2004.

Dwyer, Michelle. Michelle Dwyer grew up in Lewisporte, where she was inspired to write by her parents and the other interesting characters in her family. She currently lives in St. Anthony, Newfoundland, where she teaches English and social studies and continues to write as much as possible in her spare time.

Earle, Derrick. Derrick Earle is a nineteen-year old student at Memorial University of Newfoundland and hails from the tip of the Northern Peninsula of Newfoundland in St. Lunaire-Griquet. He can be reached at derricke218@gmail.com.

Elliott, David. David Elliott (1923-1999) grew up in a succession of Newfoundland outport communities. At fifteen, he left school to become a telegraph operator. At twenty-five, he entered Memorial University of Newfoundland where he became the first honours graduate in English. He was a civil servant, soldier, clinical psychologist, editor and, finally, at Sir Wilfred Grenfell College, university professor. His poetry was collected in *The Edge of Beulah* (Breakwater, 1988).

Elliott, Rosalie. Rosalie Elliott (1941-2006) was a teacher of literature, history and music in St. John's and Corner Brook. Her poems were published and republished in various magazines and anthologies, most recently in *The Backyards of Heaven* (2003). She was at work on a collection of poems when she died in October 2006.

Ennis, John. John Ennis has published thirteen books of poetry. Head of the School of Humanities at the Waterford Institute of Technology in Ireland, he also chairs WIT's Centre for Newfoundland and Labrador Studies. His collection, *Goldcrest Falling* (Scop Productions), was launched at the Corner Brook March Hare in 2006. In August 2006, he published *Oisin's Journey Home*, a long poem on the Newfoundland Railway.

Ferncase, Anne. Anne Ferncase, winner of the Hilroy Fellowship Award in 1989, is a poet, playwright, environmentalist, and wordsmith. Her children's play, *Running With Dragons*, has been produced both in Vancouver, British Columbia and Newfoundland. Born in California, she sojourned in France, then immigrated to Canada, and has lived in Newfoundland since 1984.

Fogwill Porter, Helen. Helen Fogwill Porter was born and grew up in St. John's, where she still lives. Her book publications include *Below the Bridge* (1980), *January, February, June, or July* (1988) and *A Long and Lonely Ride* (1991). All were published by Breakwater. Her new novel, *Finishing School*, has recently been accepted by the Pottersfield Press in Halifax, Nova Scotia.

Fowler, Adrian. Adrian Fowler's work has appeared in various magazines and collections of Canadian writing. He was co-editor with Al Pittman of the poetry anthology *31 Newfoundland Poets*, published in 1979. He lives in Corner Brook, Newfoundland, where he teaches English at Sir Wilfred Grenfell College.

Garvey, Alan. Alan Garvey's work has been published in *The Backyards of Heaven* and *However Blow the Winds*. He has three chapbooks: *Dear Whoever, The Devil and the Deep Blue Sea* and *Play Dead*. He received Arts Council grants to read in Toronto and Newfoundland. He is doing an M.A. in Creative Writing at the Waterford Institute of Technology.

Gillis, Susan. Susan Gillis is the author of two books of poetry, including *Volta*, which won the A.M. Klein Prize for Poetry in 2003. Originally from Halifax, Susan lived on Vancouver Island for many years before settling in Montreal, where she teaches English literature at John Abbott College.

Goh, Poh Seng. Goh Poh Seng, born in Malaya in 1936, received his medical degree from University College in Dublin. He has authored four novels, three full-length plays and five books of poetry, including *The Girl from Ermita: Selected Poems* (1998) and *As Though the Gods Love Us* (2002), both published by Nightwood Editions. He divides his time between Vancouver, British Columbia, and Lark Harbour, Newfoundland.

Halfe, Louise (Sky Dancer). Louise Bernice Halfe, also known as Sky Dancer, is a Cree writer originally from the Saddle Lake First Nations, Alberta. Married with two adult children and two grandsons, Louise now lives happily with her husband in a strawbale house outside of Saskatoon, Saskatchewan. She is the author of two books of poetry, and her third *The Crooked Good* will be released in 2007.

Hehir, Kevin. Kevin Hehir is a writer, performer and educator living in St. John's. His writing is available online at ubu.com and blazevox.org and in various printed things. He has developed *The Exploding Language Poetry Workshop for Young Writers* and taught children at the Anna Templeton Centre for Craft, Art and Design.

Helfgott Hyett, Barbara. Barbara Helfgott Hyett has published four collections of poetry: *In Evidence: Poems of the Liberation of Nazi Concentration Camps, Natural Law, The Double Reckoning of Christopher Columbus,* and *The Tracks We Leave: Poems on Endangered Wildlife of North America.* Her new collection, *Rift,* is due in 2007. She directs POEMWORKS: The Workshop for Publishing Poets, in Brookline, MA, USA.

Hobbs, Carol. Carol Hobbs, originally from Notre Dame Bay in Newfoundland, is a writer and teacher in Massachusetts. Her work has appeared in various journals and anthologies in Canada, the United States and Ireland. Her poetry manuscript, *New Found Lande,* was awarded a New England PEN Discovery Prize.

Hollett, Matthew. Matthew Hollett is a poet and visual artist from Pasadena, Newfoundland. His work has previously appeared in *Shift & Switch: New Canadian Poetry* and *The Backyards of Heaven.* He maintains a website of artwork and writing at matthewhollett.com.

Hynes, Ben. A syllable dropped from the mouth of the Humber River, Ben Hynes has lived his whole life in Corner Brook. His work has appeared in *Humber Mouths* (2002). He won a prize the Newfoundland and Labrador Arts & Letters Competition Senior Poetry Division in 2005.

Hynes, Joel. Joel Hynes is the author of *Down to the Dirt,* shortlisted for the Winterset Award and winner of the Percy Janes First Novel Award. He is also an award-winning playwright and actor. Currently, he appears in the CBC's *Hatching, Matching and Dispatching,* and is also a contributing writer for the show. His new novel, *Right Away Monday,* will soon be released. He lives in St. John's, Newfoundland.

Johnston, Wayne. Wayne Johnston was born in Newfoundland and now divides his time between Toronto and Virginia. He is the author of seven novels and one memoir. His new novel, *The Custodian of Paradise,* was released in Canada by Alfred A. Knopf in September of 2006.

Lane, Patrick. Patrick Lane has published more than twenty books of poetry, fiction, and non-fiction since 1965. His recent memoir, *There Is A Season,* won the $25,000 British Columbia Award for Canadian Non-Fiction in 2005. A novel, *Red Dog Red Dog,* will be published in 2008.

Lawrence, Ruth. Ruth Lawrence is an actor/writer from St. Jacques, Fortune Bay. Her poetry has appeared in several anthologies including *The Backyards of Heaven* (WIT and SCOP) and *Land, Sea, and Time* (Breakwater) as well as the literary magazine, *TickleAce.* *The House Wife* (co-written with Sherry White) is published in *Two Hands Clapping* (Signature Editions), an anthology of two-person plays.

Leggo, Carl. Carl Leggo is a professor at the University of British Columbia where he teaches courses in writing. He is the author of four books: *Growing Up Perpendicular on the Side of a Hill, View from My Mother's House, Teaching to Wonder: Responding to Poetry in the Secondary Classroom,* and *Come-By-Chance.*

Lush, Laura. Laura Lush has published three collections of poetry and a collection of short stories. She read at the 2004 March Hare with a cast of lively writers including Alistair MacLeod to whom she would like to extend her sincere apologies for stealing his last piece of fruit cake. She lives in Toronto with her son, Jack-Curtis and teaches in The English Language Program at the University of Toronto.

MacLeod, Alistair. Alistair MacLeod was born in Saskatchewan in 1936 and lived on the Prairies until he was ten, when his parents moved back to the family farm on Cape Breton. His publications include *Lost Salt Gift of Blood* (1976), *As Birds Bring Forth the Sun and other Stories* (1986), *No Great Mischief* (1999) – winner of the International IMPAC Dublin Award – and *Island: The Collected Stories of Alistair MacLeod* (2000).

Maggs, Randall. A member of Grenfell College's English Department, Randall Maggs succeeded Al Pittman as Artistic Director of The March Hare in 2002. With John Ennis and Stephanie McKenzie, he edited *However Blow the Winds,* an anthology of Irish and Newfoundland poems. His last collection of poems, *Timely Departures,* was published by Breakwater in 1994. His latest, *Night Work: The Sawchuk Poems,* will be brought out by Brick Books in 2008.

McBreairty, Sheldon. Sheldon McBreairty was born in 1954 at Bath, New Brunswick, but grew up in Corner Brook, and now lives in Gander. He has released two CDs of original music and is an award winner in the Newfoundland and Labrador Arts and Letters Music Competition. He assisted Eric Norman in the organizing of the first Gander March Hare in 2002 and has been involved ever since.

McGrath, Carmelita. Carmelita McGrath is a poet, fiction writer, children's author, freelancer and editor. Her most recent books are the *The Boston Box* (picture book, 2003) and *Vistas* (2005), a poetry chapbook excerpted from a new collection in progress. She lives in St. John's.

McKenzie, Stephanie. Stephanie McKenzie (PhD, Toronto) is Assistant Professor of English at Northern Michigan University. Her book *Before the Country: Native Renaissance, Canadian Mythology* is forthcoming with the University of Toronto Press. McKenzie is also an editor and poet. *Cutting My Mother's Hair* (Cliffs of Moher: Salmon, 2006) is her first book of poetry.

Miyashita, Emiko. Emiko Miyashita writes haiku, a traditional Japanese short poetry with a touch of seasonal element found in nature and in human life, both in Japanese and in English. Her haiku collection, *a mime's perpendicular pause,* is edited by Nick Avis. She lives in Kawasaki, Japan.

Moore, Lisa. Lisa Moore is the author of two collections of short stories, *Degrees of Nakedness* and *Open,* and the novel *Alligator.* She lives in downtown St. John's and is currently working on another novel.

Morgan, Bernice. Author of two novels, *Random Passage* and *Waiting for Time,* Bernice Morgan has received both the Canadian Author's Literary Prize for Fiction and the Thomas H. Raddall Atlantic Fiction Award. Her collection of short stories, *The Topography of Love,* was published in 2000 and a new novel, *Shadowdancers,* will be released in 2007.

Murphy, Liam. Born in Waterford in 1948, Liam Murphy is a storyteller, poet, actor, teacher and sometime journalist. His publications include *Occasion of Watershed* (Gallery, 1970), *Irish Poets, 1924-1974* (Pan, 1975), and *Poets of Munster* (Brandon/Anvil, 1985). With Anne Farrell he founded Cuala Verbal Arts in 1998 to revive storytelling and verbal work. Cuala have worked in the U.S., Canada, England and Wales, and toured extensively in Ireland.

Musgrave, Susan. Susan Musgrave has received awards in five different genres: poetry, fiction, creative non-fiction, children's writing and for her work as an editor. She teaches in the Low Residency Creative Writing MFA Programme at the University of British Columbia. Her most recent book is "YOU'RE IN CANADA NOW... A Memoir of Sorts."

Ní Chuilleanáin, Eiléan. Eiléan Ní Chuilleanáin was born in 1942 and she has taught for forty years at Trinity College, Dublin. She has written academic books and articles and translated poetry from various languages, most recently *After the Raising of Lazarus*, from the Romanian of Ileana Malancioiu (Cork, 2005). She has published seven collections of poetry, most recently *The Girl Who Married the Reindeer*, Wake Forest University Press (North Carolina), 2002.

O'Donoghue, Bernard. Bernard O'Donoghue was born in County Cork in 1945. He has published five volumes of poetry, of which *Gunpowder* (Chatto & Windus 1995) won the Whitbread Poetry Prize. He teaches Medieval English at Oxford University.

Ollerhead, Pamela. Pamela Ollerhead has a degree in Canadian literature and anthropology from Sir Wilfred Grenfell College. She has traveled extensively in North America and Europe and lived in Italy for six years where she worked at a Canadian research centre and then as an English teacher and translator.

Ondaatje, Michael. Michael Ondaatje was born in Sri Lanka and has lived in Canada since 1963. His works include *The Conversations: Walter Murch and the Art of Editing Film*, *Anil's Ghost*, *The English Patient*, *In the Skin of a Lion*, *Coming Through Slaughter*, *The Collected Works of Billy the Kid*, and his memoir, *Running in the Family*. His collections of poetry include *Secular Love*, *The Cinnamon Peeler* and *Handwriting*.

O'Sullivan, Leanne. Leanne O'Sullivan is from the Beara peninsula in West Cork and is currently completing an M.A. in English at University College, Cork. Her poems have been widely published in magazines and journals, including *The Backyards of Heaven*. Her first collection of poetry, *Waiting for My Clothes*, was published in 2004 by Bloodaxe Books.

Pittman, Al. Born in St. Leonard's, Placentia Bay, Al Pittman (1940-2001) was the author of six books of poetry, two plays, one dramatic collage, three children's books and a collection of short stories. In 2001, a Newfoundland production of his play, *West Moon*, was enthusiastically received in a tour of Ireland. For over twenty years, he taught English at Sir Wilfred Grenfell College, where he helped to build a culture supportive of creative writing. He was the heart and soul of The March Hare.

Pittman, Kyran. Kyran Pittman is a Newfoundland poet and essayist living in the southern United States. She has published and performed her work in the U.S., Canada and Ireland.

Pratt, Christopher. Born in 1935, Christopher Pratt studied art at the Glasgow School of Art, Scotland, and Mount Allison University. His major exhibitions include the 2005-2007 Touring Retrospective organized by National Gallery of Canada, Ottawa, and a 30th Anniversary Show at the Mira Godard Gallery, Toronto, 1999. A Companion of the Order of Canada, he lives and works in Salmonier, St. Mary's Bay, Newfoundland.

Redhill, Michael. Michael Redhill's latest book is the novel, *Consolation*. His previous works include *Martin Sloane*, the play, *Goodness*, and numerous collections of poetry. He lives and works in Toronto.

Reid, Stephen. Stephen Reid's *Jackrabbit Parole* is the autobiographical story of a bank robber who escaped once too often. A biography of his life, *The Stopwatch Gang*, written by Greg Weston, was published by MacMillan in 1992. His prison memoir will be published by Knopf.

Rodgers, Gordon. Gordon Rodgers is author of the novel, *A Settlement of Memory*, and two books of poetry, *Floating Houses* and *The Pyrate Latitudes*. He is writing a second novel.

Rose, Clyde. Clyde Rose was born on Fox Island on the south coast of Newfoundland. After several years teaching English at Memorial University of Newfoundland, he founded Breakwater Books in 1973. He edited the anthologies *The Blasty Bough*, *Baffles of Wind and Tide*, and *East of Canada*, and co-edited the *Land, Sea and Time* Series. His first poetry collection, *Christ in the Pizza Place*, was published by Jesperson Publishing in 2002.

Ruste, Arne. Arne Ruste, born in 1942 in southern Norway, has published nine collections of poetry, two of them awarded (and one short-listed for) the Norwegian Literature Prize (Brage). Most recent titles are: *Indre krets* (*Internal Zodiac*), 1999, and *Søsken for en tid* (*Siblings for a While*), 2001. He has also published a volume of essays and translated into Norwegian the work of Ted Hughes and Roald Dahl.

Shaw, David J. Born in England, a Canadian by accident and a Newfoundlander by choice, David J. Shaw lives in Glenwood. Married to his wife Janet for forty-seven years, he has three children and two grandchildren. For twenty-five years he was in the Royal Canadian Navy as a Communications Researcher. His interests are family, scouting, beachcombing, fishing, hiking, writing, gardening and computers.

Small, Larry. Larry Small was born on Twillingate Island and grew up in Moreton's Harbour, the home of his ancestors for two centuries. He did an M.A. in Folklore at Memorial University and a Ph.D. in Folklore and Anthropology at the University of Pennsylvania, after which he taught at Memorial until his retirement. His first collection of poetry will be released in February 2007.

Sorestad, Glen. Glen Sorestad is a well-known Saskatoon poet who was Saskatchewan's first Poet Laureate (2000-2004). He is the author of more than fifteen books of poems, the most recent being *Blood & Bone, Ice & Stone* (2005). He has given public readings of his poems all over North America and in several European countries.

Steffler, John. Originally from Ontario, John Steffler moved to Corner Brook in 1975. He is the author of a novel, *The Afterlife of George Cartwright*, and five collections of poems including *The Grey Islands*, *That Night We Were Ravenous* and *Helix: New and Selected Poems*.

Strowbrige, Nellie. Nellie P. Strowbridge's work has been published nationally and internationally. Among her publications are: *Widdershins: Stories of a Fisherman's Daughter*, *Doors Held Ajar* (tri-author), *Shadows of the Heart*, *Dancing on Ochre Sands* (short-listed for the 2005 E. J. Pratt Award), *Far from Home: Dr. Grenfell's Little Orphan* (a young adult novel), and *The Gift of Christmas*.

Walsh, Agnes. Agnes Walsh was born in Placentia. A theatre artist as well as poet, she is artistic director of the The Tramore Theatre Troupe on the Cape Shore of Placentia Bay. Her first collection of poems, *In the Old Country of My Heart* (Killick Press, 1996), sold out and was reprinted in 2003. Her new collection is due out the spring of 2007 with Brick Books.

Walsh, Des. Des Walsh has published four collections of poetry, including *The Singer's Broken Throat* and *Love and Savagery*. He co-wrote the TV drama *The Boys of St. Vincent* for which he received a Gemini (Canada), the Umbriafiction (Italy), the FIPA Grand d'Or (France), and the Peabody Award (USA). His eight-hour TV adaptation of the novel, *Random Passage*, has aired internationally.

Warner, Patrick. Patrick Warner is the author of two collections of poetry. His first collection, *All Manner of Misunderstanding*, was short-listed for the Atlantic Poetry Prize in 2002. His second collection, *There, there*, was published by Signal Editions (Montreal) in 2005. Patrick Warner lives in St. John's, Newfoundland.

Watts, Enos. Born in Long Pond, Manuels in Conception Bay, Enos Watts is one of Newfoundland's most respected poets. He has published three collections of poetry, *After the Locusts* (Breakwater, 1974), *Autumn Vengeance* (Breakwater, 1986) and *Spaces Between the Trees* (Pennywell, 2005), which was short-listed for the Winterset Award and long-listed for the ReLit Award.

Winter, Michael. Michael Winter is the author of two novels and two collections of short stories. He has won the CBC literary prize and the Winterset Award. He lives in Toronto and Western Bay.

IMAGES

Photographic reproductions of March Hare Images by David Morish

CREDITS

Every reasonable effort has been made to trace the ownership of material reprinted in this book and to make full acknowledgments for its use. The publisher would be grateful to know of any errors or omission so they may be rectified in subsequent editions.

Nick Avis "now that you are living" – Reprinted with permission of the author. "you aim to love" – Reprinted with permission of the author.

Isabel Blackmore "Tounges and Common Sense" – Reprinted with permission of the author.

Archibald Bonnell "Helpless" – Reprinted with permission of the author.

Stephen Brunt Excerpted from *Searching for Bobby Orr* by Stephen Brunt. Copyright © 2006 Stephen Brunt. Reprinted with permission of Knopf Canada.

Bill Butt "Keepers of Time" – Reprinted with permission of the author.

Mark Callanan "Turk's Gut Wolf" – Reprinted with permission of the author. "Wheelbarrow" – Reprinted with permission of the author.

Boyd Chubbs "For the Creature" – Reprinted with permission of Breakwater Books Limited. "I Met a Saint" – Reprinted with permission of Breakwater Books Limited.

Joan Clark Excerpted from *Latitudes of Melt* by Joan Clark. Copyright © 2000 by Joan Clark. Repritned by permission of Knopf Canada.

Lynn Coady Excerpted from *Mean Boys*. Reprinted with permission of the author.

Tony Collins "Disqualified" – Reprinted with permission of the author.

Libby Creelman "Landscape" – Reprinted from *Walking in Paradise* by Libby Creelman by permission of the Porcupine's Quill. Copyright © Libby Creelman, 2000.

Lorna Croizer "When I Come Again to My Father's House" from *Everything Arrives at the Light* by Lorna Crozier, © 1995. Published by McClelland & Stewart. Used with permission of the publisher. "Leaving Home" from *Whetston* by Lorna Crozier, © 2005. Published by McClelland & Stewart. Used with permission of the publisher. "The Dark Ages of the Sea" from *Everything Arrives at the Light* by Lorna Crozier, © 1995. Published by McClelland & Stewart. Used with permission of the publisher. "Sand from the Gobi Desert" from *Whetstone* by Lorna Crozier, © 2005. Published by McClelland & Stewart. Used with permission of the publisher.

Michael Crummey "Women's Work" – Reprinted with permission of the author. "Patience" – Reprinted with permission of the author. "Birding, Cape St. Mary's" – Reprinted with permission of the author.

Kerri Cull "red" – Copyright © 2006 by Kerri Cull. "houses" – Copyright © 2006 by Kerri Cull.

Mary Dalton "Headlong" – originally published in *The Newfoundland Quarterly*. "Ravished" – originally published in *TickleAce*. "Kitchen" – Reprinted with permission of Breakwater Books Limited. "In the Wide Room" – Reprinted with permission of the author.

Tom Dawe "Elsewhere: a Poem to Emily" — Reprinted with permission of the author. "Slips" – Reprinted with permission of the author. "Frog-Prince" – Reprinted with permission of the author. "Xantippe" – Reprinted with permission of the author.

Paul Dean "Melvin" – Reprinted with permission of the author.

Don Downer "Last Nail" – Reprinted with permission of the author.

Stan Dragland "Come All Ye" – Reprinted with permission of Pedlar Press."Mr. Iceberg" – Reprinted with permission of Pedlar Press.

Paul Durcan "Mr. and Mrs. Talbot" – Copyright © Paul Durcan 2004. Reproduced by permission of the author c/o Rogers, Coleridge & White Ltd., 20 Powis Mews, London W11 1JN. "The Far Side of the Island" – Copyright © Paul Durcan 2004. Reproduced by permission of the author c/o Rogers, Coleridge & White Ltd., 20 Powis Mews, London W11 1JN. "The 12 O'Clock Mass, Roundston, County Galway" – Copyright © Paul Durcan 2004. Reproduced by permission of the author c/o Rogers, Coleridge & White Ltd., 20 Powis Mews, London W11 1JN.

Michelle Dwyer "Oliver's Cove, 29 September" – Reprinted with permission of the author.

Derrick Earle "The Flagman" – Reprinted with permission of the author.

David Elliott "Talking to Trees" – Copyright © David Elliott 1988. Reprinted with permission of the Estate of Rosalie Elliott. "After the Snake" – Copyright © David Elliott 1988. Reprinted with permission of the Estate of Rosalie Elliott. "Bamboos Flowering" – Copyright © David Elliott 1988. Reprinted with permission of the Estate of Rosalie Elliott. "River IV" – Copyright © David Elliott 1988. Reprinted with permission of the Estate of Rosalie Elliott

Rosalie Elliott "I Ran So Fast" – Copyright © Rosalie Elliott 2006. Reprinted with permission of the Estate of Rosalie Elliott. "The Honourable Bird" – Copyright © Rosalie Elliott 2006. Reprinted with permission of the Estate of Rosalie Elliott.

John Ennis "Pool Ice" – Reprinted with permission of Scop Productions and John Ennis. "Boy Amongst Sparrows" – Reprinted with permission of Scop Productions and John Ennis.

Anne Ferncase "Catching the Klong Boat" – © Anne Fercase 2001

Adrian Fowler "The Russians Are Coming" – Copyright © Adrian Fowler 2006. Reprinted with permission of the author.

Alan Garvey "No Longer New" – from *Herself in Air* by Alan Garvey, © 2006. Published by Lapwing Publications, Belfast. "Never Mind" – from *Herself in Air* by Alan Garvey, © 2006. Published by Lapwing Publications, Belfast.

Susan Gillis "Love as Stone" – Reprinted with permission from *Volta*, published by Signature Editions in 2002. "Kitchen Floor– Reprinted with permission from *Volta*, published by Signature Editions in 2002. "Love as Pure Desire" – Reprinted with permission from *Volta*, published by Signature Editions in 2002.

Goh Poh Seng "Summer in Lark Harbour" – Reprinted with permission of the author. "Vietnam 1967" – Reprinted with permission of the author. "Cemetery by the Sea" – Reprinted with permission of the author.

Louise Skydancer Halfe "Dear Magpie" – Reprinted with permission of the author. "White Island" – Reprinted with permission of the author. To appear in new book in Fall 2007, *The Crooked Good*.

Kevin Hehir "Reasons to Celebrate" – Reprinted with permission of the author. "Lexicon Lake" – Reprinted with permission of the author.

Barbara Helfgott Hyett "In the Ring of Twenty Signs" – First published by Agni Review. Reprinted with permission of the author. "The Keeper of the Light" – Published in Natural Law, 1989. Reprinted with permission of the author. "The Lightkeeper's Daughter" – Reprinted with permission of the author. Written at Trinity Bay. "In the Woods near Munich" – Published in Natural Law, 1989. Reprinted with permission of the author.

Carol Hobbs "Steady Goods" – Reprinted with permission of the author. "Iceberg" – Reprinted with permission of the author. "Late at Bannerman Park" – Reprinted with permission of the author.

Matthew Hollett "Poem for a Found Paper Crane" – Reprinted with permission of the author.

Ben Hynes "We Spoke Only With Our Feet" – Reprinted with permission of the author.

Joel Hynes "Homecoming" – Reprinted with permission of the author.

Wayne Johnston The excerpt by Wayne Johnston is reprinted from *The Story of Bobby O'Malley* by permission of Oberon Press.

Patrick Lane "For Al Pittman" – Reprinted with permission of the author. "Hope and Love" – Reprinted with permission of the author. "Not going to the Nitobi Gardens, Choosing Poetry Instead" – Reprinted with permission of the author. "August Light" – Reprinted with permission of the author.

Ruth Lawrence "First Prize" – Reprinted with permission of the author. "The Scavenger" – Reprinted with permission of the author.

Carl Leggo "West Coast Prairie" – Reprinted with permission of Breakwater Books Limited. "Come-by-Chance" – Reprinted with permission of Breakwater Books Limited.

Laura Lush "The Other Side of the Lake" from *Faultline* are used by permission of Signal Editions, Véhicule Press. "How Trees Grow" – Reprinted with permission of the author. "Witness" from *Faultline* are used by permission of Signal Editions, Véhicule Press. "Riverside Heights" from *Faultline* are used by permission of Signal Editions, Véhicule Press.

Alistair MacLeod From *No Great Mischief* by Alistair MacLeod © 1999. Published by McClelland & Stewart Ltd. Used with permission of the publisher.

Randall Maggs "Berbers" – Reprinted with permission of Breakwater Books Limited. "Narrow Gauge" – Reprinted with permission of the author. "Game Days" – Reprinted with permission of the author.

Sheldon McBreairty "Jabberwock Envy" – Reprinted with permission of the author.

Carmelita McGrath "As Persephone" – Reprinted with permission of the author. "Watering at Dawn" – Reprinted with permission of the author. "My Father's Ghost" first published in *Ghosts Poems*, Running the Goat Books and Broadsides, 2001. Reprinted with permission of the author. "Hearts of Pain" – Reprinted with permission of the author.

Stephanie McKenzie "Cutting My Mother's Hair" published in *Cutting My Mother's Hair* (Cliffs of Moher, Ireland: Salmon Poetry, 2006). "The Fruitpicker" published in *Cutting My Mother's Hair* (Cliffs of Moher, Ireland: Salmon Poetry, 2006).

Emiko Miyashita "Haiku" – Reprinted with permission of the author.

Lisa Moore From *Alligator* – copyright © 2005 by Lisa Moore. Reprinted with permission from House of Anansi Press.

Bernice Morgan From *Topography of Love* – Reprinted with permission of Breakwater Books Limited.

Liam Murphy "Me Mam" – A version of this was first printed in *The Munster Express*. Reprinted with permission of the author. "Little Hurler or Even Smaller Ballerina" – Reprinted with permission of the author.

Susan Musgrave "Magnolia" – Reprinted with permission of the author. "*No Hablo Ingles*" – Reprinted with permission of the author. "The Room Where They Found You" – Reprinted with permission of the author. "Understanding the Sky" – Reprinted with permission of the author.

Ní Chuilleanáin, Eiléan "On Lacking the Killer Instinct" – Reprinted with permission of the author. "The Sister" – Reprinted with permission of the author.

Bernard O'Donoghue "A Nun takes the Veil" from THE WEAKNESS by Bernard O'Donoghue, published by Chatto & Windus. Reprinted with permission of The Random House Group Ltd. "Anmnesis" from THE WEAKNESS by Bernard O'Donoghue, published by Chatto & Windus. Reprinted with permission of The Random House Group Ltd. "Stay, You Imperfect Speakers" – Reprinted with permission of the author. "The Starling's Lament" – Reprinted with permission of the author.

Pamela Ollerhead "One November in Mexico" Reprinted with permission of the author.

Michael Ondaajte "The Great Tree" and "To a Sad Daughter" Copyright © 1987,1984 by Michael Ondaate. Reprinted with permission of Ellen Levine Literary Agency/Trident Media Group.

Leanne O'Sullivan "The Fisherman" – Reprinted with permission of the author. "About Midnight" – Reprinted with permission of the author. "River" - Reprinted with permission of the author. "The Lights of New York" – Reprinted with permission of the author.

Al Pittman Excerpt from *West Moon*. Reprinted with permission from Breakwater Books Limited. "Lupines" – Reprinted with permission from Breakwater Books Limited. "Atlantis" – Reprinted with permission from Breakwater Books Limited. "Her Portrait of Me" – Reprinted with permission from Breakwater Books Limited. "Final Farewell" – Reprinted with permission from Breakwater Books Limited.

Kyran Pittman "Launch" – Reprinted with permission of the author.

Helen Fogwill Porter "Hot Night in July" –- originally published in *TickleAce*. Reprinted with permission of the author. "Sunday Best" – originally published in *TickleAce*. Reprinted with permission of the author.

Christopher Pratt "I Had Already Written Poetry for You" – Copyright © C. Pratt 1986. Reprinted with permission from Breakwater Books Limited.

Michael Redhill "My Grandfather's Empire" from *Asphodel* by Michael Redhill © 1997, published by McClelland & Stewart. Used with permission of the publisher. "Viewing Detroit" from *Asphodel* by Michael Redhill © 1997, published by McClelland & Stewart. Used with permission of the publisher.

Stephen Reid "There Are No Children's Books in Prison" – Reprinted with permission of the author.

Gordon Rodgers From "Emergency Roadside Assistance" – Reprinted with permission of the author.

Clyde Rose "Morning in Bologna" – Reprinted with permission of Breakwater Books Limited.

Arne Ruste From "Post-it Notes, Just in Case" ("On the Bathroom Mirror Cabinet," "By the Telephone," and "Under the Apple Tree") – published in Sosken for en tid (Siblings for a While) 2001.

David J. Shaw "Beachcombing" – Reprinted with permission of the author.

Larry Small "The Bay from Long Point" – Reprinted with permission of Breakwater Books Limited. "Christmas" – Reprinted with permission of Breakwater Books Limited.

Glen Sorestad "Mid-March Riot in Beacon Hill Park" – Reprinted with permission of the author. "The Lady who Loved Shrimp" – Reprinted with permission of the author. "Dear Kyran" – Reprinted with permission of the author.

John Steffler "Cook's Line" from *That Night We Were Ravenous*, by John Steffler © 1998. Published by McClelland & Stewart. Used with permission of the publisher. "Cedar Cove" from *That Night We Were Ravenous*, by John Steffler © 1998. Published by McClelland & Stewart. Used with permission of the publisher.

Nellie Strowbridge "Emerald Island 2003" – Reprinted with permission of the author. "The Fisherman's Wife" – Reprinted with permission of the author.

Agnes Walsh "Homecoming to the End" – Reprinted with permission of the author. This poem will published in Spring 2007 by Brick Books. "The Cows Were There" – Reprinted with permission of the author. This poem will published in Spring 2007 by Brick Books.

Des Walsh "Talamh an éisc (Land of the Fish)" – Reprinted with permission from *The Singers' Broken Throat* by Des Walsh, copyright © 2003, Talon Books Ltd., Vancouver, BC. "Puis Power..." – Reprinted with permission from *The Singers' Broken Throat* by Des Walsh, copyright © 2003, Talon Books Ltd., Vancouver, BC. "Antibiotics" – Reprinted with permission from *The Singers' Broken Throat by Des Walsh*, copyright © 2003, Talon Books Ltd., Vancouver, BC. "I Knew You Then" – Reprinted with permission of the author. "She Imagines Herself Forgetting" - Reprinted with permission of the author.

Patrick Warner "Mormon" from *There, there* is used by permission of Signal Editions, Véhicule Press. "Gumshoe" from *There, there* is used by permission of Signal Editions, Véhicule Press.

Enos Watts "Rocky Mountain Bighorn" – Reprinted with permission from Pennywell Books. "For One Who Died Alone in the Night" – Reprinted with permission of Breakwater Books Limited. "Margaret Lawrence's *Manawaka*" – Reprinted with permission from Pennywell Books.

Michael Winter "The Point David Made Earlier" – Reprinted with permission of the author.

www.ingramcontent.com/pod-product-compliance
Lightning Source LLC
Chambersburg PA
CBHW060425030726
47495CB00003B/739